力得文化
Leader Culture

THE GOLDEN TICKET
TO YOUR CAREER

贏得百大企業的黃金入場券

99_%百大企業
會問的 英文面試題

王郁琪 ◎著

打敗英文面試恐懼症，打造面試最大贏面！
讓面試官一見傾心，當天就錄取！

考前必Check！

☑ 60題經典面試題→見招拆招，談吐自然又大方
☑ 題解+評解→分析問題的隱藏版涵義與答題策略
☑ 短回答+長回答→簡單與進階說法，完全推銷自己
☑ 用句型勝出→必備英文表達句型使用簡單明瞭
☑ 換個說法讓人眼睛一亮→拿捏得宜，應對有條理

外師精準錄音MP3

PREFACE 作者序

　　作者曾在美國工作，歷經多場英文面試，深知面試的表現良好與否與自身的準備工作息息相關。準備越充分，面試時越能從容應答。隨著台灣朝著世界經濟邁進與市場的多元趨向，求職者的英文能力越顯重要。

　　本書的第二部份針對 60 個面試常見問題提供回答方向、基本版與進階版的短回答、長回答，並附上回答中的重要單字、句型、文法說明。這些說明除了可增進讀者的英語文基本能力外，說明中的例句與換句話說也讓讀者可就面試中的應答有更多的參考範例，期望這些範例可幫助應徵者準備與演練面試Q&A。本書的第一部分除了詳列面試基本守則與面試地雷，提醒讀者在面試前的準備、面試中、面試後三階段應該與不應該做的事以外，也提供 18 個應徵者常見提問範例可供讀者參考。在本書在最後一部份作者根據面試實境對話提醒台灣求職者英文常講錯的地方。

　　希望藉由這本書讓讀者成為英文面試的箇中好手。

王郁琪

WORDS FROM THE EDITOR

編者序

　　隨著企業越來越重視英文能力，越來越多企業在面試時會有英文面試。身為非英文為母語的我們，在面試時突然要轉換成英文，的確是一個不小的挑戰。這時候，所要依靠的就是面試之前的練習了。

　　本書依面試常見題目分為 14 大類共 60 題精選面試題，供讀者可自行練習。每一個題目，都涵蓋題解、簡答與詳答。故讀者可以了解題目的涵義與答題的方向。再者，依個人程度，練習短回答或長回答。使答題思路清晰，言詞達意讓主考官知道您的才能與對這份工作的熱情。

　　試想在面試時，面試官突然話鋒一轉開始問您：

　　你打算做多久？

　　你願意外派嗎？

　　為什麼我們要雇用你？

　　會不會一時間答不出來，在腦中搜尋單字句型，而還沒講出來，時間已經過了三秒鐘了。

　　本書的目標就是希望可以幫助您在面試時，先做好準備。面對各種奇怪又試探的題目，能從容面對、自然對答，提高更多錄取心儀的工作機會。Good Luck!

倍斯特編輯部

使用說明 ✒ Instructions

精選60題面試常問考題，
有準備就不用怕

更仔細的回答題目
讓面試官更了解面試者

可參考兩種回答的優點
並提供的建議

 面 試 英 文 Hire Me!

2-14 敏感問題

01 If hired, how long do you plan on working here?

How long do you expect yourself to work here if we hire you?
如果錄取了，你預計在這裡工作多久？

▶ 題解

這是較敏感的問題，但很多面試官會問。回答前提是「誠實」。如果你知道兩年內你會搬到另一城市，就直接說「在那之前我會希望在這裡穩定工作。」如果你希望長期在這間公司耕耘，附帶說明這個職位這個公司有那些優勢使你希望這會是一份長期的工作。

▶ 短回答 —— 基本版 🎧

I have always been looking to establish and settle my career in a company where I will be challenged to take more responsibilities and my good work will be appreciated. Here if I find those opportunities then I would definitely work for a long time.

我一直希望能在一個能讓我面對挑戰負起更多責任且欣賞我工作的公司建立和穩定我的職業。如果在這裡我可以有這機會，我肯定會長期在這工作。

▶ 短回答 —— 進階版

As far as I am concerned, the company offers some excellent

解析這個問題
要怎麼回答更切中重點

分為基本版
與進階版讓回答簡單有力

▶ 評解

兩個回答都表達強烈的動機為公司奉獻，進階
與職位。

▶ 長回答 🎧

I can see a long tenure with this comp
opportunities across the spectrum of r
heard good things about your training
which is perfect for my own studies. I
company that is willing to invest on em
a promotion, and get the broad experi
industry, I'll be here for a long perio
make significant contributions to you.

我可以在貴公司看到一個長遠的終身職業。我
機會。我聽說您們的培訓和研究支持計畫非
的。我一直夢想在一個願意投資在員工訓練的
並且獲得在這個產業要進步所需要的廣泛知識
顯著貢獻給公司。

▶ 評解

這個回答不僅說明這個公司有那些優勢讓人想
與積極在工作上有所表現的動機。

🏆 單字 🎧

❶ tenure [`tɛnjʊr] n. 終身職位
❷ spectrum [`spɛktrəm] n. 系列；範圍

與主題相關
好用單字補充

好用句型，
讓你答題舉一反三

選擇一個念的最順口
的答案，反覆練習

✍ 用句型取勝

as far as sb. / sth. + be concerned 對... 來說, 就...而言, 關於....方面

📝 要注意

1. be動詞要用現在簡單式。
2. as far as I am concerned= as for me=in my opinion=from my point of view, 通常都放在句首。

例句

· As far as I am concerned, what the job applicant said doesn't make

💡 換個說法令人眼睛一亮

(1)I've heard good things about
support programs, which is perfe
我聽說您們的培訓和研究支持計畫非常
益的。

= Your training and study support
and are very good to my own studie
= Your training and study suppo
perfect for my studies.

模擬實際面試情況，
提高流暢度

Engineer

工程師

3-1

角色

D: David, the hiring manager. 面試者
H: Henry, the job applicant. 求職者

情景

Henry is applying for the senior computer programmer position at ABC company.
Henry 應徵ABC公司的資深電腦程式設計師一職。

-14 敏感問題

了解目標公司

a range of
is firm. I've
programs,
rking for a
can achieve
gress in the
my best to

範圍內的各種
究是很有助益
升遷機會，
並我所能提供

露強烈的學習

特別設置容易
講錯的地方，
預防講錯或詞
不達意

面試時別講錯

我在研究所的訓練，加上多年的專業經驗，使我適合這份工作。

（✗）I graduate school training and many yearsprofessiona
experiences, I am suitable for this job.

（○）My graduate school training combined with my years c
professional experiences should qualify me for thi
particular job.

錯誤的句子是中文式英文，很多人都會犯這樣的錯誤。研究所英文説「gradua
school」，有些人會説成「research school」。多年的專業經驗英文應説「man
years of professional experiences」而非「many years professiona
experiences」。錯誤的句子裡沒有連接詞，可以改為「Because of my gradua
school training and many years of experiences, I am suitable for this job
」。正確句子中的「combined with」就等於「and」，因此「A and B= A

常用表達的延
伸說法，應對
合宜

延伸說法

(1) I have never involved in fundraising and therefore this job is
quite challenging for me. However, this is also a chance for me
to grow.
我從來沒有從事過募款，所以這個工作是蠻具挑戰性的。然而這也是
一個成長機會。

(2) I am not afraid of making mistakes. I am only afraid that I
can't learn anything from the mistake itself.
我不怕犯錯。我只怕我沒有從錯誤本身學習到東西。

d study
dies.
是很有助

reputation

popular and

Part
2
面試常見問題

目錄

CONTENTS

Part **1** 面試前準備
Prepare for a Job Interview

Part **2** 99%會問的面試題
Job Interview FAQs

Part 3 實際面試對答
The Interview Scenarios

Part 1

面試前準備
Prepare for a Job
Interview

Job Interview Basic Rules

1-1

面試基本守則

1. 面試前的準備

- 透過網路或其他管道（例如該公司員工）研究你要應徵工作的公司，詳細閱讀該公司網站，了解其企業組織、經營理念、業務範圍、未來願景、公司文化等。也要對你所應徵的職位的工作內容與職責有一定的了解。對公司與目標職位相關資訊清楚明白有助於回答「為何你想來本公司工作？」或「為何你認為你可以勝任這個工作？」相關問題。

- 在面試前一個星期左右的時間裡，積極思考可能會被問到的問題與相對應的答案（詳細閱讀本書可讓你的準備工作事半功倍）。面試的問題不出以下幾個類別：

  ⑴ 和緩緊張問候性問題　　⑻ 執行能力

  ⑵ 求職目的與動機　　　　⑼ 管理能力

  ⑶ 學歷與教育訓練　　　　⑽ 社交能力

  ⑷ 工作經驗與技能　　　　⑾ 創造能力

  ⑸ 業績　　　　　　　　　⑿ 領導能力

  ⑹ 未來目標　　　　　　　⒀ 個人事務

  ⑺ 解決問題能力　　　　　⒁ 敏感問題

　　要知道大多數人無法在面試的緊張氣氛下，確切地回答未經準備的問題。因此，強烈建議多花時間閱讀本書充分準備面試 Q&A。也可請親人朋友扮演面試官幫助你針對可能被問到的問題進行事前演練。

- 準備一份有效的自我介紹，重點要擺在藉由自我介紹讓面試官清楚明白你的專長與興趣。專長必須是和目標職位有直接相關的。

- 利用這個機會好好思考自我生涯規劃，準備一份明確的講稿。記得職涯的規劃必須與目標職位結合在一起。

- 雖然你的履歷中已列你的學經歷，針對即將來臨的面試要確保自己可以完整且具體地將你的學經歷說明清楚。
- 詳讀自己的履歷表，清楚了解內容，避免在面試時出現與履歷表不符的說詞。
- 事先勘查交通與地點，規畫好路線，當天提早出門，確保自己能在面試前五到十分鐘抵達，不要把時間算得剛剛好。

2. 面試當天的行為儀態

- 要有基本禮貌，不要忘了說請、謝謝、對不起。點頭與微笑也不可少。
- 姿勢與動作要優雅，讓面試官對你有良好的第一印象。
- 根據你應徵工作的屬性決定當天的搭配穿著，穿著要得體，儀容要端正。
- 展現自信與積極的態度，要讓面試官覺得你對自己的專業與才能是有自信的且對於目標職位的爭取是積極與誠懇的。
- 展現自己對工作與職涯發展的企圖心。
- 用平常心面對面試，越是緊張越容易表現失常。如果有充分的準備與練習，自然能以輕鬆的心情與面試官互動。
- 多用過去工作經驗舉實例來具體展現個人優點。例如，如果你說「我的工作表現很好」，不如說「我在上一份工作替部門增加百分之三十的業績」。
- 如果被問到敏感或令你感到不愉快的問題，盡量用幽默感化解尷尬。

3. 面試結束後的後續詢問

- 可寫一張小卡片表達對面試官的感謝寄到公司。
- 面試後一週如未收到任何回音，可主動打電話詢問結果。如果被錄取，可向其請教報到應注意事項，若未被錄取，可委婉請教原因，以做為改進自己的參考，並表示如果未來還有相關職缺也會希望能應徵，表現出自己對該公司的強烈興趣與動機。

Common Questions from Job Applicants　1-2

應徵者常見提問

1. 貴公司對這項職務最大的期望是什麼？有沒有什麼部分是我可以努力的地方？

   What do you expect the most about this position? Is there any part I can work on?

2. 如果我有機會作為貴公司員工，要如何超越您的期待？

   If I have the opportunity to be one of your employees, how do I do to go beyond your expectations?

3. 請問您對我個人的背景有沒有任何不清楚之處？我很樂意現在詳加闡述。

   Is there anything about my background that I didn't make it clear? I would love to elaborate on it now.

4. 貴公司是否有正式或非正式在職訓練？

   Do you have any formal or informal on-job training?

5. 我可以多了解貴公司的升遷系統嗎？

   Could I know more about your promotion system?

6. 就我了解貴公司多角化經營，而且在海內外都設有分公司，將來是否有輪調或海外工作的機會？

   I know that you have diversified businesses along with branches in and outside the country. Is there any chance of job rotation or working overseas?

7. 請問你認為這職位所面對的最大挑戰是什麼？

   What do you think the most challenging part of this job is?

8. 你們希望在未來的員工身上看到什麼性格特質？

   What personal qualities are you expected to see in prospective employees?

9. 我想知道是甚麼讓您公司的優秀員工有別於其他人。

I would like to know what make your outstanding employees different from others.

10. 在選擇未來的員工時，公司考慮的第一要素為何？

What's your first factor to consider when selecting the prospective employees?

11. 是甚麼讓貴公司在這個行業保持競爭力？

What makes you remain competitive in the industry?

12. 部門（或團隊）合作的方式是怎麼進行的？

How do people in the department (team) cooperate to get the work done?

13. 我知道貴公司強調團隊合作，可否請問團隊成員的特性為何？

I know that your company emphasizes team work. May I ask what the members' characteristics are?

14. 貴公司在人事管理上的規定和作法如何？

May I ask what the regulations and practices are about your personnel management?

15. 能否為我介紹一下工作環境，或者是否有機會能參觀一下貴公司？

Is it possible for you to introduce the work environment to me or do I have the chance to visit your company?

16. 您認為我今天的表現如何？

What do you think of my performance today?

17. 貴公司的績效評估主要包含哪些要素？

What factors are included in your performance evaluation?

18. 如果我這次未符合您的要求，請問我失敗的原因是什麼呢？

If I don't reach your requirements this time, what will be the reasons for my failure?

"Don's" in an Interview

面試的地雷不要碰

1. 儀態方面

　　要注意不要穿露腳趾頭的鞋子，不要穿不合時宜的服裝或不修邊幅，身上不要有太多配件（例如耳環、戒指、手環、項鍊等），切忌化濃妝。面試前不要抽菸，也不要噴香水（不要讓身上的味道成為焦點）。肢體動作不要顯得過度緊張與僵硬。

2. 行為方面

　　要注意絕對不要遲到，但也不要太早到。避免有家屬陪同，這會讓人覺得你還未能獨立自主、獨當一面。 如果等待時間長也不要顯露不耐煩。不要忘了帶筆，面試開始時不要主動坐下，除非面試官請你先坐下。面試進行時不要看手錶，手機不要開機。肢體動作要注意不要抖腳或蹺腳，身體不要往後傾，不要聳肩，手不要玩弄東西（如手機、頭髮、手指等），不要一直低著頭，不要左顧右盼，擺動身體。不要在面試完成的一刻顯露出鬆一口氣的模樣。

3. 應答部分

- 不要打斷面試官的話，別急著回答面試官的問題，或急著想表達意見。太快搶著說，會給人輕率的印象，面試官甚至會覺得你在跟他／她爭辯。
- 注意不要答非所問。
- 說話速度不要太快，最忌諱連珠炮般講話，這會讓面試官神經緊張，聽不進去你說的話。
- 避免語調平板，欠缺節奏，這會讓面試官對你說的內容提不起興趣。聲音太小或聲調太低會讓人覺得應徵者缺乏自信。
- 回答不要長篇大論，滔滔不絕只會讓面試官覺得他／她是來聽你演說的。

- 不要使用不確定的字眼如「可能吧」、「都可以吧」、「應該是」等。

- 避免負面或批判的字眼如「我受夠了」、「真討厭他」、「浪費我時間」等。

- 在回答面試官問題後不要反問他／她問題，除非對方邀請你問問題。反問面試官他／她的經驗或請其陳述某些觀念是被認為不禮貌的表現。

- 避免談論自己專業外的領域，如果是回答自己屬於自己專業，非常有信心，非常熟悉的話題時，不要一時興奮加快說話速度。

- 應答時不要顯得強勢，應由面試官主導對話。　應答態度不要自傲也不要自卑。也就是不要過於吹噓自己的強項或太過謙虛，說自己甚麼都不會，甚麼都做不好等。

- 不要談論與面試無關的問題或吐露個人隱私，除非面試官要求。

- 如果遇到令你不太愉快的問題例如「你畢業那麼久為何還找不到工作？」，不要表現出過度的情緒反應如羞愧或憤怒。

- 不要刻意攀親帶故，如果真有人情關係，也應該讓面試官主動提及，而非由求職者說出。

- 應答時不要顯得不在乎或漫不經心，更不要情緒化，要避免難過地訴說之前工作的不順利，氣憤地指責前主管的不是，或慷慨激昂地說明自己的豐功偉業等。

- 在面試的談話中，不要對其他公司做出評價，不要出現與你的履歷不合的應答，更不要談論政治，也不要強調之前面試的失敗經驗或工作上的不順遂與懷才不遇等。

- 回答問題時不要一直想著自己這樣答對不對，或逃避表達自己的立場。沒犯錯不等於拿滿分。

- 不要主動打探薪資福利，除非被問及。

- 面試結束時不要忘了跟面試官說謝謝。

Part 2

99％會問的面試題
Job Interview FAQs

01 Q Tell me about yourself.

Would you please introduce yourself first?

談談你自己吧。

▶ 題 解

這很可能是面試中的第一個題目，但面試官並不是要你描訴你的整個人生，或把你履歷的內容從頭到尾重複一次。回答時可以先說明你過去的工作經驗，再強調你有的優勢與技能，最後表達強烈希望能有機會被錄取。

▶ 短回答 —— 基本版 🎧 MP3 001

I'm happily married and originally from Denver. My family settled down in our new home last month. I'm now ready to go back to work. I've worked in a variety of jobs, usually customer service related. I'm looking for a company like you that offers growth opportunities.

我婚姻美滿，從丹佛來的。我們家上個月在新家安頓下來了。我現在已經準備好回到工作職場。我做過各種工作，通常與客戶服務相關。我在尋找像貴公司一樣提供我成長機會的公司。

▶ 短回答 —— 進階版

Well, I'm currently an account executive at Smith, where I handle our top performing client. While I really enjoyed the work, I'd love the chance to work for one specific healthcare company, which is why I'm so excited about this opportunity with you.

嗯，我目前在史密斯擔任客戶經理，我在那裡負責我們表現最出色的客戶。雖然我很喜歡這個工作，但我很想有機會能為一個特定的醫療保健公司工作，這就是為什

麼我很高興能有這次面試的機會。

> **⊙評 解**

回答都先從目前的工作（經驗）談起，接著表達很希望能為貴公司工作。

> **⊙長回答** 🎧 **MP3 002**

I have been in the customer service industry for the past five years. My most recent experience has been handling incoming calls in the high tech industry. In my last job, I formed some significant customer relationships resulting in a 30 percent increase in sales in three months. My real strength is my attention to detail. I pride myself on my reputation for following through and meeting deadlines. <u>When I commit to doing something, I make sure it gets done on time.</u> What I am looking for now is a company like you that values customer relations, where I can join a strong team and have a positive impact on customer retention and sales.

過去的五年我一直在客戶服務行業工作。我最近的經驗是負責高科技產業的來電。在我的上一份工作，我塑造顯著的客戶關係因此在三個月內銷售增長30％。我的真正實力是我對細節的關注。我很自豪自己在按時完成任務的聲譽。我承諾做的事情，我一定確保它按時完成。我現在所尋找的是一家像貴公司一樣重視客戶關係的公司，在這裡我可以加入一個強大的團隊並對客戶維繫和銷售產生積極的影響。

> **⊙評 解**

回答中藉由談到之前工作的良好表現加深面試官對自己的印象。

> **單字** 🎧 **MP3 003**

❶ **incoming** [ˋɪnˌkʌmɪŋ] *adj.* 進來的
❷ **form** [fɔrm] *v.* 形成；構成；塑造
❸ **pride** [praɪd] *v.* 以……自豪
❹ **reputation** [ˌrɛpjəˋteʃən] *n.* 名譽，名聲
❺ **commit** [kəˋmɪt] *v.* 使承擔義務

用句型取勝

a variety of ~ 多種多樣的～

👉 要注意

1. a variety of ~ =varieties of ~兩者都可修飾可數與不可數名詞。
2. a variety of + 可數複數名詞時，動詞要用複數動詞；a variety of + 不可數名詞，動詞要用單數動詞。
3. varieties of +可數複數名詞時，動詞要用複數動詞。

例句：

· My previous company has a variety of product lines.
  = My previous company has varieties of product lines.
  我之前的公司有各式各樣的產品線。
· A variety of factors account for my resignation.
  = Varieties of factors account for my resignation.
  種種因素解釋了我為何離職。

sb commit to (doing) sth 某人承諾做好某事

👉 要注意

1. 這裡指的 sth 可以是名詞或動名詞。
2. sb commit to (doing) sth= sb commit oneself to (doing)sth。

例句：

· I commit myself to each job task I was assigned to.
  = I commit to accomplishing every job I was assigned to.
  我承諾做好我被指派的每一個工作任務。
· I told my clients that we can commit to placing orders for twelve months.
  我告訴我的客戶我們承諾十二個月內都跟他們訂貨。

換個說法令人眼睛一亮

(1) I've worked in a variety of jobs, usually customer service related.

我做過各種工作，通常與客戶服務相關。

= A variety of jobs I have done are usually about customer service.

= I've done many different jobs and most of them are customer service related.

---

(2) In my last job, I formed some significant customer relationships resulting in a 30 percent increase in sales in three months.

在我的上一份工作，我塑造顯著的客戶關係因此在三個月內銷售增長30%。

= In my last job, I increased sales by 30% in three months by forming some significant customer relationships.

= In my last job, some significant customer relationships I formed brought in a 30 percent increase in sales.

---

(3) When I commit to doing something, I make sure it gets done on time.

我承諾做的事情，我一定確保它按時完成。

= When I determine to do something, I always get it done on time.

= Things I commit to are always done on time.

What interests you about this job?

Why do you want to apply for this position?

你為何對這個職位感興趣（為何想應徵這個工作）？

▶ 題 解

這個問題測試你對所應徵的公司與職位的了解程度與是否有很強的求職動機。回答可從幾個方向著手：這個工作可以給我新的學習經驗、可以應用與改進我目前擁有的技能、讓我進入全新的專業領域、符合我的興趣等、提供很好的職涯發展機會。注意「薪資」不應該是動機。

▶ 短回答 —— 基本版 🎧 MP3 004

This vacancy will allow me to practically use the knowledge and skills I have obtained through my education and previous work experiences, and learn and improve new and/or existing skills. Therefore, I am sincerely interested in this job and will be motivated to perform if hired.

這個職缺可實務應用我從學校和之前工作經驗獲得的知識和技能，並學習新技能與改進現有技能。因此，我誠摯地對這個工作感興趣，如果錄取會積極表現。

▶ 短回答 —— 進階版

Well, I like your company's software products and I would welcome the opportunity to work with the best in the business. Besides, the role excites me because I love the idea of helping develop cutting-edge software products and I know I could start contributing to the company from Day 1.

我喜歡您們公司的軟體產品，希望有機會能為最好的公司工作。除此之外，這個工作讓我很興奮因為我喜歡開發尖端軟體產品。我知道從第一天工作我就可開始對公司有所貢獻。

▶ 評解

基本版的回答是比較一般的說法，進階版較更好是因為有說明對該公司有一定程度的了解並陳述工作符合自己的興趣與將為公司貢獻所學。

▶ 長回答 🎧 MP3 005

I have worked in the real estate investment/financing field for six years and the reason I apply for this position is that this is an opportunity which will help me to develop further in this career field. I have previously worked in the similar type of working environment and responsibilities. I have developed a good national and international real estate financing/developing network, which I believe will create new business opportunities for my employer. Hence, my gained experience/ knowledge in investment sector will help me perform the associated responsibilities to a professional level. <u>In conclusion, I am not only highly interested in this position, but also a good fit for it.</u>

我在房地產投資／金融領域已工作六年。我應徵這個職位是因為這是一個可以幫助我在這個職場領域進一步發展的機會。我已在類似的工作環境和工作責任就業並開發了一個良好的國內和國際房地產融資／發展網絡。我相信這可以為我的雇主創造新的商機。因此，我在投資領域的經驗／知識將幫助我在執行相關職責時達到專業水平。總括來說，我不僅對這個職位有高度興趣，也非常適合這個工作。

▶ 評解

此回答不僅表達高度興趣與動機，也陳述了自己擁有目標職位所需的經驗和知識，將對公司有所貢獻。

 單字 🎧 MP3 006

❶ **real estate** [`riəl] [ɪs`tet] *n.* 房地產
❷ **investment** [ɪn`vɛstmənt] *n.* 投資

❸ **financing** [faɪˋnænsɪŋ] *n.* 財政；金融
❹ **career** [kəˋrɪr] *n.* （終身的）職業
❺ **associated** [əˋsoʃɪˏetɪd] *adj.* 相關的

用句型取勝

contribute+to 主要有兩個意思：
1. 貢獻、有助於　**2.** 捐（款）、把（時間）投入、投（稿）

要注意

1. to 後加名詞或動名詞。
2. contribute+to = make a contribution to。

例句：

· I believe my suggestion will contribute to solving the problem.
= I believe my suggestions will make a contribution to solving the problem.
我相信我的建議將有助於解決這個問題。

· It is a great honor to be invited to contribute to your business magazine.
= It is a great honor to be invited to make a contribution to your business magazine.
能應邀為您的商業雜誌寫稿我感到非常榮幸。

In conclusion　最後；總結來說

要注意

1. in conclusion 通常放在句首，後加逗號。
2. in conclusion 的同義詞有：finally, last, lastly, to conclude。

例句：

· In conclusion, I would like to thank you for giving me the opportunity for this interview.

最後，我要謝謝你給我這次的面試機會。

💡 換個說法令人眼睛一亮

(1) Well, I like your company's software products and I would welcome the opportunity to work with the best in the business.

我喜歡您們公司的軟體產品，希望有機會能為最好的公司工作。

= Well, you are the best in business and your software products are the ones I like. Hence, I would like to have this opportunity to work with you.

= Not only do I like your company's software products, but I honor the opportunity to work with the best in the business.

(2) I have developed a good national and international real estate financing/developing network, which I believe will create new business opportunities for my employer.

我開發了一個良好的國內和國際房地產融資／發展網絡。我相信這可以為我的雇主創造新的商機。

= The good national and international real estate financing/developing network I developed can provide my employers new business opportunities.

(3) Hence, my gained experience/ knowledge in investment sector will help me perform the associated responsibilities to a professional level.

因此，我在投資領域的經驗／知識將幫助我在執行相關職責時達到專業水平。

= I believe I can perform the associated responsibilities in a professional manner as a result of my experience/knowledge in investment sector.

= My experience/knowledge in investment sector makes it possible for me to do the associated jobs in a professional manner.

Part

2

99％會問的面試題

25

2-2 求職目的與動機

Why are you leaving your job?

Why did you resign from your last position?

你為何會離職？

▶ 題解

雇主通常都會好奇求職者為何會離職。回答時避免負面的原因如工作表現不佳或和主管同事有衝突等，也不可抱怨之前的雇主。回答要正面，例如為了在職涯上有更好的發展，追求更多專業上的成長等。或是因一個外在原因（不可抗拒的因素），例如公司重組或縮編。

▶ 短回答 — 基本版　🎧 MP3 007

Frankly speaking, I am grateful to my previous company because they created a good platform for me to perform when I was just starting out. I have learned lot from my previous employer. Now I want to improve my professional growth and I'm ready to face new challenges.

老實說，我很感激我之前的公司，因為他們在我職涯開始時替我創造了一個很好的平台讓我表現。我從我之前的雇主學到很多。現在我要更多的專業成長，我已做好面對新挑戰的準備。

▶ 短回答 — 進階版

I resigned because my organization has gone through multiple restructurings and unfortunately I was shifted to a job that doesn't match my interests and skills. After serious consideration I decided to leave to pursue a better match and reignite my passion!

我辭職因為公司經歷了幾波重組。不幸地我被轉調到一個不符合我興趣和專長的工作。慎重考慮之後我決定離開去追求更符合我興趣的工作重新點燃我的熱情！

▶ 評 解

二個回答都因相對正面的理由離職，例如想面對新挑戰，需要有更多專業成長和符合興趣的工作。

▶ 長回答　🎧 MP3 008

I've worked for many years with an organization where work never seems to be a burden and a healthy office environment is an additional advantage. It's hard for me to leave such a wonderful organization where my supervisor understands my qualities and utilizes them for the best use and my skills got sharper with time. Even so, at this stage, with good experience and developed skills, I seek a senior position. However it was difficult for me to replace my seniors in my previous organization as they have worked best at their posts. So I am seeking a job opportunity for this position in your company.

我在之前的公司工作多年，在那工作從來就不是負擔，健康的工作環境是另一項優點。我的主管了解我的特質，善用我的專長，隨著時間過去我更精進了我的技能，要離開這樣的公司是很困難的。然而在現階段以我的資歷和專長，我尋求一個更高的職位。但我很難取代我之前公司的資深前輩因為他們都在工作崗位上做得很好。因此我尋求在你們公司的這個職位。

▶ 評 解

此回答優點在於除了陳述正面的離職原因外，也說明在上一個工作的良好表現。

單字　🎧 MP3 009

❶ **burden** [`bɝdn] *n.* 重負，重擔；負擔
❷ **utilize** [`jut!ˌaɪz] *v.* 利用
❸ **replace** [rɪ`ples] *v.* 取代
❹ **post** [post] *n.* 職位；職守
❺ **seek** [sik] *v.* 尋找；追求

用句型取勝

frankly speaking 坦白說

✍ 要注意

1. speak要加ing。
2. 同義詞有：to be honest；in fact；actually；as a matter of fact。
3. frankly speaking 與 generally speaking 不同。general speaking 指「通常來說」。

例句：

- Frankly speaking, I don't always agree with my previous boss.
  坦白說，我並不是總是和我之前的老闆意見相同。
- Frankly speaking, I think she is the person who has the best qualifications needed for this open position.
  坦白說，我認為她有這個職缺需要的最好條件。

be+grateful+to+sb 感激某人

✍ 要注意

1. be grateful to sb for sth（名詞或動名詞），或者後面接 to+原形動詞或 that+完整子句。
2. be grateful to sb= thank sb=appreciate sb，用 be+grateful (adj) 表現，後面要加 to。

例句：

- I am grateful to have this opportunity to work for you.
  我很感激有這個機會為您工作。
  I am grateful for having this opportunity to work for you.
  =I thank(appreciate) for having this opportunity to work for you.

💡 換個說法令人眼睛一亮

(1)I resigned because my organization has gone through

multiple restructurings and unfortunately I was shifted to a job that doesn't match my interests and skills.

我辭職因為公司經歷了幾波重組。不幸地我被轉調到一個不符合我興趣和專長的工作。

= The multiple restructurings my organization has gone through made me resign because I was shifted to a job that doesn't match my interests and skills.

= After several corporate restructurings, I left my previous job because I was shifted to a job that doesn't match my interests and skills.

⑵ I've worked for many years with an organization where work never seems to be a burden and a healthy office environment is an additional advantage.

我在之前的公司工作多年，在那工作從來就不是負擔，健康的工作環境是另一項優點。

= The organization I have worked for many years offered me a healthy office environment in which work never seems to be a burden.

= For many years, I have worked in a healthy office environment and work never seems to be a burden to me.

⑶ I am grateful to my previous company because they created a good platform for me to perform when I was just starting out.

我很感激我之前的公司，因為他們在我職涯開始時替我創造了一個很好的平台讓我表現。

= My previous company offered me opportunities to perform when I was a freshman, and therefore I am grateful to them.

= I am thankful for the good platform my previous company created for me to perform when I was just starting out.

2-2 求職目的與動機

03 What will you do if you don't get this job?

How will you react if you are not offered the job?

如果你沒有被錄取，你會怎麼做？

▶ 題 解

不是每位應徵者都會被錄取，這個問題在問你對在目標公司工作的動機有多強與對自己取得這個工作有多少信心。回答重點要說明會改進自己，讓自己更具競爭力，也要表達相信自己是這個職位的最佳人選與對目標公司的高度動機。

▶ 短回答 —— 基本版 🎧 MP3 010

I will try to improve my interview skills and my weak points so that in the next interview I can perform better. However, I do feel that my experience in the department and with the team would make me the best candidate for this position.

我會試著改進自己的面試技巧和我的不足之處，以便在接下來的面試中我可以表現良好。不過，我真的覺得我在部門和團隊的經驗讓我成為這個職位的最佳候選人。

▶ 短回答 —— 進階版

I believe that the committee seeks for the best fit in the position. So if you don't hire me, I will wait for constructive feedback to improve myself for the next opportunity. However, I am sure that I am the one you seek, both as I am and as I will develop.

我相信委員會旨在為這個位置尋找最合適的人選。所以，如果您沒有僱用我，我會等待建設性的回饋意見為下一個機會改進自己。不過，我相信，我就是您尋找的人，無論是現在的我或是將來更好的我。

ⓞ 評 解

回答中都有說明會改進自己與對自己有自信。

ⓞ 長回答 🎧 MP3 011

Every experience is an opportunity for growth. First, with your permission, I would like to learn what I could have done to make my application more compelling. Secondly, I am convinced that this is the company that I'd like to work for. So, I ask your permission to check with you in 3 months to see if any other opportunities have arisen. Finally, if you were impressed by my candidacy but unable to place me at this time, I'd ask if you might be able to introduce me to a colleague who works in an area that you think might be more suited to my talents so that I might ask that person how I can best prepare myself for any opportunities that arise in that department.

Part 2 99%會問的面試題

每一次經歷都是成長的機會。首先，有您的允許下，我希望可以知道我可以做甚麼來讓我的工作申請更令人信服。其次，我確信這是我想工作的公司。所以，我想請求您的許可，讓我在3個月內看看是否有任何其他的機會。最後，如果你對我的候選資格印象深刻，但這次還不能給我合適的位子，我會請求你也許可以把我介紹給你認為可能是在更適合我的才華領域裡工作的同事，讓我能問那個人，我如何能夠為該部門的任何機會更佳地準備自己。

ⓞ 評 解

內容重點在說明會透過管道了解自己不足之處並進而改進自己。

🍎 單 字 🎧 MP3 012

❶ **permission** [pə`mɪʃən] *n*. 允許，許可，同意
❷ **application** [ˌæpli`keiʃən] *n*. 申請，請求；申請書
❸ **compelling** [kəm`pɛlɪŋ] *adj*. 令人信服的
❹ **convinced** [kən`vɪnst] *adj*. 確信的
❺ **candidacy** [`kændɪdəsɪ] *n*. 候選資格

用句型取勝

人 beV +convinced that ~ 某人確信～

要注意

1. that 後加完整句子。
2. 也可用人 beV +convinced of ~表示，但 of 後加名詞。

例句：

· You will soon be convinced that I am the right person for this position.
  = You will soon be convinced of my qualification for this position.
  你一定會相信我是這個職位的適當人選。

· I was convinced that we were doing the right thing.
  = I was convinced of the rightfulness of the thing we are doing.
  我堅信我們做的事是對的。

人 beV + impressed with/ by + N：對～印象深刻

要注意

1. impress 除上述用法外，還有以下三種用法：
   impress A with B：用 B 使 A 印象深刻。
   Ex: You impress me with your extensive experience in marketing.
   你在行銷的廣泛經驗使我印象深刻。
   A + make/ leave an impression on B：A 給 B~印象。
   Ex: You made a great first impression on me.
   你給我很好的第一印象。
   impression of + N：對...的印象。
   Ex: My impression of this company is very good.
   我對這個公司的印象非常好。
2. 這四種不同的用法要注意不同的介係詞。

例句：

· I hope you will be impressed with/ by my resume.
我希望你會對我的履歷印象深刻。

· My previous boss was impressed with the work I had done.
我之前的老闆對我所做的工作非常滿意。

💡 換個說法令人眼睛一亮

⑴ If you don't hire me, I will wait for constructive feedback to improve myself for the next opportunity.
如果您不僱用我，我會等待建設性的回饋意見為下一個機會改進自己。

= If I am not offered the job, I hope you can give me constructive feedback for improving myself for the next opportunity.
= If you don't hire me, I will wait for constructive feedback that I can use for improving myself when the next opportunity arrives.

⑵ With your permission, I would like to learn what I could have done to make my application more compelling.
有您的允許下，我希望可以知道我可以做甚麼來讓我的工作申請更令人信服。

= If you agree, I would like to know how my application could have been to make myself more competitive.
= With your permission, I would like to learn how I can improve my application to make it more compelling.

⑶ I am convinced that this is the company that I'd like to work for.
我確信這是我想工作的公司。

= I strongly believe that this is an ideal company for me.
= Your company is the one I always want to work for.

2-3 學歷與教育訓練

Besides academic knowledge, what else did you learn in your college days?

In addition to academic knowledge, what do you think you have learnt in college?

除了學業知識外,你在大學時期還學到了甚麼?

▶ 題 解

大多的面試官都希望錄取的人不是只會死讀書,而是會多方學習的人。這樣的問題可以辨識出你是哪種人。回答著重在闡述求學中獲得的寶貴經驗,包括時間管理、人際相處、獨立思考、團隊合作、解決問題的能力等。這些也通常是很多行業所要求的特質與技巧。

▶ 短回答 —— 基本版 🎧 MP3 013

I learned how to conduct a project, how to collect and analyze data, and how to complete the project on time with my team members. The process of doing a project itself is a very meaningful learning experience for me.

我學習到如何做專題,如何收集與分析資料,與如何和團隊成員在期限內完成這個專題。做專題的這個過程本身就是一個非常有意義的學習經驗。

▶ 短回答 —— 進階版

In college, we had many chances of conducting a team project. I was trained to work effectively and efficiently in a team. During teamwork, I also improved my interpersonal skills, independent thinking skills, and problem-solving skills.

在大學裡我們有很多做團隊專題的機會。我被訓練在團隊中有效率地工作。在團隊合作的過程中,我也改進了我人際交往的能力、獨立思考的能力、與解決問題的能力。

評 解

這兩個回答都點出有學到職場上須具備的技能如團隊合作、人際交往與獨立思考。不足之處在是可以再多著墨如何學習到獨立思考與解決問題的能力。

長回答 🎧 MP3 014

The biggest challenge I had was to produce a fifteen-thousand-word paper. I had to collect data from libraries, government offices, and local business centers. I learned how to persuade others and therefore obtained meaningful data. Despite deadline pressure, I couldn't hasten those people who provided data to me in order to maintain good relationships with them. This experience made me confident about my capability to organize and carry out a big project. Furthermore, I was assigned as a student representative in my sophomore year to provide services to other students in my department. I created a good channel of communication, listened to my fellow students' needs, and found ways to satisfy their needs. I learned so much by serving others.

最大的挑戰應該算是撰寫一萬五千字的論文。當時我必須到圖書館、政府部門、當地商務中心蒐集資料。我學習到如何說服對方才能拿到有意義的資料。雖然我有期限的壓力，可是又不能催促那些提供我資料的人，才能和他們維持良好的關係。這個經驗使我對自己組織和執行大型專案的能力感到有信心。再者，我在大二那年被指派為學生代表，為我們系上的同學們提供服務。我建立一個良好的溝通管道，傾聽同學們的需求並找方法滿足他們的需求。藉由服務他人，我學習到很多。

 評 解

這個回答詳細敘述了完成一個論文在課業之外所需要的人際溝通技巧與擔任學生代表為同學服務的態度精神。這些都是職場上所需的技能和特質。

🍎 **單字** 🎧 MP3 015

❶ **challenge** [ˋtʃælɪndʒ] *n.* 挑戰
❷ **persuade** [pɚˋswed] *v.* 說服
❸ **capability** [ˌkepəˋbɪlətɪ] *n.* 能力

Part

2

99
％
會
問
的
面
試
題

❹ **assign** [ə`saɪn] *v.* 分派、指定
❺ **representative** [rɛprɪ`zɛntətɪv] *n.* 代表

用句型取勝

Despite + N. ~ 雖然（儘管）～

要注意

1. 介係詞「雖然；儘管」despite (= in spite of)，用於承接語意有所轉折的句子，後方都需搭配「名詞」。而「雖然；儘管」despite the fact that 和 in spite of the fact that 為「連接詞」，後方需連接「句子」（主詞+動詞）。

例句：

· Despite not having related working experiences, being a quick learner makes me confident that I am qualified for this job.
儘管沒有相關工作經驗，學習速度快的我有自信可以勝任這份工作。

A + makes+ B + adj. A 使 B 變得如何～

要注意

1. make 在這當「使役動詞」，意思是「使」或「讓」或「叫」，後可加形容詞或原形動詞。加形容詞表示「A 使 B 變得（感覺）如何」；加動詞表示「A 叫 B 做甚麼事」。
2. 使役動詞接過去分詞：使役動詞後面接的受詞（多為事物，也可為人）表達了接受其後的動作，也就是被動地完成了某事時，受詞後接的是過去分詞。

例句：

· The opportunities you offer for newly graduates make me very interested in this position.
您提供給應屆畢業生的機會讓我對這個職位非常感興趣。

· Having no chance of advancement made me decide to leave my previous employment.

沒有升遷機會讓我決定離開之前的工作。

💡 換個說法令人眼睛一亮

⑴ The biggest challenge I had was to produce a fifteen-thousand-word paper.

最大的挑戰應該算是撰寫一萬五千字的論文。

= Producing a fifteen-thousand-word paper was the biggest challenge I've ever had.

= The most challenging thing I've ever done was to produce a fifteen-thousand-word paper.

⑵ Despite deadline pressure, I couldn't hasten those people who provided data to me in order to maintain good relationships with them.

雖然我有期限的壓力，可是又不能催促那些提供我資料的人，才能和他們維持良好的關係。

= Although I was under deadline pressure, I had to be patient with those people who provided data to me in order to maintain good relationships with them.

= In order to maintain good relationships with those people who provided data to me, I never hastened them in spite of deadline pressure.

⑶ I was assigned as a student representative in my sophomore year to provide services to other students in my department.

我在大二那年被指派為學生代表，為我們系上的同學們提供服務。

= Being assigned as a student representative in my second year of college, I provided services to other students in my department.

= In my sophomore year, I got the chance to serve other students in my department because I was assigned as a student representative.

You are a newly graduate, and therefore lack of working experience. Do you think you are qualified for this position?

A newly graduate like you usually doesn't have sufficient working experience. How do you think you are capable of doing this job?

你是應屆畢業生，缺乏工作經驗。你認為你能勝任這份工作嗎？

▶ 題解

這樣的面試題目很常見，目的在瞭解應屆畢業的應徵者如何彌補自身在工作經歷上的不足。應徵者的回覆最好是提到可以彌補工作經驗不足的個人特質。例如學習力強、誠懇、負責任、團隊精神、善於溝通、勤奮等。如果有打工兼職的經驗也可説明，主動提及在兼職中良好的工作表現。

▶ 短回答 — 基本版 🎧 MP3 016

As a newly graduate, there's no doubt that I am lack of full-time working experience. However, I had some part-time jobs during my summer and winter vacations. I did learn a lot from these experiences and because I am good in teamwork and communication, I got very good feedbacks from my supervisors.

作為一個應屆畢業生、毫無疑問地我缺乏正職工作經驗。然而我在寒暑假期間都有兼職打工。 我從這些工作經驗學到很多且因為我擅長團隊合作與溝通，我的主管對我有很好的評價。

▶ 短回答 — 進階版

I know one of the disadvantages newly graduates have is lacking full-time working experience. Consequently, I worked part-time during my summer and winter breaks. These working experiences are invaluable to me. I not only learned a lot but also received very positive feedbacks from my supervisors due to my superior work performance.

我了解應屆畢業生的弱點之一就是缺乏正職工作經驗。因此我在寒暑假期間都有兼職工作。這些工作經驗對我來說是非常寶貴的。我不但學到很多而且我優異的工作表現贏得主管非常正面的評價。

▶ 評 解

兩個簡答的優點是有提到可以彌補工作經驗不足的個人特質或是兼職經驗。不足之處是可以再多著墨在兼職經驗中學到了甚麼。

▶ 長回答　🎧 MP3 017

Knowing that lacking full-time work experience will be my weakness when I am looking for a job right after graduation, I worked part-time during summer and winter breaks. These work experiences made me realize that a real job in the real world is far more complicated than what we learned from books. But since I am ambitious, diligent, and have a strong sense of responsibility, I learned very practical knowledge and professional skills while doing these jobs. I successfully fulfilled every job task assigned to me. These valuable experiences benefited me a lot. As a result, I am confident that what I learnt from school and my part-time work experiences makes me qualified for this position.

了解到沒有正職工作經驗會是我大學畢業時找工作的弱點，我在寒暑假都有做兼職工作。我從中發現在現實世界裡的真實工作遠比書本上的知識複雜許多。但是因為我企圖心強，勤奮、並有很強的責任心，我從這些工作經驗中學到很多實用的知識與專業的技能。我成功地完成每項指派給我的任務；這些寶貴的經驗讓我受益匪淺。因此我有信心從學校所學的知識及兼職所獲得的經驗使我能勝任這個職位。

▶ 評 解

應徵者先正面回應缺乏正職工作經驗本來就是應屆畢業生都要面對的問題。接著用自己的兼職經驗補足自身的缺點。

單字 🎧 MP3 018

❶ **newly graduate** [`njulɪ] [`grædʒʊˌet] *n.* 應屆畢業生
❷ **supervisor** [sjupəˈvaɪzə] *n.* 主管
❸ **invaluable** [ɪnˈvæljəbl] *adj.* 寶貴的，非常有價值的
❹ **ambitious** [æmˈbɪʃəs] *adj.* 有企圖心的
❺ **diligent** [`dɪlədʒənt] *adj.* 勤奮的

用句型取勝

There is no doubt that …… 毫無疑問地，……

🖐 要注意

1. 相同意思不同的表示方法有：
   There is no doubt that ……
   = It is without doubt ……
   = Certainly, ……
   = No doubt (that) ……

2. There is no doubt that + 完整句子
   There is no doubt about + 名詞或動名詞

例句：

- There is no doubt that I am able to complete the marketing plan in one week.
  毫無疑問地，我能夠在一週內完成行銷計畫。

- No doubt I learned a lot from my part-time work experiences, and therefore I am confident that I am capable of doing this job.
  毫無疑問地，我從兼職工作學到很多，因此我有自信我能勝任這份工作。

Knowing that + 完整句子，S + V …… 得知（瞭解到）……

🖐 要注意

1. 要以動名詞（knowing）開頭，而非原型動詞或不定詞。也就是說
   （○）Knowing that ……

（×）Know that ......

（×）To know that ......

2. **Knowing that** 後要加完整句子而非名詞或動名詞。

例句：

- Knowing that I had done my best, I never feel nervous before an examination.

  知道我已盡全力，我在考試前從不緊張。

- Knowing that a master degree is helpful for my career, I went back to school after two year of working.

  了解到碩士學位對我的職業是有幫助的，我在工作兩年後回到學校。

💡 換個說法令人眼睛一亮

⑴ I not only learned a lot but also received very positive feedbacks from my supervisors due to my superior work performance.

我不但學到很多，而且我優異的工作表現贏得主管非常正面的評價。

= I learned a lot and my supervisors had given very positive feedbacks on my superior work performance.

= Not only did I learn a lot, but I also received very positive feedbacks from my supervisors due to my superior work performance.

⑵ Do you think you are qualified for this position?

你認為你能勝任這份工作嗎？

= Do you think you have the qualification for this job?

= Do you think you have the capability of doing this job?

⑶ These valuable experiences benefited me a lot.

這些寶貴的經驗讓我受益匪淺。

= I benefited greatly from these valuable experiences.

= These valuable experiences are very beneficial to me.

Part

2

99％會問的面試題

Why did you choose your university?

Why did you choose to attend this university?

你當初為何選擇就讀這所大學？

▶ 題解

關於教育方面的問話重點之一是為何選擇某所大學，答案應該導向這所學校能提供應試者準備應徵的目標職位所需的技能。回答的方向有：學校的整體聲望很好、某個科系特別強、學校資源多、師資設備研究能力等為全國一流、提供健全的教育訓練，尤其強調某些課程對目標職位特別有幫助。

▶ 短回答 — 基本版 🎧 MP3 019

I chose National Cheng Kung University because the graduates from this university have been rated as domestic business' favorite employees for years. Furthermore, its faculty and facilities are one of the best among universities. Therefore, I never regret choosing National Cheng Kung University.

我選擇國立成功大學因為它所教育出來的畢業生多年來都被評比為國內企業界最愛的員工。除此之外，它的師資和設備是國內數一數二的學校。因此我從沒後悔過我選擇了國立成功大學。

▶ 短回答 — 進階版

I have always wanted to be a civil engineer. The main reason I decided to attend National Cheng Kung University was that its outstanding faculty and facilities provided adequate training on practical knowledge and skills needed to be a professional civil engineer.

我一直都希望成為一個土木工程師。我決定就讀國立成功大學最主要是因為這所學校擁有傑出的師資和設備,能提供作為一個專業土木工程師所需的實務知識和技能方面足夠的訓練。

▶ **評解**

兩個回答都指出優秀的師資設備是選校的主要原因。進階版回答較優之處在於強調選校的決定對目標職位(土木工程師)上的幫助。

▶ **長回答** 🎧 MP3 020

I chose Shih Chien University because I like their module options, work experience opportunities, and extra-curricular activities. In addition, my career goal is to become a fashion designer and their fashion design department is one of the best in Taiwan. The courses and internship opportunities they offered equipped me with the practical skills needed in the fashion design industry. Under my tutor's guidance, I also participated in some fashion design competitions and won several awards. As a result, choosing Shih Chien University was one of the best decisions I have made.

我選擇實踐大學是因為我喜歡他們提供的課程選項、工作機會、課外活動。再者,我的職涯目標是成為一個服裝設計師,而他們的服裝設計系在台灣是數一數二的。他們提供的課程和實習機會讓我具備了服裝設計產業所需的實務技能。在導師的輔導下,我也參加一些服裝設計競賽並贏得幾個獎項。因此,選擇實踐大學是我做過最好的決定之一。

▶ **評解**

這個回答不只說明了選校動機,也陳述自己具備目標職位(服裝設計師)所需的專業知識與技能。

🍎 **單字** 🎧 MP3 021

❶ **faculty** [`fækltɪ] *n.* 大學教師

❷ **facility** [fə`sɪlətɪ] *n.* 設備,設施

❸ **extra-curricular** [ˌɛkstrəkə`rɪkjələ] *a.* 課外的;業餘的

❹ **internship** [`ɪntɝn͵ʃɪp] *n.* 實習

❺ **award** [ə`wɔrd] *n.* 獎,獎品;獎狀

Part

2

99％會問的面試題

用句型取勝

regret +Ving 後悔做過～事

👉 **要注意**

1. regret後加動名詞的一般式或完成式都表示對已經做過的事感到後悔。
2. regret後加 that+子句同樣表示對已經做過的事感到後悔。
3. 但regret後接不定詞，表示「對要做的事感到遺憾」，這時常用 to say, to tell you, to inform you 等，相當於 I'm sorry to say/ tell/ inform you that...。

例句：

· Do you think Bill will regret quitting the job?
  =Do you think Bill will regret that he quitted the job?
  你認為 Bill 會後悔辭去這個工作嗎？

· I never regret telling my boss the truth.
  = I never regret that I told my boss the truth.
  我從沒後悔跟老闆說實話。

participate in 參加～

👉 **要注意**

1. participate in 參與；參加（某項活動），常與 in 連用。
2. participate in = take part in = join in

例句：

· I recommended one of my colleagues to participate in the new project.
  我推薦我的一位同事參與這項新專案。

· I participated in evaluating the performances of all the contractors and suppliers.
  我參與對所有承包商和供應商的表現評估。

換個說法令人眼睛一亮

(1) The main reason I decided to attend National Cheng Kung University was that its outstanding faculty and facilities provided adequate training on practical knowledge and skills needed to be a professional civil engineer.

我決定就讀國立成功大學最主要是因為這所學校擁有傑出的師資和設備，能提供作為一個專業土木工程師所需的實務知識和技能方面足夠的訓練。

= I decided to attend National Cheng Kung University because its outstanding faculty and facilities provided adequate training on practical knowledge and skills needed to be a professional civil engineer.

Part

2

99%會問的面試題

(2) The courses and internship opportunities they offered equipped me with the practical skills needed in the fashion design industry.

他們提供的課程和實習機會讓我具備了服裝設計產業所需的實務技能。

=I obtained the practical skills needed in the fashion design industry from the courses and the internship opportunities they offered.
=They offered the courses and internship opportunities that trained me to be a professional fashion designer.

(3) As a result, choosing Shih Chien University was one of the best decisions I have made.

因此，選擇實踐大學是我做過最好的決定之一。

= Therefore, one of the best decisions I have made was choosing Shih Chien University.
= So, I'd say I never regret choosing Shih Chien University and this was a very good decision I made in life.

04 How would you plan your academic study if you have the second chance?

How would you plan your academic study differently?

你如果你有第二次機會，你會如何重新規劃你的學業？

▶ 題 解

這個問題在應徵基礎工作(或針對大學畢業生的工作)時是很常見的。回答時要注意不要講到犯了甚麼嚴重的錯誤，讓你非常遺憾且對目標職位是非常不利的。回答是可以多朝希望多拿點不同的課，或開發自己課餘的興趣等對應徵工作較無殺傷力的答案。

▶ 短回答 —— 基本版　🎧 MP3 022

The majority of my coursework, excluding core curriculum requirements, is in science. While I am doing what I love, I wish I had taken advantage of a wider variety of courses so I could have graduated with a more well-rounded education.

我的大部分課程，不包括核心課程的要求，都是在科學。雖然我是學我喜歡的，我還是希望我當初有採取了更多元化的課程優勢，在畢業時完成更全面的教育。

▶ 短回答 —— 進階版

I always wanted to learn music and I regret I didn't use college as a vehicle to explore that passion. When I was in grade school, I played saxophone. I would try to fall in love again with music if I had another chance to do so in college.

我一直想學音樂，我後悔我沒有利用大學時期來探索這個熱情。當我在研究所就讀時，我才會吹薩克斯風。如果我再有一次機會上大學的話，我會嘗試再次愛上音樂。

▶ 評 解

兩個回答（希望採取了更多元化的課程優勢、學音樂）都不會成為應徵工作時的個人缺點。

▶ 長回答 🎧 MP3 023

The only regret I have during my time in college is that I wasted too much time for personal needs and other stuff rather than studying. If I had a chance once more, I would spend the whole 4 years of college studying my most interested subjects which I had only 2 years in fact to understand its meaning. I also wish I had pursued a master degree in my field. I believe education is a key to personal success. That's why nowadays I attend night classes to acquire professional knowledge needed in the job market.

我在大學時唯一的遺憾是我浪費了太多的時間在個人需要和其他東西，而不是讀書。如果我有再一次機會，我會花整整4年大學時光研讀我感興趣的科目，我其實只有花 2 年去理解最感興趣的科目的含義。我還希望當時在我的領域我攻讀碩士學位。我相信教育是個人成功的關鍵。這就是為什麼現在我參加晚間課程來獲得在就業市場所需的專業知識。

▶ 評 解

後悔當時沒有好好讀書，或追求更高學位是很多人會有的遺憾，只要表明現在求知若渴就可彌補缺憾。

🍎 單字 🎧 MP3 024

❶ **regret** [rɪ`grɛt] *v.* 懊悔；因……而遺憾
❷ **waste** [west] *v.* 浪費；濫用；未充分利用
❸ **personal** [`pɝsn!] *adj.* 個人的，私人的
❹ **stuff** [stʌf] *n.* 物品，東西
❺ **acquire** [ə`kwaɪr] *v.* 取得，獲得

Part

2

99％會問的面試題

用句型取勝

regret that ...... 對～感到後悔

👆 要注意

1. that 後面的子句要用過去式，表示對做過的事感到後悔。
2. 也可用 regret + Ving 表示對做過的事感到後悔。

例句：

· I regret that I didn't work part-time to gain some working experience in college.
· I regret not working part-time to gain some working experience in college.
  我後悔大學時沒有打工以增加工作經驗。
· I regret that I made such a silly mistake.
  我後悔犯了那樣一個愚蠢的錯誤。

I wish (that) ...... 與過去事實相反

👆 要注意

1. I wish (that) + S + 過去式動詞/ were... → 與現在事實相反
2. I wish (that) + S + had + PP... → 與過去事實相反
3. 也可用 if 來表示與過去事實相反的句子。
   If + S1 + 過去完成式 (had+P.P.) ···, S + would/ should/ could/ might + have + P.P. ···

例句：

· Retrospectively, I wish I hadn't done that.
  回想起來，我要是沒有那樣做就好了（與過去事實相反。事實是他當時是那樣做了）。
· I wish I had listened to my parents and pursued my studies abroad. Then I could have had better foreign language skills.

· If I had listened to my parents and pursued my studies abroad, I could have had better foreign language skills.

我希望我當初有聽我父母的話去海外讀書，這樣我就會有較佳的外語能力了（與過去事實相反。事實是他當時沒有聽父母的話去海外讀書）。

💡 換個說法令人眼睛一亮

(1) The majority of my coursework, excluding core curriculum requirements, is in science.

我的大部分課程，不包括必修的核心課程都是在科學。

= Excluding core curriculum requirements, most of the courses I have taken are about science.

= Except for core curriculum requirements, the majority of my coursework is in science.

(2) I wish I had taken advantage of a wider variety of courses so I could have graduated with a more well-rounded education.

我希望我當初有採取了更多元化的課程優勢，在畢業時完成更全面的教育。

= I wish I had taken more different courses and so I could have received a more well-rounded education when I graduated.

= I regret that I didn't take advantage of a wider variety of courses. If I had done so, I could have graduated with a more well-rounded education.

(3) I believe education is a key to personal success.

我相信教育是個人成功的關鍵。

= I believe good education leads to personal success.

= I believe a person can have more chances to be successful if he/she received good education.

2-3 學歷與教育訓練

05 How do you prepare for exams?

What would you do to perform well on tests?

你如何準備考試？

▶ 題解

這個問題常用來詢問社會新鮮人（剛從學校畢業的應徵者）。剛從學校畢業的人通常沒有太多工作經驗，於是面試官會著重在了解其在學校的表現，以預測此人的工作能力。學校如何準備考試會反映在將來工作上會如何執行專案以達到主管的要求。

▶ 短回答 ── 基本版 🎧 MP3 025

I like to study with a group. Typically, I get together with a few classmates and study. We review notes, quiz each other, and provide moral support. I have always worked better in groups and that is reflected in my study habits.

我喜歡和一群人一起學習。通常情況下，我會找幾個同學一起學習。我們複習筆記，考考對方，並提供精神上的支持。我一向在團體裡的工作效率會更好，這也反映在我的學習習慣。

▶ 短回答 ── 進階版

When preparing for a test, I always review section by section until I have mastered all of the concepts presented. I also like to make charts, graphs, illustrations and use real life examples to comprehend difficult concepts.

在準備考試時，我總是一部分一部分地複習，直到我掌握了所有的概念。我也會畫圖表、曲線圖、圖解和利用現實生活中的例子來真正理解複雜的概念。

▶ 評 解

基本版回答説明善於團隊合作，進階版強調會利用圖表等還理解複雜概念，這都是對工作有益的技能。

▶ 長回答　🎧 MP3 026

When preparing for exams, I design my own time-table which directs all the material that has to be covered and tells myself how much is needed to be studied each day. I make a schedule of every subject with different priorities. I give tough subjects and the ones I'm weak at more hours, and easier ones are given fewer hours with sufficient intervals between each subject. Very importantly, my time-table has breaks in between. On the day before the exam, I relax myself without doing any study, have a good night of sleep, and then I usually perform well on the next day.

當準備考試，我設計我自己的時間表，時間表會涵蓋所有必須讀的資料，並告訴自己每天需要研讀多少資料。每一個科目的時間表應有不同的優先順序。我給棘手的科目和我比較弱的科目較多時間，而比較容易的科目分配到的時間較少，各學科之間有足夠的間隔。重要的是我的時間表都有包括休息時間。在考試的前一天，我放鬆自己沒有做任何學習，有一個良好的睡眠，然後我通常在第二天表現良好。

▶ 評 解

回答中闡述如果作時間分配來準備考試代表自己是會規劃好時間的人，這對工作也是很有幫助的。

🍎 單 字　🎧 MP3 027

❶ schedule [`skɛdʒʊl] *n.* 計畫表；日程安排表
❷ priority [praɪˋɔrətɪ] *n.* 優先，重點；優先權
❸ tough [tʌf] *adj.* 棘手的，費勁的
❹ sufficient [səˋfɪʃənt] *adj.* 足夠的，充分的
❺ interval [ˋɪntɚv!] *n.* 間隔；距離

用句型取勝

prepare for ~ 為～作準備

☞ 要注意

- prepare 和 prepare for 兩者在用法上一般都可以互相轉換，但是從本質上看它們還是有差別的。prepare for sth 為了 sth 而做準備工作，prepare sth 是準備 sth。

例句：

- I have been preparing for the presentation for the whole week.
  這整個禮拜我都在為這個簡報作準備。
- I always hope for the best and prepare for the worst.
  我總是抱最好的希望，最壞的打算。

till/ untill ~ 直到

☞ 要注意

1. 當主句是否定句時，它引出的意思是「直到（某時）（某動作）才（發生）」，如果將 not until... 的結構放在句首，那麼主句要寫成倒裝句。
2. 另外，until 可以放在句首而 till 則不行。

例句：

- I usually study till/ until midnight in order to perform well on the test the next day.
- I usually study all day and don't sleep until midnight in order to perform well on the test the next day.
  為了要在隔天的考試有好的表現，我通常讀書讀到午夜。
- I always say to myself: Never put off till tomorrow what you can do today.
  我總是告訴自己：今日事今日畢。

換個說法令人眼睛一亮

(1) I also like to make charts, graphs, illustrations and use real life examples to comprehend difficult concepts.

我也會畫圖表、曲線圖、圖解和利用現實生活中的例子來真正理解複雜的概念。

= I comprehend difficult concepts by making charts, graphs, illustrations, and using real life examples.

= Charts, graphs, illustrations and real life examples are helpful for me to comprehend difficult concepts.

(2) When preparing for a test, I always review section by section until I have mastered all of the concepts presented.

在準備考試時，我總是一部分一部分地複習，直到我掌握了所有的概念。

= In order to do well on tests, I fully review each section and make sure I comprehend all the concepts.

= When preparing for a test, I make sure all the sections are reviewed and all the concepts are comprehended.

(3) I give tough subjects and the ones I'm weak more hours, and easier ones are given fewer hours with sufficient intervals between each subject.

我給棘手的科目和我比較弱的科目較多小時，而比較容易的科目分配到的時間較少，各學科之間有足夠的間隔。

= I spend more time on tough subjects and the ones I'm weak, while fewer hours on easier ones. Besides, there are sufficient intervals between each subject.

= More hours are assigned to tough subjects and the ones I'm weak, while easier subjects are given less time. There are sufficient intervals between each subject.

Part

2

99％會問的面試題

2-3 學歷與教育訓練

Q 06 What college subjects did you like best? Why?

What was your favorite subject in college? Why?

大學甚麼科目你最喜歡，為什麼？

▶ 題 解

這個問題常用來詢問社會新鮮人（剛從學校畢業的應徵者）。你大學最喜歡的科目最好和目標職位相關。如果無確切相關，也要說明拿這門課為你帶來甚麼益處，而這個益處是對工作有幫助的。

▶ 短回答 — 基本版 🎧 MP3 028

My English courses were most beneficial for me. I love to write. I enjoy writing a creative narrative or poetry. The skills I have developed in my English classes have been extremely beneficial to my other coursework.

我修的英語課程是對我最有幫助的。我熱愛寫作。我喜歡寫原創的故事或詩。我在英語課所學到的技能對我學習其他課程幫助很大。

▶ 短回答 — 進階版

I knew nothing about music or art when entering college, but when I took my first class, I fell in love. They act as a getaway from the strenuous world of academia. It also allows me to express myself creatively, which I never knew I could do.

進入大學時，我對音樂或藝術一無所知，但是當我上了第一次課，我就愛上它了。他們讓我從繁重的學術世界逃離。它還允許我表達自己的創造性，這是我從來不知道我能做到的。

▶ 評 解

基本版回答適用於應徵與寫作相關且須英語能力的工作。進階版説明除了自己的專業外也具備創造力。

▶ 長回答 🎧 MP3 029

I really enjoyed majoring in electrical engineering and it really helped me to prepare for my career, but the class I enjoyed the most is probably a couple of psychology classes I took. Although it didn't help me in any technical way, I learned some knowledge about human behavior and learned how the brain works. I started to understand the reasons for my strengths and weaknesses instead of just knowing them. Also, it helped me to understand people who are different from me.

我真的很喜歡主修電機工程,它對我的職業生涯幫助很大,但我最喜歡的是幾門我修的心理學課程。,雖然它並沒有對我的技術有幫助,但我學習到一些關於人類行為的知識,並理解大腦如何運作。我開始明白為何我自己有這些長處和弱點,而不是只知道自己的優劣勢為何。此外,它也幫助我了解與我不同的人。

▶ 評 解

技術人員通常人際互動技巧較差。所以當一位要應徵工程師類別職位的人陳述最喜歡的科目是心理學時等於向面試官説明他同時具備技術與人際互動技巧。

🍎 單字 🎧 MP3 030

❶ **electrical** [ɪˋlɛktrɪk!] *adj.* 電機的
❷ **psychology** [saɪˋkɑlədʒɪ] *n.* 心理學
❸ **technical** [ˋtɛknɪk!] *adj.* 工藝的;技術的;科技的
❹ **behavior** [bɪˋhevjɚ] *n.* 行為,舉止;態度
❺ **brain** [bren] *n.* 腦,腦袋

用句型取勝

sth is beneficial for sb/ sth 某事物對某人（某事物）是有幫助的

要注意

1. 介係詞也可用 to 取代。
2. beneficial 也可用 helpful 取代。

例句：

- Sometimes I asked myself: Are part-time Jobs beneficial/ helpful to / for college students?
  有時我問自己：打工對大學生有益嗎？
- I think joint venture will be beneficial/ helpful to/ for both of us.
  我認為合資經營對我們雙方都有好處。

sth allows sb to do sth 某事物讓某人可以（允許某人）做某事

要注意

1. 也可用被動句表示：sb is allowed to do sth。

例句：

- My previous job at ABC Company didn't allow me to have afternoon tea breaks.
  = I was not allowed to have afternoon tea breaks when I worked for ABC Company.
  我之前在 ABC 公司工作時不被允許有下午茶休息時間。
- I never allow myself to be ruled by emotion.
  我從不允許自己感情用事。

換個說法令人眼睛一亮

(1) The skills I have developed in my English classes have been extremely beneficial in my other coursework.
我在英語課所學到的技能對我學習其他課程幫助很大。

= The training I received in my English classes has been very helpful for my other coursework.
= The skills I have developed in my English classes helped me to learn well in other coursework.

(2) The class I enjoyed the most is probably a couple of psychology classes I took.
我最喜歡的是幾門我修的心理學課程。

= My favorite courses are related to psychology.
= Those psychology courses I took are my favorite.

(3) I really enjoyed majoring in electrical engineering and it really helped me to prepare for my career
我真的很喜歡主修電機工程，它對我的職業生涯幫助很大。

= I like my electrical engineering major very much and it helped me a lot when preparing for my career.
= I enjoy my electrical engineering major very much and this major is helpful for my career.

Part

2

99％會問的面試題

2-3 學歷與教育訓練

07 Please describe your most rewarding college experience.

What is your most rewarding college experience?

請描述大學時你有過對你最有幫助的經驗。

▶ 題 解

這個問題常用來詢問社會新鮮人（剛從學校畢業的應徵者）。回答時要強調這個經驗給你帶來甚麼成就或益處。而這個成就或益處必須是對工作有幫助的，例如語言能力、社交能力等。義工服務也會獲青睞因那代表你對社會人群的付出。

▶ 短回答 — 基本版 🎧 MP3 031

During my senior year, I volunteered to be a tutor at my college's writing center. It was such a rewarding experience to see students who came to us stressed and anxious, leaving the center feeling confident in themselves as writers.

在我四年級時，我自願擔任我大學寫作中心的助教。這是一個有益的經驗讓我看到原本前來求助的焦慮、緊張的學生，離開中心時的自信並自豪自己是作者。

▶ 短回答 — 進階版

Getting my diploma was my most rewarding college experience. I was challenged everyday by my courses, and I worked very hard to earn my degree. I have never felt as proud as I did at my college graduation.

得到我的文憑是我最有意義的大學經驗。我的課程每天都給我很多挑戰，我很努力取得我的學位。我在大學畢業時感到非常自豪。

▶ 評解

兩個回答都強調成就的部分，基本版回答說明自己寫作能力強並願意幫助別人。進階版回答陳述自身努力取得學位。

▶ 長回答　🎧 MP3 032

I joined the exchange student program at my university in my sophomore year. Then I was given the chance to study in America for one year. The experience promoted personal and social growth within me. Particularly, I developed many useful qualities. For instance, my proficiency in English increased after living in America. Moreover, I built life-long connections with people from other cultures. During the program, I lived with a family who provided me food and shelter. Even until now, the bond is still strong and we are still keeping in touch with each other. The experience is so rewarding that I will never forget.

我在大二的時候參加了我大學的交換生計劃，然後我得到了在美國學習一年的機會。這個經驗促進在我個人和社交方面的成長。尤其是，我養成了很多有用的個人特質。舉例來說，我的英語程度在美國生活之後成長很多。此外，我建立了與來自其他文化背景的人終身的連接（友誼）。在交換生計劃期間，我和美國家庭住在一起，他們提供我食物和住所。甚至到現在為止，我們還是時常保持聯繫。這個經驗是如此的有意義，我永遠不會忘記。

▶ 評解

回答中說明經驗帶給個人的正面成長包含社交能力，語言能力等，這些都是職場不可或缺的能力。

🍎 單字　🎧 MP3 033

❶ **particularly** [pəˋtɪkjələlɪ] *adv.* 特別，尤其

❷ **proficiency** [prəˋfɪʃənsɪ] *n.* 精通；熟練

❸ **connection** [kəˋnɛkʃən] *n.* 連接；聯絡；銜接

❹ **shelter** [ˋʃɛltə] *n.* 遮蓋物；躲避處；避難所

❺ **bond** [bɑnd] *n.* 結合力；聯結，聯繫

用句型取勝

sb volunteer to + V 某人自願（不求金錢待遇）做～事

📖 要注意

1. sb volunteer to + V 的 volunteer 做動詞。volunteer 也可做「名詞」，指義工。

2. 至於 voluntary (adj.)，絕大多數用在形容「義務性的活動、行為」、「義務性的組織、團體、系統」、「自動退休」、「自動自發的服從」、「自動自發的召回某上市的商品等」，而甚少用來指「義工人員」，例: A voluntary action/act; A voluntary program/association/organization/group; A voluntary retirement/compliance/recall。

例句：

- During my college years, I volunteered to work in community service and day care centers.
  = During my college years, I was a volunteer in community service and day care centers.
  大學時，我是社區服務和日間照護的義工。

- The biggest satisfaction I have ever had comes from volunteer work.
  = The biggest satisfaction I have ever had comes from being a volunteer.
  我有過最大的滿足感是來自義工工作。

such a + 名詞，某事物讓某人可以（允許某人）做某事

📖 要注意

1. 修飾單數名詞時，放於不定冠詞 a (an) 之前。

2. 在such ... that ...，such ... as ... 句型中，that 後加完整句子，表示「如此…以至於」；as 後加名詞，表示「像…」。

例句：

· This is such a meaningful experience that I'll never forget.
這是一個如此有意義的經驗，以至於我永遠不會忘記。

· The university I attend is such a good school just as I expect.
正如我所預期，我讀的這所大學是一所好學校。

換個說法令人眼睛一亮

(1) I have never felt as proud as I did at my college graduation.
我在大學畢業時感到非常自豪。

= I was very proud of myself when I graduated from college.
= I have never been so proud of myself when graduating from university.

(2) I built life-long connections with people from other cultures.
我建立了與來自其他文化背景的人終身的連接（友誼）。

= I make friends with people from other cultures and we established a life-long friendship.
= I make life-long friends with people from other cultures.

(3) I joined the exchange student program at my university in my sophomore year.
我在大二的時候參加了我大學的交換生計劃

= I took part in the exchange program in my second year of college.
= When I was a sophomore, I participated in the exchange student program at my university.

Part

2

99％會問的面試題

2-3 學歷與教育訓練

08 What was your biggest challenge as a student?

What was the biggest challenge you faced when you were a student?

作為一個學生時，你面對過最大的挑戰為何？

▶ 題 解

人在每一階段都會面臨若干挑戰，因次當面試官問到這個問題時（通常針對大學畢業生），她／他期待的不是否定的答案，而是希望應徵者誠摯描述面臨過的挑戰及如何克服，自我成長。回答時要強調自己從這個挑戰學習到什麼。

▶ 短回答 — 基本版 🎧 MP3 034

Acquiring successful time management skills was the biggest challenge I faced as a student. However I tried my best to acquire these skills. I will continue to use the skills I gained in the workplace and managed my time well.

我當學生時最大挑戰是取得成功管理時間的技巧。不過，我盡我所能學習這些技能。我會繼續在工作場合使用這些技能良好管理自己的時間。

▶ 短回答 — 進階版

I faced my biggest challenge as a student in my freshman year. I had never lived away from home before and I experienced severe homesickness. Nevertheless, I decided to try to overcome my homesickness, which I did. <u>Since then, I can easily adapt to a new environment.</u>

作為一名大一學生是我面對過最大的挑戰。我從未離開家，我經歷了嚴重的思鄉之情。不過，我決定嘗試克服我的鄉愁，我做到了。從那時起，我可以很容易地適應新的環境。

▶ 評解

成功管理時間的技巧和適應新環境的能力都是職場必要技能。

▶ 長回答 🎧 MP3 035

I was most challenged during the first month of studying abroad. I felt like an outsider; I had to overcome the language barrier, get used to currency difference, cope with cultural misunderstandings, meanwhile being far away from my support system. But all of these didn't really discourage me. I tried to improve my language skills by attending language courses and making friends with local people. I avoided many cultural misunderstandings by observing what others do, and how they do it. If there's any doubt, I just asked! I no longer felt like an outsider. I built up a new support network after a year or so.

出國念書的第一個月是我最被挑戰的時候；我感覺自己就像一個局外人；我必須克服語言障礙，習慣貨幣的差異，處理文化上的誤解，同時遠離我的支持系統。但所有這些並沒有真正讓我沮喪。我試圖透過參加語言課程，廣交當地人朋友來提高我的語言技能。透過觀察別人怎麼做，以及他們如何做可以避免很多文化上的誤解。如有任何疑問，我就問！我再也不覺得自己像個局外人。在大約一年後，我建立了一個新的支持網絡。

▶ 評解

很多企業偏好留學過的人，因他們面臨的挑戰很多，也會學習到很多。回答的重點在如何克服這些挑戰。

🍎 單字 🎧 MP3 036

❶ **outsider** [`aʊt`saɪdɚ] *n.* 外人；門外漢；局外人
❷ **currency** [`kɝ-ənsɪ] *n.* 通貨，貨幣
❸ **meanwhile** [`min͵hwaɪl] *adv.* 其間；同時
❹ **discourage** [dɪs`kɝ-ɪdʒ] *v.* 使洩氣，使沮喪
❺ **attend** [ə`tɛnd] *v.* 出席，參加

用句型取勝

adapt to~ 適應～

要注意

1. adapt 有「使適合、適應」的意思。而 adopt 有幾個常見的意思如「採取、採用、收養」，這兩個動詞在使用時因為字型相像，所以經常會不小心混用，但事實上，這兩者的用法和意義可是大不相同。例如: I try to adopt a positive attitude towards everything, and I find that life is not as hard as I think.（我試著對所有事採取正向的態度，我發現生活並不如我所想的那麼艱難。）adapt 當「適應」時，後要加 to。

例句：

- I keep learning to adapt to every change.
  我持續學習著適應每一個改變。
- I adapt myself to the new environment in an open-minded manner.
  我用一種開放的態度來讓自己適應新環境。

no longer 不再

要注意

1. no longer 意為「不再」，通常放在行為動詞前，be 動詞的後面。 no longer 可用 not ... any longer 代替。

例句：

- I am no longer afraid of being in a new environment.
  我不再害怕身處新環境中。
- I no longer waste time on unnecessary things.
  = I don't waste time on unnecessary things any longer.
  我不再浪費時間在不必要的事情上。

💡 換個說法令人眼睛一亮

⑴ Acquiring successful time management skills was the biggest challenge I faced as a student.

我當學生時最大挑戰是取得成功管理時間的技巧。

= Acquiring successful time management skills was the most challenging thing I faced when I was a student.

=Being a student, I was most challenged when I had to acquire successful time management skills.

⑵ I tried to improve my language skills by attending language courses and making friends with local people.

我試圖透過參加語言課程，廣交當地人朋友來提高我的語言技能。

= Attending language courses and making friends with local people are helpful to improve my language skills.

= The language courses I attended and local friends I made improved my language skills.

⑶ I had never lived away from home before and I experienced severe homesickness.

我從未離開家，我經歷了嚴重的思鄉之情。

= That was my first time living away from home and I had bad homesick.

= My first experience of living away from home made me severely homesick.

Part

2

99％會問的面試題

65

2-4 工作經驗與技能

 **01**

How was your job performance in your last position?

Do you think you have done a good job in your last position?

你之前的工作表現如何?

▶ 題 解

這類問題不只對應徵者的工作表現有興趣,也想探究其對價值觀的判斷。回答要領是仔細想想是否有讓自己與眾不同,且與招募職位相關的事蹟,例如讓營運轉虧為盈,業績加倍成長,或成功開啟一條生產線等等。應答者必須凸顯這些成就的貢獻與效益儘量提出數據加以量化與具體化。

▶ 短回答 — 基本版 🎧 MP3 037

Five years ago, I started as a junior engineer, and I became a senior engineer in only three years. The outcome of my yearly performance appraisal was satisfactory and even the general manager knew about my outstanding performance.

五年前我從初級工程師做起,但在三年內我就成為高級工程師。每年我的績效考核結果都非常令人滿意,連總經理都知道我的工作表現非常出色。

▶ 短回答 — 進階版

My supervisor and colleagues are all positive about my job performance. The outcome of my yearly performance appraisal says that I am willing to learn/improve, good at communication and leadership, and have positive attitudes and extensive job-related knowledge.

我的主管和同事都對我的工作表現持肯定態度。我每年的績效考核結果都說明了我

會自發性的學習／改進，擅長溝通和領導，並有正面的態度與廣泛的工作知識。

▶ **評解**

藉由績效考核來說明工作表現是較有公信度的。短回答－基本版只說明考績的結果優良稍嫌不足。進階版就敘述了在哪些方面表現優異。

▶ **長回答** 🎧 MP3 038

The fact that I have improved my department's productivity by 35% last year shows my excellent job performance. Last year our department was running more projects than before. In order to implement these projects on time using limited human capital, I designed an incentive program in which employees got extra bonuses when their productivity was improved. In the end, the projects were successfully carried out and the overall profits were increased by 20% despite the higher expense in employee bonuses. Consequently, I assured others of my ability in problem-solving and leadership and I was promoted as a general manager of the company.

我優異的工作表現可以從去年我為我的部門提升了百分之三十五的產能看出。去年我們部門執行比以往還多的計畫，所以為了能運用有限的人力如期進行這些計畫，我設計了一個獎勵方案，只要員工的個人產值增加就可得到額外的獎金。最後，計畫都成功地執行，而且即使增加員工獎金的花費，整體利潤還增加了百分之二十。因此，我向他人證明了我解決問題與領導的能力且被晉升為公司的總經理。

▶ **評解**

這個回答凸顯了為部門增加產值所帶來的效益，並提供數據讓內容更具說服力。

🍎 **單字** 🎧 MP3 009

❶ **performance appraisal** [pɚˋfɔrməns] [əˋprez!] *n.* 績效考核
❷ **productivity** [͵prodʌkˋtɪvətɪ] *n.* 生產力
❸ **implement** [ˋɪmpləmənt] *v.* 執行
❹ **human capital** [ˋhjumən] [ˋkæpət!] *n.* 人力
❺ **incentive** [ɪnˋsɛntɪv] *n* 鼓勵；獎勵

用句型取勝

The fact that ...（名詞子句）+ V.（句子的主要動詞）

這個句型的主詞就是「這個事實」，事實的內容在 that 後的名詞子句中說明，主要動詞接在名詞子句之後。

要注意

1. 主詞是 the fact，所以對應的主要動詞應是單數動詞。

例句：

- The fact that I don't speak any foreign languages became my big disadvantage when I am applying for this position.
  我不會說任何外國語言的這個事實在我應徵這個職位時變成我的大弱點。
- The fact that there is a sharp decline in sales this quarter worried every one of us.
  本季業績大幅下滑的這個事實使我們每一個人都非常憂心。

assure +sb + of+ sth 向某人保證某事；使某人確信某事

要注意

1. assure +sb +of 後接名詞，assure+sb+that 後接完整句子。

例句：

- I assured the clients of my best services at all times.
  = I assured the clients that I will provide best services at all times.
  我向客戶們保證我能隨時提供最好的服務。
- John tried to assure the supervisor of his willingness to work in this department.
  = John tried to assure the supervisor that he is willing to work in this department.
  = John 試著讓主管相信他是樂意在這部門工作的。

💡 換個說法令人眼睛一亮

(1) The outcome of my yearly performance appraisal was satisfactory

每年我的績效考核結果都非常令人滿意。

= Every year I got good performance appraisal.
= I am always proud of my yearly performance appraisal results.

---

(2) I designed an incentive program in which employees got extra bonuses when their productivity was improved.

我設計了一個獎勵方案，只要員工的個人產值增加就可得到額外的獎金。

= I gave those employees whose productivity was improved extra bonuses as an incentive.
= The way I motivated staffs was to give extra bonuses to those employees who had better productivity.

---

(3) In the end, the projects were successfully carried out and the overall profits were increased by 20% despite the higher expense in employee bonuses.

最後，計畫都成功地執行，而且即使增加員工獎金的花費，整體利潤還增加了百分之二十。

= The outcome is that the projects were successfully completed and we also raised overall profits by 20% even though we spent more on employee bonuses.
= In the end, the projects were successfully implemented with increased profits of 20% although there were higher expenses in employee bonuses.

Part

2

99％會問的面試題

02 How would people you have worked with describe you?

How would your past coworkers describe you?

曾經跟您共事的同事會怎麼形容您？

▶ 題解

這個問題想了解你和同事與主管的人際和工作關係。回答時舉實際正面的例子說明，公司都希望尋找在工作上有良好人際關係的員工，能和主管和諧相處，與同事同心協力完成工作。但記得要誠實回答，因有時面試官會詢問您之前的雇主相關問題。

▶ 短回答 — 基本版 🎧 MP3 040

My supervisor Steven always said he was impressed with how organized and professional I am. In fact, he even volunteered to write a letter of recommendation in which he shared a few more insights about me and highly recommended me.

我的主管 Steven 總是說他對我的專業度和組織能力印象深刻。事實上，他甚至自願幫我寫推薦信，在信中他分享了很多對我深刻的了解並強力推薦我。

▶ 短回答 — 進階版

Colleagues who worked close to me (or from my team) always tell others that I am friendly, loyal to friends, cooperating, respectful, honest, empathetic, caring and ready to help. I and my team members cooperate well to accomplish every job task we are assigned.

和我工作很親近的同事（或我團隊裡的同事）總是對別人說我很友善、對朋友忠實、很配合，有禮貌的，誠實的，有同理心，照顧人的，且樂於助人。我和團隊裡

的成員合作無間地完成每個被指派的工作任務。

▶ 評解

進階版較優因陳述了很多正面的個人特質。

▶ 長回答 🎧 MP3 041

My managers would describe me as someone who would rather tirelessly overcome obstacles on my own than continuously seek managerial guidance. I make my managers' lives easier in this way. For example, when I first started working at firm xxx, I was asked to figure out ways to cut costs. Instead of relying on my manager, who had other projects to oversee, I decided to better understand the possibility of reducing transportation costs and negotiating prices with our suppliers. After seeing what worked best and what could be improved, I took this information to my manager, who was grateful for the initiative I took.

我的主管會形容我是一個寧願不屈不撓靠自己克服障礙也不願一直尋求主管的指導。這樣的方式會讓我的主管比較輕鬆。例如，當我剛開始在xxx公司工作時，我被要求找到方法降低成本。為了不要太依賴我的主管（他有其他專案要監督），我決定要更加了解降低運輸成本與和供應商議價的可能性。了解了何種方法最有效與可改善處，我把資訊告知我的主管，主管也非常感激我的主動積極。

▶ 評解

這個回答陳述了一個實際的例子提高說服力。

🍎 單字 🎧 MP3 042

❶ **tirelessly** [ˋtaɪrlɪslɪ] *adv.* 不屈不撓地；堅忍地

❷ **overcome** [͵ovɚˋkʌm] *v.* 戰勝；克服

❸ **obstacle** [ˋɑbstək!] *n.* 障礙（物）；妨礙

❹ **guidance** [ˋgaɪdns] *n.* 指導；引導；領導

❺ **negotiate** [nɪˋgoʃɪ͵et] *v.* 談判，協商，洽談

用句型取勝

be impressed with~ 對~印象深刻

要注意

1. be impressed with ~ = be impressed by~
2. impress 也可當及物動詞。用法：sth impress sb。表「某事物讓某人留下深刻印象」。

例句：

- I am greatly impressed with (by) the new products your company present and therefore I look forward to the opportunity to work for you.
  我對貴公司呈現的新產品印象深刻，因此很期待能為您工作。
- My colleagues and my supervisor all told me that they are most impressed with (by) my efficiency.
  = My colleagues and my supervisor all told me that my efficiency impressed them the most.
  我的同事和主管都告訴我他們對我的工作效率印象深刻。

figure out~ 解決，理解~

要注意

1. figure out 與 find out 意思上不同。find out: 是找出；發現；查明的意思。"find out" 多與 "who"，"what"&"when" 一起用。把握 "figure out" 是要用腦筋想和理解，而 "find out" 是「發現，查明」就比較容易區別。

例句：

- It didn't take us long to figure out the correct answer.
  我們沒有花太多時間就理解出正確答案。
- I can't figure out why my supervisor ridicules this constructive suggestion.
  我不能理解我的主管為何嘲笑這個有建設性的建議。

換個說法令人眼睛一亮

(1) My supervisor Steven always said he was impressed with how organized and professional I am.

我的主管 Steven 總是說他對我的專業度和組織能力印象深刻。

= My supervisor Steven always said I am very organized and professional, which impressed him.

= My supervisor said to me that he appreciate my organization and professional skills.

---

(2) My managers would describe me as someone who would rather tirelessly overcome obstacles on my own than continuously seek managerial guidance.

我的主管會形容我是一個寧願不屈不饒靠自己克服障礙也不願一直尋求主管的指導。

= My managers said that I am the person who, instead of continuously seeking managerial guidance, would tirelessly overcome obstacles on his own.

= According to my managers, I would tirelessly overcome obstacles by myself instead of seeking managerial guidance continuously.

---

(3) I decided to better understand the possibility of reducing transportation costs and negotiating prices with our suppliers.

我決定要更加了解降低運輸成本與和供應商議價的可能性。

= I was trying to find ways to reduce transportation costs and negotiate prices with our suppliers.

= I was seeking the possibility of reducing transportation costs and negotiating prices with our suppliers.

03 Q What are your strengths?

Why are you the best person for the job?
你的優勢為何？

▶ 題解

詢問應徵者個人的優勢是非常常見的面試題目。回答方向應著重在對應徵職位有助益的個人優點。優點可以是個人特質例如學習能力強、善於溝通、對工作有熱情、有耐心、正面思考等。也可以是目標職位所需的技能例如善於統計分析、能提供良好客戶服務等。注意不要聽起來太自滿或太謙虛。

▶ 短回答 —— 基本版 🎧 MP3 043

<u>I'd say my biggest strength is that I am passionate about my job, which allows me to produce the best performances.</u> In addition, I have years of experiences and expertise in marketing, and therefore I am good at writing marketing proposals and doing market research.

我會說我最大的優勢是我熱愛我的工作，因此我可以有最好的工作表現。除此之外，我在行銷領域有多年經驗與專長，因此我擅長寫行銷計畫與做市場調查。

▶ 短回答 —— 進階版

One of my strengths is that I commit to a deadline and do whatever it takes to deliver. For example, last week I had a report due, but I got some numbers back late from our team members. I stayed up for two nights to finish the spreadsheet because I knew my client had to receive the report on time.

我的優點之一是我對我承諾的期限負責，並盡一切可能完成工作。例如，上週我必

須完成一份報告，但我團隊的成員遲交一些數字，我熬夜兩晚完成表格因為我知道我的客戶必須如期收到這份報告。

▶ 評解

兩個回答都指出對工作有益的個人特質或技能。進階版回答較優之處在於有實際例子佐證可以增加說服力。

▶ 長回答 🎧 MP3 044

In the past five years of working, I have been organized and followed through to accomplish assignments, usually within deadlines. I was flexible in meeting new tasks or using new methods. I was always persistent and worked to get the things done, and I've been told and tried to be a quick study with new processes. I worked to keep my superiors posted so there weren't any surprises. I trust in this way I contribute successfully to my supervisors and the department's (company's) needs and I consequently learn a lot and continue improving myself.

在過去五年的工作經驗中，我做事一直都很有組織，在期限內按部就班完成工作。我對新任務與使用新方法適應力高。我總是執著地完成每一項工作任務。我也曾經被要求並試著快速學習新的工作流程。我隨時向主管回報工作進度避免任何突發狀況。我相信這樣的工作方式能成功對主管、部門、與公司有所貢獻。我也因此學習到很多並持續自我改進。

▶ 評解

這樣的回答講述了很多個人優點並舉例過去的工作經驗與表現使人信服。

🍎 單字 🎧 MP3 045

❶ **organized** [ˈɔrgənˌaɪzd] *adj.* 有組織的
❷ **accomplish** [fəˈsɪlətɪ] *v.* 完成，實現，達到
❸ **flexible** [ˈflɛksəb!] *adj.* 可變通的；靈活的；易適應的
❹ **persistent** [pɚˈsɪstənt] *adj.* 堅持不懈的；執著的
❺ **process** [ˈprɑsɛs] *n.* 程序；流程

用句型取勝

sth+ allow(s)+ sb+to+v 某事（物）使某人能夠做（達到）～

👆 要注意

1. to 後面要加原型動詞。
2. 人物要用受詞而非主詞。
3. （○）It allows me ....
   （×）It allows I ......

例句：

- Working overtime for three days allowed me to finish the proposal within the deadline.
  加班三天讓我能在期限內完成計畫書。
- We are all happy that new regulations allow us to have better employee benefits.
  我們都很開心新規定讓我們能有更好的員工福利。

keep+sb+posted 隨時通報某人；讓某人隨時了解～

👆 要注意

1. keep+sb+posted 後可加 about+某事，作為隨時通報某人～事；讓某人隨時了解～事。

例句：

- I have to keep the vice-president posted about how the job is progressing.
  我必須隨時通報總經理工作的進展狀況。
- In my previous job, my supervisor requested me to keep her posted about the stock prices every day.
  在我的上一份工作我的主管要求我讓她隨時瞭解每天的股票價格。

換個說法令人眼睛一亮

(1) I'd say my biggest strength is that I am passionate about my job, which allows me to produce the best performances.

我會說我最大的優勢是我熱愛我的工作，因此我可以有最好的工作表現

= I'd say my biggest strength is that I am passionate about my job and therefore I produce the best performances.

= I produce the best performance because I am passionate about my job, which is my biggest strength.

(2) I have years of experiences and expertise in marketing, and therefore I am good at writing marketing proposals and doing market research.

我在行銷領域有多年經驗與專長，因此我擅長寫行銷計畫與做市場調查。

= Due to years of experiences and expertise in marketing, I can do well in writing marketing proposals and market research.

= I perform well in doing market research and writing marketing proposal, which owes to my years of experiences and expertise in marketing.

(3) I stayed up for two nights to finish the spreadsheet because I knew my client had to receive the report on time.

我熬夜兩晚完成表格因為我知道我的客戶必須如期收到這份報告。

= Staying up for two nights, I completed the spreadsheet to make sure that my client receives the report on time.

= I made sure there was no delay in sending the report to my client by staying up for two nights to finish the spreadsheet.

Part

2

99％會問的面試題

2-4 工作經驗與技能

What is your weakness?

What area you think you should work on to improve yourself?

你的劣勢為何？

▶ 題 解

人無完美，這樣的題目測試應徵者在面對自己的缺點時如何改進。回答時注意這個缺點必須對求職沒有大的殺傷力。你可以陳述一個缺點但你因此學習並改進自己，或把這項缺點轉化為優點，例如太注重細節，承接太多工作無法把責任適時下放等。

▶ 短回答 —— 基本版 🎧 MP3 046

I like to make sure that my work is perfect, so I tend to spend more time checking it. However, I've come to a good balance by learning to do everything correctly the first time.

我喜歡確認我完成的工作是完美的，所以我會花多一點時間檢查。然而，我藉由學習在第一次就把事情做好在兩者中取得平衡。

▶ 短回答 —— 進階版

Sometimes I take on tasks personally that could easily be delegated to someone else. Though I still finish all my work on time, I should make an effort to know when to move on to the next task, and to be confident when assigning others work.

有時候我把應該可以委派給其他人的工作攬在身上。雖然我還是如期完成工作，我仍要努力適時地做下一個工作並自信地把工作指派給別人。

▶ 評解

要求工作完美或承接太多工作都是聽起來像優點的缺點。講述完缺點並說明因應這個缺點的自我改進辦法。

▶ 長回答 MP3 047

I would say public speaking is an area that I could work on. I am the first to stand up and present in small meeting, but I tend to get nervous when presenting to a large group of people. I actually spoke to my manager about this and we set it as one of my development goals for this year. I took an internal presentation skills class. With practices, I started to feel more confident. Last month, I even volunteered to represent our team to present at the city hall and got great feedback!

我會說公開演講是我要努力的一塊。在小型會議中我是第一個站起來發表意見的人，但當對一大群人演講時我會很緊張。事實上我有和我主管聊過，我們一起把這訂為我當年度的發展目標。我去上公司內部訓練簡報技巧的課程。練習過後我開始比較有自信。上個月我甚至自願代表我們團隊去市政廳做簡報並得到很好的回饋意見！

▶ 評解

這樣的缺點殺傷力不大因對大眾演講是很多人的弱點。重點是陳述了應徵者如何努力克服這項缺點並有良好的改進效果。

單字 MP3 048

❶ **public speaking** [ˋpʌblɪk] [ˋspikɪŋ] *n.* 公眾演說
❷ **actually** [ˋæktʃʊəlɪ] *adv.* 事實上
❸ **presentation** [ˌprizɛnˋteʃən] *n.* 簡報
❹ **volunteer** [ˌvɑlənˋtɪr] *v.* 自願（做）
❺ **represent** [ˌrɛprɪˋzɛnt] *v.* 代表

用句型取勝

tend+to 傾向於～

要注意

1. to後面要加原型動詞。
2. tend+to 不同於intend+to：tend to...表「有……傾向；易於 / 往往會……」的意思，而 intend to ... 表「有意要……；打算要……」的意思。

例句：

- I tend to be well prepared for each presentation I will make.
  我往往會為我將做的每一個簡報做足準備。
- Do you intend to be an architect in five years?
  你有打算在五年內成為一個建築師嗎？
- As usual, the new assistant tends to make such mistakes.
  如同往常，這個新助理傾向於犯這樣的錯誤。
- We tend to have regularly meetings every Monday morning.
  我們傾向每週一開例行會議。

make an effort to～ 努力去達成某事；努力去做～

要注意

1. effort 在這裡可做單數或複數。
2. effort 因是母音開頭的字，冠詞要用 an，而非 a。

例句：

- It means that I make an effort to be a person with a conscience.
  = It means that I make efforts to be a person with a conscience.
  這意味著我努力成為一個有良知的人。
- I made efforts to improve my reading comprehension.
  = I made an effort to improve my reading comprehension.
  我努力提高我的閱讀能力。

換個說法令人眼睛一亮

(1) Sometimes I take on tasks personally that could easily be delegated to someone else.

有時候我把應該可以委派給其他人的工作攬在身上。

= Sometimes I should have delegated tasks to someone else, rather than taking all those jobs myself.

= I admit that I shouldn't take on tasks personally that could easily be delegated to others.

(2) I would say public speaking is an area that I could work on.

我會說公開演講是我要努力的一塊。

= I think I need to work on my public speaking skills.

= I've always wanted to improve my public speaking skills.

(3) I tend to get nervous when presenting to a large group of people.

對一大群人演講時我會很緊張。

= Presenting to a large group of people always makes me nervous.

= I felt nervous when I was presenting to a large group of people.

Part

2

99％會問的面試題

 **How do you handle stress/ pressure in your previous job(s)?**

How did you reduce and manager work stress?

你如何處理工作上的壓力？

▶ 題 解

壓力管理是職場的必修課。雇主會希望員工在面對壓力時保持冷靜，正面積極處理壓力，例如深呼吸，從事健康的休閒活動等。回答重點在於說明自己如何管理壓力，並把壓力轉換成對工作有益的正面能量，避免述說自己被壓力擊倒的經驗。

▶ 短回答 —— 基本版 🎧 MP3 049

I actually work better under pressure and I've found that I enjoy working in a challenging environment. From a personal perspective, I manage stress by visiting the gym every evening. It effectively reduces my pressure and refreshes myself.

事實上我在壓力下工作得更好，我也發現自己喜歡在富有挑戰性的環境裡工作。就我個人來說，我藉由每晚去健身房來管理我的壓力。它有效地減輕我的壓力，讓我恢復精神。

▶ 短回答 —— 進階版

Whenever I feel overwhelmed and stressed out, what I do is to concentrate on remaining calm, maybe taking a few deep breaths. Then I mentally break the stressful task into smaller steps, and just focus on reaching each one on the way to accomplish the larger task.

每當我感到很有壓力不知所措時，我會專注在保持冷靜，或許先深呼吸幾下。然後我在心裡把很有壓力的工作分成幾個部分，只專注達成每一個小任務，然後完成更大的任務。

評解

這兩個回答都明白陳述如何面對與處理壓力並積極完成工作任務。

長回答 🎧 MP3 050

If I start to feel nervous or stressful, I try to stay focused on the task at hand, or step back from the situation, take a deep breath and try to approach from a different angle. In my daily life, I reduce stress by going hiking, spending quality time with my family and friends, and try to get plenty of sleep at night. Furthermore, I've found that if I'm well prepared and know my job, stress isn't much of a factor. Therefore I would learn as much as possible about the task so I can complete it and eliminate the stress.

如果我開始覺得緊張或有壓力，我試著專注在手邊的工作，或先抽離出來，深呼吸，然後試著從另一個角度著手。在日常生活中，我藉由健行、和朋友家人一起度過有品質的時間、晚上有充足的睡眠來減輕壓力。再者，我發現如果我做好充足的準備，充分了解我的工作，壓力就不是太大的因素。因此我對自己的工作任務盡可能學習，就能消除壓力並完成工作。

評解

這個回答提供了很多正面處理壓力的技巧，並闡述積極學習也可以減輕壓力，這點是雇主會喜歡聽到的答案。

單字 🎧 MP3 051

❶ approach [ə`protʃ] *v.* 著手處理
❷ reduce [rɪ`djus] *v.* 減少；縮小；降低
❸ plenty [`plɛntɪ] *n.* 豐富；充足；大量
❹ factor [`fæktɚ] *n.* 因素；要素
❺ eliminate [ɪ`lɪməˌnet] *v.* 排除；消除；消滅

✏️ **用句型取勝**

I've found that~ 我發現（了解到）

👉 **要注意**

1. 可用現在完成式或過去式。
2. that 後接完整子句，陳述了解到甚麼。
3. 也可以説 I've realized that~；I've conceived that~。

例句：

- I've found /realized/ conceived that practice makes things perfect, so I always rehearse several times before I actually make a presentation.
  我了解到熟能生巧，所以我總是在做簡報前排練幾次。
- I've found that my manager don't necessary like those employees who are either too modest or too ambitious.
  我發現到我的主管並不一定喜歡那些太謙虛或太有企圖心的員工。

from a personal perspective 就個人的角度來看

👉 **要注意**

1. from a personal perspective 通常放在句首。
2. from a personal perspective = personally = take myself as an example。

例句：

- From a personal perspective, I make a difficult decision by weighing the risk vs. the gain.
  就個人的角度來看，我藉由權衡風險與收益來做一個困難的決定。
- From a personal perspective, I never doubt about the feasibility of the project.
  就我個人來説，我從未懷疑這個計畫的可行性。

💡 **換個說法令人眼睛一亮**

⑴ I actually work better under pressure and I've found that I enjoy working in a challenging environment.

事實上我在壓力下工作得更好，我也發現自己喜歡在富有挑戰性的環境裡工作。

= In fact pressure motivates me to work better and I like the challenging working environment.
= Stress actually enhances my work productivity and what I like is working in a challenging environment.

⑵ Whenever I feel overwhelmed and stressed out, what I do is to concentrate on remaining calm, maybe taking a few deep breaths.

每當我感到很有壓力不知所措時，我會專注在保持冷靜，或許先深呼吸幾下。

= The way I cope with work stress is to concentrate on remaining calm, maybe taking a few deep breaths.
= Concentrating on remaining calm, maybe taking a few deep breaths reduces my stress.

⑶ I've found that if I'm well prepared and know my job, stress isn't much of a factor.

我發現如果我做好充足的準備，充分了解我的工作，壓力就不是太大的因素。

= Stress wouldn't interfere with my job when I'm well prepared and know about my tasks.
= I can still work productively if I'm well prepared and know my job.

Part

2

99％會問的面試題

2-4 工作經驗與技能

06 Do you prefer working alone or in teams?

Do you work better in teams or individually?

你偏好獨立工作或團隊合作？

▶ 題 解

工作性質不同固然會影響這個問題的答案，但通常來說雇主會偏好能夠獨立工作也能團隊合作的人，因為在大部分的職場上這兩種能力都是必須的。例如如果要應徵程式設計類的工作，你必須展現你有獨立思考作業的能力，但千萬不要讓面試官覺得你不擅團隊合作。

▶ 短回答 —— 基本版 🎧 MP3 052

I enjoy working as part of a team, but also on my own. I read the job description and your web site, and found that there are going to be opportunities to do both. I look forward to each one. The bottom line is to meet the goals.

我喜歡在團隊中工作，也喜歡獨立工作。我讀過這個職缺的工作敘述和你們網站，了解到獨立工作和團隊合作都是可能的。我對兩者都很期待，最重要是達成任務。

▶ 短回答 —— 進階版

It depends on the task. When it comes to brainstorming, teams produce great ideas with multiple inputs. Certainly I enjoy working on my tasks as an individual as well since in many ways it takes the ability to work alone for the team to fully succeed.

這要視任務而定。當需要腦力激盪時，團隊裡各式不同的聲音可以產生出很好的構

想。當然我也喜歡獨立作業，因為在很多方面能獨立完成工作的能力是團隊能成功的要素之一。

▶ 評解

兩個回答都闡述了應徵者擁有獨立工作與團隊合作的能力與其對達成工作任務的重要性。

▶ 長回答 🎧 MP3 053

My previous job required me to work with a team, and I certainly enjoyed that. I worked for an international trading company, and I had to cooperate with people from countries in different parts of the world. It was always so interesting and educational to work as a team with people of different nationalities and cultures. My experiences had told me that cooperation really is the basis for mutual benefits. However, I also enjoy working alone because it gives you more peace and concentration with the tasks that is given to you. So, for me, I both like working in a team and working alone.

我之前的工作團隊合作是必須的，而我也非常喜歡。我之前在一家國際貿易公司上班，我必須和世界各地不同國籍的人合作。和來自不同國家和文化的人們一起團隊合作是很有趣且富教育意義的。我的經驗告訴我合作真的是互利的基礎。然而我也喜歡獨立作業，因為我會有安靜的環境能專注在被指派的任務。因此對我來說，我喜歡團隊合作也喜歡獨立作業。

▶ 評解

舉之前工作的例子說明自己具備團隊合作與獨立作業的能力，說服力提高。

 單字 🎧 MP3 054

❶ cooperate [ko`ɑpə‚ret] v. 合作
❷ nationality [‚næʃə`nælətɪ] n. 國籍
❸ mutual [`mjutʃʊəl] adj. 相互的，彼此的
❹ benefit [`bɛnəfɪt] n. 利益，好處；優勢
❺ concentration [‚kɑnsɛn`treʃən] n. 專心，專注

用句型取勝

look forward to~ 期待～

👉 要注意

1. 後面一律接名詞或動名詞，不可接原型動詞。
2. 和expect (v.) 用法不同：

expect (v) 有下列三種意思：

期待，期望

Ex: I expect (that) I'll pass the exam.

我期望通過考試。

認為，指望，希望

Ex: The train leaves at 8:30. I'm expecting you all to be at the station before then.

火車於 8：30 出發。我認為你們在這之前都應該在車站

想，認為

Ex: "Who broke that cup ?" "I expect it was the dog."

「誰打破杯子？」「我想是那隻狗。」

例句：

· I look forward to hearing from you in the near future.
  希望能早日得到您的回覆。
· I look forward to working here in the near future.
  希望能早日在這裡上班。

cooperate with 和～合作

👉 要注意

1. 和～合作 介係詞用 with。
2. 在甚麼事情上合作，介係詞用 on。

例句：

· The two groups agreed to cooperate with each other on this matter.
兩方人同意在這件事情上彼此合作。

· I cooperated with my previous team members well to solve any problem that occurred.
我和我之前的團隊成員合作無間解決任何發生的問題。

換個說法令人眼睛一亮

(1) I enjoy working as part of a team, but also on my own.
我喜歡在團隊中工作，也喜歡獨立工作。

= I like both working in a team and on my own.
= I enjoy cooperating with others as well as depending solely on myself.

---

(2) It was always so interesting and educational to work as a team with people of different nationalities and cultures.
和來自不同國家和文化的人們一起團隊合作是很有趣且富教育意義的。

= I always have fun and learn a lot when I work as a team with people of different nationalities and cultures.
= Working as a team with people of different nationalities and cultures is a both interesting and educational experience.

---

(3) My experiences had told me that cooperation really is the basis for mutual benefits.
我的經驗告訴我合作真的是互利的基礎。

= I learnt from my experiences that mutual benefits are really based on cooperation.
= My experiences had told me that cooperation leads to mutual benefits.

Part

2

99％會問的面試題

What did you like or dislike about your previous job?

What did you like best/ least about your previous job?

對於你以前的工作你有什麼喜歡或不喜歡的地方？

⊙ 題 解

當被問到你不喜歡之前的公司什麼，千萬別説太負面的批評。原因是你不會想讓面試官覺得你將來會批評他們的公司。回答的重點應該在正面的評價與你希望在新工作能達到什麼（如個人專業成長、升遷的機會等）。

⊙ 短回答 — 基本版　🎧 MP3 055

Through my experience in my previous job, I learned about strategies for maintaining cooperation in a large group project setting. However, I am looking forward to working on more specialized projects where I will have the opportunity to be more of a leader.

藉由我之前的工作經驗，我學習到在一個大專案裡團隊合作的策略。然而我期待在較專業分工的專案裡工作，有機會接觸比較有領導性質的工作。

⊙ 短回答 — 進階版

While the people at my previous job were terrific to work with, I felt that the opportunities for me there were limited by the structure and size of the company. I believe that a larger company can offer challenges and opportunities unavailable at a smaller firm.

雖然和我之前的同事共事是很棒的，我覺得我的機會因公司的結構和大小而有了限制。我相信較大型的公司可以給我小公司所無法提供的挑戰和機會。

▶ 評 解

兩個回答都正面肯定了之前的公司，也等於肯定自己在那工作的經驗。雖然有提到不滿意之處，但都是相當正面的原因（例如期待挑戰和機會）。

▶ 長回答 🎧 MP3 056

One of the reasons I am leaving is that I felt the job was not challenging enough. As a new employee, the company offered a great opportunity for a good entry level position. However, after being there for several years, I felt I was not able to reach my full potential because of the lack of challenge and there was no room for advancement in the company. While I did enjoy working there and appreciate the skills I developed while with the company, I feel my skill set can be better utilized elsewhere, where my capabilities are more recognized and there is the opportunity for growth.

我會離職的原因之一是我覺得那個工作不夠有挑戰性。作為一個新員工，公司提供一個很好的初階工作的機會。然而，在那工作了幾年後，我覺得我無法達到我全部的潛力因為缺乏挑戰且無升遷機會。雖然我真的享受在那工作也感激我在那學習到的技能，我覺得我的技能可以在其他地方得到更好的利用，我的能力也能更被認同，並且有機會成長。

▶ 評 解

回答肯定了自己之前的工作表現，也表明強烈想要自我成長的動機。

🍎 單 字 🎧 MP3 057

❶ **offer** [ˋɔfɚ] *v.* 給予，提供
❷ **potential** [pəˋtɛnʃəl] *adj.* 潛在的，可能的
❸ **utilize** [ˋjut!ˏaɪz] *v.* 利用
❹ **elsewhere** [ˋɛlsˏhwɛr] *adv.* 在別處
❺ **recognize** [ˋrɛkəgˏnaɪz] *v.* 承認；認同

用句型取勝

> **while** 當連接詞，表「雖然；儘管」.。

要注意

1. 當「雖然；儘管」時，可用 although 代換，用以強調前後兩件事情的對比或差異。
2. While+S1+V1, S2+V2 與 Although+S1+V1, S2+V2 皆不可與 but 同用。

例句：

- While I don't have relevant work experiences in this field, I did take several courses about it in college.

  雖然我在這個領域沒有相關的工作經驗，但我在大學時有修過相關的課程。

  （×）While I don't have relevant work experiences in this field, but I did take several courses about it in college.

- While I have never met the new president, I know him from hearing so much about him.

  雖然我還沒見過新總裁，但因聽到很多關於他的事，好像已經認識他了。

  （×）While I have never met the new president, but I know him from hearing so much about him.

> **sb's + sth + beV+recognized** 某人的～事物被認同

要注意

1. sb's +sth+ beV+recognized = Sb+ beV+ recognized +for+ sth

例句：

- The designer's creativity is recognized by all of us.

  = The designer is recognized by all of us for his creativity.

  這個設計師的創造力是我們所有人所認可的。

· I don't think my talent is recognized by my supervisor and therefore I am looking for new opportunities elsewhere.

我不認為我的才能是被主管所認可的，因此我想在別處找尋新機會。

換個說法令人眼睛一亮

(1) I am looking forward to working on more specialized projects where I will have the opportunity to be more of a leader.

我期待在較專業分工的專案裡工作，有機會接觸比較有領導性質的工作。

= I expect to work on more specialized projects and be given a chance to be a project leader.

= I always want to involve and take a leading role in more specialized projects.

(2) While the people at my previous job were terrific to work with, I felt that the opportunities for me there were limited by the structure and size of the company.

雖然和我之前的同事共事是很棒的，我覺得我的機會因公司的結構和大小而有了限制。

= Although I had great experiences of working with my previous colleagues, I lost some opportunities because the company I worked for was not big enough.

= Despite the nice colleagues in my previous job, I felt the structure and size of the company had limited my opportunities.

(3) I believe that a larger company can offer challenges and opportunities unavailable at a smaller firm.

我相信較大型的公司可以給我小公司所無法提供的挑戰和機會。

= I believe I can be challenged more and offered more opportunities in a big firm than in a small firm.

= I believe a large company can offer me more challenges and opportunities than a small company can do.

Part

2

99％會問的面試題

93

2-4 工作經驗與技能

08 Q Have you completed any internship? What did you gain from the experience?

Have you ever been an intern? What did your learn from it?
你實習過嗎？從中學習到甚麼？

▶ 題 解

這個問題通常針對大學應屆畢業生，且他／她的打工經驗也很有限。面試官就會想知道應徵者是否有實習經驗，也希望其在實習時有養成或學到對職場有幫助的特質或技能，以彌補工作經驗的不足。如果有實習經驗就加強說明自己學到了什麼，如果沒有可用志工服務或社團經驗來取代。

▶ 短回答 — 基本版 🎧 MP3 058

This past summer, I completed an internship with a major marketing firm in the city. I learned to watch what my coworkers do. <u>They can be my best resource to learn both what to do and what not to do in the office.</u>

今年夏天我在城市裡一家大型行銷公司實習。我學會觀察我的同事做些什麼。他們可以是我最好的資源，學習在辦公室裡什麼該做，什麼不該做。

▶ 短回答 — 進階版

My university required all fashion design majors to complete an internship. The internship helped me focus more specifically on what part of fashion design I was interested in. <u>Without it, I may have had to go back to square one if I was not happy with my career choice.</u>

我的大學要求所有主修服裝設計的學生都要實習。這次實習幫助我更專注於服裝設

計中我感興趣的哪一部分,沒有它,我可能不得不回到原點,如果我不滿意我的職業選擇。

▶ 評 解

兩個回答都說明實習學習到甚麼。

▶ 長回答 🎧 MP3 059

I did not complete any internship during college, but I did use my last two summers to volunteer at a local homeless shelter. At the shelter, I worked with the social workers on a daily basis. I was able to assist with home visits, life skills, and employment issues, along with all other resources and services offered to the unemployed at the shelter. Although this job didn't offer me formal internship title, it served the same purpose and gave me the same hands on experience I would have gotten by doing a social service internship with the government.

我在大學期間沒有完成任何的實習,但是我利用我大學的最後兩個夏天在當地的無家可歸者收容所擔任志工。在庇護所,我每天和社工一起工作。我針對家訪,生活技能和就業問題,以及提供給失業者的避難所的所有其他資源和服務等方面提供協助。雖然這個工作沒有給我正式的實習生頭銜,但它和在政府擔任社會服務實習生的目的相同,給了我同樣的實務經驗。

▶ 評 解

用志工服務取代實習經驗,並說明學到些甚麼。

單字 🎧 MP3 060

❶ internship [`ɪntɝnˌʃɪp] *n.* 實習
❷ homeless [`homlɪs] *adj.* 無家的,無家可歸的
❸ unemployed [ˌʌnɪm`plɔɪd] *adj.* 失業的,無工作的
❹ formal [`fɔrml̩] *adj.* 正式的
❺ purpose [`pɝpəs] *n.* 目的,意圖

用句型取勝

both A and B　A 和 B 兩者都是

要注意

1. A 和 B 中間加的是 and。
2. A 和 B 必須是相同詞性。
3. both A and B = A as well as B = not only A but also B。
4. 須和 either A or B（不是 A 就是 B），neither A nor B（不是 A 也不是 B）分辨清楚。相同處是這裡所有的 A 和 B 都必須是相同詞性。

例句：

- I learnt a lot both in my high school years and in my college years.
  =I learnt a lot in my high school as well as college years.
  =I learnt a lot not only in my high school years but also in my college years.
  我在高中和大學時期都學到很多。
- I have been both studying at the university and working part-time at the restaurant for five years.
  =I have been studying at the university as well as working part-time at the restaurant for five years.
  =I have been not only studying at the university but also working part-time at the restaurant for five years.
  我已經一邊在大學唸書一邊在餐廳打工五年了。

go back to square one 回到原點

要注意

1. go back to square one = start all over again。
2. go 可用 be 動詞 is 或 are 代替。

例句：

- Our project failed, so it's back to square one.
  我們的專案失敗了，所以一切回到原點。

- I thought everything was settled, but then my clients said they're not happy with the deal, so I went back to square one again.

  我以為一切都已成定局，然後我客戶説不滿意這個交易，所以我又回到原點了。

💡 換個說法令人眼睛一亮

(1) This past summer, I completed an internship with a major marketing firm in the city.

今年夏天我在城市裡一家大型行銷公司實習。

= This past summer, I worked as an intern at a big marketing firm downtown.

= My internship was completed this summer at a major marketing company downtown.

---

(2) My university required all fashion design majors to complete an internship.

我的大學要求所有主修服裝設計的學生都要實習。

= All fashion design majors at my university are required to complete an internship.

= At my university, an internship is a requirement for all students majoring in fashion design.

---

(3) I did not complete any internship during college, but I did use my last two summers to volunteer at a local homeless shelter.

我在大學期間沒有完成任何的實習，但是我利用我大學的最後兩個夏天在當地的無家可歸者收容所擔任志工。

= I have never been an intern during my college years, but I was a volunteer at a local homeless shelter during my last two summers.

= I have never been an intern during my college years; instead, I volunteered at a local homeless shelter in my last two summers.

Part

2

99％會問的面試題

2-4 工作經驗與技能

09 Have you accomplished something you're proud of at work?

What's something good you've done or accomplished that you're proud of?

你曾經在工作上完成某事是讓你自豪的嗎？

▶ 題 解

藉由這個問題，面試官想知道關於你的工作最好的部分，不論是你的技能、動機、或團隊合作的能力等。不一定要回答大成就，任何正面的事蹟都可陳述。只要這個事蹟說明了你擁有任何對工作有益的技能或態度。

▶ 短回答 —— 基本版 🎧 MP3 061

While I was doing research for my graduate thesis, my adviser, a leading authority in the field, asked me to guest lecture in one of her senior undergraduate classes on my thesis topic.

當我在為我的畢業論文做研究時，我的指導教授是該領域的權威，她讓我在大學部高年級的課裡針對我的論文題目擔任客座講師。

▶ 短回答 —— 進階版

The manager of the department on my previous job was so impressed with my communication skills that she asked me to make a presentation to the Board of Directors about the project our department team was working on.

我之前工作的部門經理對我的溝通能力印象非常深刻，她要求我向董事會針對我們部門團隊的工作項目做一個簡報。

▶ 評解

短回答基本版可適用於還未有工作經驗的人，進階版回答強調良好溝通能力。

▶ 長回答　🎧 MP3 062

While I was a student teacher, there was one child who was having a particular difficulty grasping one of the concepts the teacher was trying to explain. I asked to take the student aside to work with her. I explained the theory in different ways and used practical examples to illustrate how the concept works. When she finally got it, it was like a candle lit her up from the inside. I knew then that I had definitely chosen the right profession. I have been teaching for over five years since then and my teaching evaluation has always been better than other teachers.

當我還是個實習老師時，有一個孩子對於老師試圖解釋的一個概念感到特別地難理解。我要求把這個學生帶到一邊並和她一起做。我用不同的方式解釋這個理論並用實際的例子來說明這個概念是如何運作的。當她終於了解了，就像一支蠟燭由內而外照亮了她。那時我就知道，我已經明確選擇了正確的行業。直至今日我已經教了五年書，我的教學評價一直比其他老師好。

▶ 評解

當應徵教學工作時，這樣的回答闡述擁有對作為一個老師很重要的技能。

🍎 單字　🎧 MP3 063

❶ **particular** [pəˈtɪkjələ-] *adj.* 特殊的；特定的；特別的
❷ **grasp** [græsp] *v.* 領會，理解
❸ **concept** [ˈkɑnsɛpt] *n.* 概念，觀念
❹ **illustrate** [ˈɪləstret] *v.* （用圖，實例等）說明，闡明
❺ **definitely** [ˈdɛfənɪtlɪ] *adv.* 明確地；明顯地，清楚地

用句型取勝

make a presentation to sb about sth 向某人針對某事做簡報

要注意

1. make a presentation = present。presentation 是名詞，present 是動詞。
2. make a presentation on sth 指的是「針對～議題做簡報」。
3. make a presentation to sb on/ about sth
   = present sth to sb
   = present to sb on/ about sth 指的是「針對～議題對某人做簡報」。
4. oral presentation=delivering an address to a public audience
   指的是「向公眾做口頭演說」。

例句：

· Representing the manufacturer, I made a presentation to possible hotel customer on our new product line.
  = Representing the manufacturer, I presented to possible hotel customer on our new product line.
  = Representing the manufacturer, I presented our new product line to possible hotel customer.
  我代表製造商向潛在的飯店客戶針對新的產品線做簡報。

· I have good presentation skills and I have made presentations on various topics to different audience.
  我有很好的簡報技巧，我針對不同主題對不同觀眾做過簡報。

take sb aside 把某人帶離開一群人，以便私下和他／她談談

例句：

· I took one of my staff aside and tried to understand what he is thinking about.
  我把我的一個員工帶開，試著了解他在想甚麼。

- I never criticized my staff in public. Instead, I took the person aside and talked to him/her.

  我從不在公共場合批評員工，而是把此人帶開和他／她談一談。

💡 換個說法令人眼睛一亮

(1) While I was doing research for my graduate thesis, my adviser, a leading authority in the field, asked me to guest lecture in one of her senior undergraduate classes on my thesis topic.

當我在為我的研究所畢業論文做研究時，我的指導教授，在該領域的權威，讓我在他大學部高年級的課裡針對我的論文題目擔任客座講師。

= While I was doing research for my graduate thesis, I guest lectured on my thesis topic in one senior undergraduate class of my adviser, who is a leading authority in the field.

(2) The manager of the department on my previous job was so impressed with my communication skills that she asked me to make a presentation to the Board of Directors about the project our department team was working on.

我之前工作的部門經理對我的溝通能力印象非常深刻，她要求我向董事會針對我們部門團隊的工作項目做一個簡報。

= Being impressed with my communication skills, the department manager on my previous job asked me to make a presentation to the Board of Directors about the project our department team was working on.

= I got the chance to present to the Board of Directors about the project our department team was working on because the department manager on my previous job was very impressed with my communication skills.

2-5 業績

01 Have you consistently met your sales goals?

Did you always reach your sales goals?

你一直持續達成你的業績目標嗎？

▶ 題 解

當應徵業務類工作時，面試官想當然耳會想知道你的業績歷史。雇主當然都希望雇用業績紀錄優良的業務。回答時要向面試官證明你可以達成或超越業績目標。在面試前想想甚麼是自己最自豪的業績紀錄，以便在面試時說明清楚，能附加數字更好。

▶ 短回答 —— 基本版 🎧 MP3 064

I have always met or exceeded my professional sales goals, and most often my personal ones too, especially in the last few years. I think with experience, I have learned to set my personal goals at an attainable level, very high, but not unreachable.

我一直都達到或超過我的專業銷售目標，而且往往是超越我個人的目標，尤其是最近幾年。我的經驗讓我學會如何設定可以達到的個人目標，這個目標非常高，但不是達不到。

▶ 短回答 —— 進階版

Yes, I have always met or exceeded my sales goals over my ten-year career in the business. For example, last year I led my team to exceed our sales projections by 25% — and this was during a very difficult market when most of the other teams in our division came up short of goal.

是的，在我 10 年的職業生涯中我一直都達到或超過我的業績目標。例如，去年我帶領我的團隊超越我們的銷售預測達25%—而這是在一個非常艱難的市場，當我們部門的大多數團隊都無法達成目標的狀態下。

▶ 評解

進階版回答較優，有數字說明增加說服力。

▶ 長回答 🎧 MP3 065

The only time I wasn't able to meet my professional sales goals was at a company where my supervisor set the goals extremely high, and none of the salesmen in our department were able to achieve them. Setting the goals so high was his method of keeping us motivated, and unfortunately it worked to demoralize the team instead. I have always at least met my personal goals, and I work very hard to exceed them. I usually go beyond the sales target by 20%. I was also elected as the "Annual Top Sales" three times at my previous job.

我唯一一次沒能滿足我的專業銷售目標是當公司的主管設定非常高的目標，而我們部門的銷售人員沒人能夠實現這些目標。設定如此高的目標是他讓我們保持積極性的方法，不幸的是這樣的方法卻使團隊士氣低落。我一直都至少有達成我個人的目標，而且我非常努力超越這些目標。我通常能超越銷售目標 20%。在我以前的工作我也曾三次當選為「年度最佳銷售員」。

▶ 評解

超越銷售目標的數字與當選年度最佳銷售員的實例加強說明自己在業務上的專長。

🍎 單字 🎧 MP3 066

❶ **extremely** [ɪk`strimlɪ] *adv.* 極端地；極其；非常
❷ **demoralize** [dɪ`mɑrəlˌaɪz] *v.* 使士氣低落；使沮喪
❹ **exceed** [ɪk`sid] *v.* 超過；勝過
❺ **beyond** [bɪ`jɑnd] *prep.* （指程度）深於；（指範圍）越出
❻ **elect** [ɪ`lɛkt] *v.* 選舉；推選

用句型取勝

at least 至少

要注意

1. at least 的意思是「至少」（指數量或程度上）也可解作「反正就是」。
   它與 at the least，at the very least 同義，可互換使用，但後兩者有強調
   意味，遠不及前者用得普遍。

例句：

· I take business trips at least once a month.
  我至少一個月出差一次。
· To be a sales representative in charge of North and South America
  regions, I have to at least master English.
  做為負責北美與南美區域的業務代表，我必須至少要精通英語。

beyond 作為介係詞的用法

要注意

1. 表示位置，意思是「在……的那一邊；在……之外；在更遠處」。
   例如：Beyond the mountain stood a power station. 過了這座山就是
   一個發電站。The sea is beyond that hill. 大海在山的那邊。
2. 表示時間，其意為「遲於；超過」。例如：
   We worked beyond midnight in the past three months.
   過去三個月我們工作到午夜 12 點。
   I don't appreciate those employee who never see beyond the
   present.
   我不欣賞那些沒有願景的員工。
3. 表示範圍、水準、限度、能力等，意思是「超出；多於；為……所不能
   及」。例如：
   These were matters beyond my understanding as yet.
   這些事情我那時候還不了解。

換個說法令人眼睛一亮

(1) I think with experience, I have learned to set my personal goals at an attainable level, very high, but not unreachable.

我認為擁有經驗讓我學會如何設定可以達到的個人目標，這個目標水平非常高，但不是達不到。

= My experience has made me learn to set attainable personal goals which are very high, but not unreachable.
= I learn from my experience about how to set very high, but reachable personal goals.

(2) Setting the goals so high was his method of keeping us motivated, and unfortunately it worked to demoralize the team instead.

設定如此高的目標是他讓我們保持積極性的方法，不幸的是這樣的方法卻使團隊士氣低落。

= He tried to keep us motivated by setting very high goals, which unfortunately demoralized the team instead.
= He thinks setting very high goals can keep us motivated, but it turned out demoralizing the team, unfortunately.

(3) I have always at least met my personal goals, and I worked very hard to exceed them.

我一直都至少有達成我個人的目標，而且我非常努力超越這些目標。

= I've not only reached my personal goals but also worked hard to exceed them.
= Not being satisfying with meeting my personal goals, I worked very hard to go beyond them.

Part

2

99％會問的面試題

105

2-5 業績

Q 02 How did you land your most successful sale?

What's your most successful sale and how did you achieve it?

你如何達成你最成功的銷售？

▶ 題解

當有業務職缺時，雇主會希望找到有具體業務績效的員工。回答時最好能舉自己成功的事蹟實例，並說明自己是如何成功地達成交易。目標是讓雇主相信你是有能力為公司帶來業績的。

▶ 短回答 — 基本版 🎧 MP3 067

One time my colleague was having a difficult time getting the client to commit to the purchase of a large motor home. When I was given the opportunity to take over the sale, I was able to give the customer some reflection time, and was ultimately able to close the sale.

有一次，我的同事遇到困難，無法讓客戶答應購買一輛露營房車。當我有機會接管這項業務時，我能夠給客戶一些思考的時間，最終能夠完成銷售。

▶ 短回答 — 進階版

My most successful one was a sale of a large number of books which had been returned after a major retailer closed. Through my contacts, I found an English language bookstore in the suburb, and I was able to offer the owner a terrific deal, which helped out my company tremendously, by not having to re-stock the items.

我最成功的一次是銷售因一家大型零售商關閉而被退回的大量書籍。透過我的聯繫，我找到了一家在郊區的英語文書店，我能夠提供老闆一個很好的交易，這幫了

我公司一個大忙，因為不必再重新庫存那些書籍。

▶ 評解

兩個回答都是具體的實例，並說明是如何成功完成交易的。

▶ 長回答　🎧 MP3 068

I would say that my most successful sales have followed a similar pattern. Once the customer has expressed interest in the product, I make myself available to answer any questions they may have. Next, I give them the details they may not be familiar with, i.e. features, benefits, etc. I believe that when a customer is making a purchase, especially a large one, they like to have time to fully understand what features the product has. By offering a high level of customer support and fair prices, I have been very successful at landing most of my sales.

我要說的是我最成功的銷售都遵循類似的模式。一旦客戶表達對產品的興趣，我讓自己可以回答他們的任何問題。接下來，我提供他們可能不熟悉的細節例如特性、優勢等。我相信，當客戶進行購買，尤其是大的項目，他們喜歡有時間充分了解這個產品有哪些功能。透過提供客戶高度支持和公平的價格，我一直很成功地完成了我的大部分銷售。

▶ 評解

此回答雖然不是特定例子，但說明了一個如何成功的銷售模式。

🍎 單字　🎧 MP3 069

❶ **pattern** [`pætɚn] *n.* 模式
❷ **available** [ə`veləb!] *adj.* 有空的，可與之聯繫的
❸ **feature** [fitʃɚ] *n.* 特徵，特色
❹ **purchase** [`pɝtʃəs] *n.* 買，購買
❺ **fair** [fɛr] *adj.* 公正的；公平的；誠實的

用句型取勝

sb +beV+ familiar with+ sth/ sb 某人熟悉某人、某物

要注意

1. sb +beV+ familiar with+ sth/ sb 需要和 sth/ sb +beV+ familiar to sb 分辨清楚。前者指的是「某人熟悉某人、某物」，後者指的是「某物、某事為某人所熟悉」。
2. 片語中的 be 動詞可改成 get (get familiar)。用 be 動詞表示狀態，和某人／某事物熟悉，get 表示動態，慢慢熟悉的過程。
3. 注意介係詞要用 with，所以接 to 是不對的。

例句：

- I am very familiar with every one of my clients.
  =Every one of my clients is very familiar to me.
  我對我的每一個客戶都很熟悉。
- I'll try to get familiar with my work content as soon as possible.
  我會儘快熟悉我的工作內容。

be successful at/in~ 在某方面很成功

要注意

1. 注意介係詞可用 at 或 in。
2. 後接名詞，故如果接的是動作必須改成動名詞。

例句：

- I am very confident to say that I am successful at/in making my customers commit to make purchases and satisfied with my service afterwards.
  我可以非常有自信地說我在讓我的客戶承諾購買並滿意我後續的服務上非常成功。
- To be successful at/ in sales, I have to treat my clients like my family.
  為了在業務上成功，我必須對待我的客戶如同我的家人。

換個說法令人眼睛一亮

(1) I would say that my most successful sales have followed a similar pattern.

我要說的是我最成功的銷售都遵循類似的模式。

= I would say that there is a similar pattern in most of my successful sales.

= I would say that I successfully close most of my sales in a similar way.

(2) Once the customer has expressed interest in the product, I make myself available to answer any questions they may have.

一旦客戶表達對產品的興趣，我讓自己可以回答他們的任何問題。

= As long as the customer has expressed interest in the product, I answer any questions they raised.

= I make myself available to answer any questions about the product which the customer is interested in.

(3) By offering a high level of customer support and fair prices, I have been very successful at landing most of my sales.

透過提供客戶高度支持和公平的價格，我一直很成功地完成了我的大部分銷售。

= A high level of customer support and fair prices I offered made me very successful at landing most of my sales.

= I have been very successful at landing most of my sales because I offer my customers a high level of support and fair prices.

Part

2

99％會問的面試題

2-5 業績

03 Do you prefer a long or short sales cycle?

What do you prefer, the longer sales cycle or shorter sales cycle?

你偏好較長的銷售週期或較短的銷售週期？

▶ 題 解

銷售週期通常有分長與短。這樣的問題沒有正確答案，只要能講出為何偏好長銷售週期或短銷售週期即可。當然也可不表達偏好，表示你兩種都喜歡，都擅長。要注意說明偏好原因時必須言之有物，讓面試官覺得你是專業的，並有能力達成銷售目標。

▶ 短回答 ── 基本版　🎧 MP3 070

I prefer a longer sales cycle because the pace can be adjusted depending on the individual clients I am dealing with. Some clients like to have a lot of information about a product and have a lot of technical questions. Others are more interested in the personal benefits of a product.

我較喜歡較長的銷售週期，因為銷售速度可以根據你所處理的各個客戶進行調整。有些客戶喜歡有很多關於產品的資訊，並有很多關於技術的問題。其他客戶對產品可提供的個人利益更感興趣。

▶ 短回答 ── 進階版

I really enjoy the quicker pace of a shorter sales cycle. I like to get right to the point about my product's features and benefits, and showcase the reasons why it's the best choice for the customer. I'm knowledgeable about what I am selling, and ready with answers to any questions my customers may have.

我真的很喜歡短銷售週期的快速步伐。我喜歡馬上進入到產品的特點和優勢點，並展示為何它是客戶的最佳選擇。我很熟悉我所販賣的東西，並準備好回答客戶所提出的任何問題。

▶ 評 解

兩個回答都陳述身為業務有的專業與技能。

▶ 長回答 🎧 MP3 071

I think there are interesting points to both types of sales. I like a longer sales cycle, as it gives me time to get to know the customers, and spend time educating them about the benefits and uses of the product. Shorter cycles are more intense, since you typically don't have too much personal knowledge of the customer, or the time for lengthy explanations. You need to hit the high priority topics rather quickly. It's challenging but I enjoy the sense of accomplishment it offers when I close a sale. I am good at both types of sales and willing to commit to them.

我覺得這兩種類型的銷售都有其有趣的點。我喜歡較長的銷售週期，因為它給了我時間去了解客戶，並花時間教育他們有關產品的好處和用途。較短週期是比較密集的，因為你通常不會有太多客戶的個人資訊，也沒有時間冗長地解釋產品。您需要相當快速地到達最優先的主題。它很有挑戰性，我很享受當我完成銷售時它所給我的成就感。我擅長這兩種類型的銷售，並願意為它們努力。

▶ 評 解

這樣的回答讓人覺得你對兩種銷售週期都有所了解並擅長。

🍎 單字 🎧 MP3 072

❶ **cycle** [ˋsaɪk!] *n.* 週期；循環

❷ **intense** [ɪnˋtɛns] *adj.* 密集的；劇烈的

❸ **lengthy** [ˋlɛŋθɪ] *adj.* 長的；冗長的

❹ **hit** [hɪt] *v.* 達到，到達

❺ **priority** [praɪˋɔrətɪ] *n.* 優先考慮的事

✎ 用句型取勝

be interested in ~ 對~感興趣

👉 要注意

1. interested 為 interest 的過去分詞，詞性為形容詞。關於興趣的意思只有「～對__感有趣、關心」一種，且須以「～ be interested + in __」方式表示。注意：能感興趣的「～」只限於擁有感情感覺的東西，例如人物，所以主詞只能是人，而非事物。

2. S +be+interesting 裡的的 interesting 為 interest 的現在分詞。意思是「__是令人感到有趣的」。所以主詞可以是人物也可以是事物。

例句：

· I think those people can be our potential customers who may be interested in our new products.
我想那些人可以是我們的潛在客戶，他們或許會對我們的新產品感興趣。

· The new TV commercial is very interesting.
這個新的電視廣告很有趣。

the reason why...... 這就是……的原因

👉 要注意

1. the reason why 後要加完整子句。

2. the reason why 也可用 the reason that 取代，that 後一樣加完整子句。

例句：

· I always try my best to understand the reason why that certain customers choose not to buy our products.
我總是盡力去了解某些客戶選擇不購買我們的產品的原因。

· I helped my sales team figure out the reason why(that) the sales figures continued to decline in the past two quarters.
我幫我的銷售團隊找出銷售數字在過去兩季持續下降的原因。

換個說法令人眼睛一亮

(1) I prefer a longer sales cycle because the pace can be adjusted depending on the individual clients I am dealing with.

我較喜歡較長的銷售週期，因銷售速度可根據所處理的各個客戶進行調整。

= I prefer a longer sales cycle because I can adjust my pace according to different individual clients I am dealing with.

= I like a longer sales cycle in which the pace can be flexible due to different clients I am dealing with.

---

(2) I like to get right to the point about my product's features and benefits, and showcase the reasons why it's the best choice for the customer.

我喜歡馬上進入產品的特點和優勢，並展示為何它是客戶的最佳選擇。

= I like to get into the point about my product's features and benefits right away and show my customers the reasons why it's the best choice for them.

= I usually talk to my customers about the product's features and benefits right away and show them the reasons why it's the best choice for them.

---

(3) I like a longer sales cycle, as it gives me time to get to know the customers, and spend time educating them about the benefits and uses of the product.

我喜歡較長的銷售週期，因為它給了我時間去了解客戶，並花時間教育他們有關產品的好處和用途。

= I like a longer sales cycle in which I have more time to get to know the customers and educate them about the benefits and uses of the product.

= I prefer a longer sales cycle because I can spend more time understanding the customers and educating them about the benefits and uses of the product.

Part
2
99％會問的面試題

2-5 業績

Q04 What makes you a good sales person?

What personality traits do you possess that make you a good sales person?

是甚麼讓你成為一個優秀的業務人員？

▶ 題解

這個問題問的是作為一個優秀業務應該擁有甚麼樣的人格特質或技能。回答時可強調個人特質部分，因為不是每一個人都適合做業務。善於社交，有雄心壯志，有耐心，願意為客戶付出等都是優秀的銷售人員會有的特質。

▶ 短回答 — 基本版 🎧 MP3 073

I'm an ambitious person, and that helps me in sales. I really like to make sure that my customers are thoroughly informed, and that I provide the best service. I feel like I've done a good job when I have made a sale that required using all my talents.

我是一個雄心勃勃的人，而這項特質幫助我的銷售。我真的很喜歡確保我的客戶徹底了解，而且我提供最好的服務。當我用我的才能完成一項銷售時我覺得我做了一件很棒的事。

▶ 短回答 — 進階版

I think that my patience helps me be a good sales person. I find that I have made some of my best sales when I have taken the time to let the customer weigh their decision carefully, ask as many questions as they wished, and not put too much pressure on them.

我覺得我的耐心幫助我成為一個優秀的銷售人員。當我抽出時間來讓顧客仔細權衡

自己的決定並提出許多想問的問題，而不是把太多的壓力加諸在他們身上時，我發現我已經達成了一些最好的銷售。

 評 解

兩個回答強調雄心勃勃與富有耐心的個人特質。

▶ 長回答 🎧 MP3 074

To be a great sales person, I'm building a business, not just trying to make a sale. When I think beyond a sale, I get other people's attention much more easily. My clients are going to be more interested in what I have to say. I never just make a sale and forget about that client. I believe the last sale I make should always open the door to new relationships and clients. When I don't close a business deal, I don't think of it as a failed attempt. I know that some attempts pay while others don't, but they're all investments in the business.

Part

2

99％會問的面試題

要成為一個優秀的銷售人員，我在建立一個生意，不只是為了做銷售。當我思考超越銷售，我更容易得到別人的關注。我的客戶會對我說的話更感興趣。我從不只是做銷售，而忘了客戶。我相信最後一次交易總會為我開啟一扇門迎接新的人際關係和客戶。如果我無法完成一筆生意，我不認為它是一個失敗的嘗試。我了解有些嘗試會有收穫而有些不會，但它們都是在業務上的投資。

 評 解

回答中陳述一些作為優秀業務的態度與做法。

🍎 **單 字** 🎧 MP3 075

❶ **interested** [`ɪntərɪstɪd] *adj.* 感興趣的；關心的
❷ **relationship** [rɪ`leʃən`ʃɪp] *n.* 人際關係
❸ **deal** [dil] *n.* 交易
❹ **failed** [feld] *adj.* 失敗了的
❺ **attempt** [ə`tɛmpt] *n.* 企圖，嘗試

用句型取勝

put pressure on sb 給某人壓力

要注意

1. put pressure on sb
   = make sb under pressure。
2. under pressure 指「在有壓力的情況下」。
3. pressure 和 stress 相同處為兩字同為名詞的「壓力、緊張」，而差異處在於：pressure 當名詞時，還有以下意思：

   ⑴按、壓、擠⑵困擾、艱難⑶大氣壓力。當及物動詞時表「對…施加壓力；迫使」[(+into)]。

   stress 當名詞則還當作以下意思：

   ⑴著重、重要性[(+on)]⑵重音；重讀[(+on)]。

   當及物動詞時則有兩個意思：

   ⑴強調，著重⑵用重音讀。而上班的壓力或是課業壓力，的確用 pressure 或 stress 都可以。

例句：

- I never force my customers to make purchases. In other words, I never put pressure on them.

  = I never force my customers to make purchases. In other words, I never make them under pressure.

  我從不強迫我的客戶購買，也就是説，我從不給他們壓力。

- Severe market competition continuously put pressure on product prices.

  市場競爭激烈令產品價格持續受壓。

think of A as B 把 A 視為 B

要注意

1. think of A as B = consider A as B。

例句：

· I think of /consider each individual client as my family member.
  我把我每一個客戶視為我的家人。

· I think of / consider every attempt as an investment in business.
  我把每一次的嘗試視為業務上的投資。

💡 換個說法令人眼睛一亮

(1) I think that my patience helps me be a good sales person.
   我覺得我的耐心幫助我成為一個優秀的銷售人員。

   = I think my patience makes me a good sales person.
   = I am a patient person, and that makes me a good sales person.

(2) To be a great sales person, I'm building a business, not just trying to make a sale.
   要成為一個優秀的銷售人員，我在建立一個生意，不只是為了做銷售。

   = To be a good sales person, I do more than just trying to make a sale. I am building a business.
   = Rather than just trying to make a sale, I want to be a great sales person by building a business.

(3) I believe the last sale I make should always open the door to new relationships and clients.
   我相信最後一次交易總會為我開啟一扇門迎接新的人際關係和客戶。

   = I believe the last sale I make can possibly bring me new relationships and clients.
   = I believe new relationships and clients can possibly come from the last sale I make.

2-6 未來目標

Where do you see yourself five years from now?

What do you want to be doing in five years?

你希望五年後成為怎樣的人？（你希望在五年內達成甚麼目標？）

▶ 題 解

面試官藉由這個問題想知道應徵者是否對自己的職涯有想法與規劃，而這樣的想法和規劃是否符合這個職缺。回答時要避免侷限在希望達到某一個特定的職稱或職位，也不要談太不切實際的夢想。重點應該擺在學習、專業與職涯發展。

▶ 短回答 ── 基本版 🎧 MP3 076

I would like to be part of the strategic team. Thus for these five years I won't be restricting myself from knowing other businesses of the organization and developing a comprehensive view of the organization along with expertise in each business I work in.

我希望成為策略團隊的一員。因此在這五年我不會限制自己學習公司的其他業務，發展對全公司業務的廣泛與全面的了解，並精進我從事的每一項業務的專門技術。

▶ 短回答 ── 進階版

I want to be a more skilled and efficient person with higher position in the company. I want to see myself become a valuable asset to the organization. One of the reasons this position excites me is that I think it will move me in that direction.

我想要成為一個更專業與更有效率的人，做到更高的職位。我希望看到自己成為公司重要的資產。我對這個職缺有高度興趣的原因之一是我相信它可以引領我達到這個目標。

▶ 評解

兩個回答的重點都在學習、專業與職涯發展並說明達成這樣的目標將為公司帶來價值。

▶ 長回答 🎧 MP3 077

I am definitely interested in making a long-term commitment to my next position. Judging by what I understand about this position, it's exactly what I'm looking for and what I am very well qualified to do. In terms of my future career path, I'm confident that if I do my work with excellence, opportunities will inevitable open up for me. It's always been that way in my career, and I'm confident I'll have similar opportunities here. I would very much like to move into a supervisory role in 5 years. I enjoy supporting my team members, and strive to set a good example for others.

我承諾對我的下一份工作長期投入。就我對這個職位的了解，這是我一直想追求的，自己也具備這份工作需要的資格條件。就我的職涯發展方面來說，我有自信只要我把事情做好，機會就會為我開啟。這也是我一直的工作態度，我確信在這裡我也會有相同的機會。我很希望能在五年內晉升到主管的職位。我喜歡支持我的團隊成員，努力樹立一個好榜樣給別人。

▶ 評解

這個回答加強對雇主說明自己對下一份工作的長期投入與正面的工作態度。應徵者不只陳述希望做到主管職，也闡述自己會是一個好主管。

🍎 單字 🎧 MP3 078

❶ **definitely** [`dɛfənɪtlɪ] *adv.* 肯定地
❷ **commitment** [kə`mɪtmənt] *n.* 承諾
❸ **inevitable** [ɪn`ɛvətəbl̩] *adj.* 不可避免的；必然（發生）的
❹ **supervisory** [ˌsupɚ`vaɪzərɪ] *adj.* 管理的
❺ **strive** [straɪv] *v.* 努力；苦幹；奮鬥

用句型取勝

make a commitment to 承諾；獻身於；致力於

要注意

1. 動詞要用 make，而不是 do。
2. to 後可接名詞或不定詞。
3. 也可用複數。make commitments to= make a commitment to
4. sb+make+a+commitment +to ～= sb+ commit+oneself+to～

例句：

- Our team made a commitment to increase the sales figure for the next quarter.

  我們團隊致力於提升下一季的銷售數字。

  = Our team made commitments to increase the sales figure for the next quarter.

  = Our team committed ourselves to increase the sales figure for the next quarter.

- They make a commitment to establish partnerships with other businesses.

  他們致力於和其他企業建立夥伴關係。

  = They make commitments to establish partnerships with other businesses.

  = They commit themselves to establish partnerships with other businesses.

in terms of 就～方面來說

要注意

1. in terms of =on the subject of=in the matter of
2. of 後接名詞或動名詞。

例句：

- The manager asked us to think of this matter in terms of an investment. 經理要求我們從投資的角度思考這件事。
- In terms of making money, my previous job was not very profitable, but I got valuable experiences from it. 就賺錢而言，我之前的工作並不是非常有利，但我從中獲取許多寶貴經驗。

💡 換個說法令人眼睛一亮

⑴ Judging by what I understand about this position, it's exactly what I'm looking for and what I am very well qualified to do.
就我對這個職位的了解，這是我一直想追求的，自己也具備這份工作需要的資格條件。

=By understanding this position, I know this is exactly what I want and what I am very good at doing.
= I've had a general understanding of this position, and believe that this is a job I always want and good at.

⑵ In terms of my future career path, I'm confident that if I do my work with excellence, opportunities will inevitable open up for me.
就我的職涯發展方面來說，我有自信只要我把事情做好，機會就會為我開啟。

=As for my future career path, I believe that opportunities come with my excellent work performance.
=On the subject of my future career path, I will have good opportunities as long as I do my work with excellence.

2-6 未來目標

02 How do you evaluate success?

What does success mean to you?

你如何定義「成功」？

▶ 題 解

這個問題在了解求職者的工作倫理，工作目標，與人格特質。回答方向要隨著所應徵的公司不同而作調整。例如，如果是應徵非營利組織的工作，其公司的目標是在社會影響而非金錢收入。因此在面試前應好好看過公司網頁，了解公司營運宗旨為何。當然也可以說明個人所定義的成功，而這個成功是對公司有幫助的。

▶ 短回答 ── 基本版　🎧 MP3 079

For me, success is the outcome of my hard work and dedication which I showed while working through my/company goals. And I believe in keep trying till we achieve success. At the end inner satisfaction is the main thing for success.

對我來說成功是我為達成工作（公司）目標而努力工作和奉獻的成果，且在過程中不斷努力直到達成目標。最終內心的成就感是成功最重要的因素。

▶ 短回答 ── 進階版

I try to set goals that meet company expectations, and work as hard as I can to complete those goals. If I make mistakes along the way, then I know I can improve, but if I reach those goals and achieve my desired outcome, I consider that a success.

我試著設定能符合公司期望的目標並努力工作來達成這些目標。如果在過程中犯錯可以讓我有自我改進的機會，但當我完成目標並達到期望的結果，這就是成功。

▶ 評解

兩個回答中成功的定義都是對公司有貢獻，這是雇主會喜歡聽到的答案。

▶ 長回答　🎧 MP3 080

I evaluate success in different ways. At work, it is meeting the goals set by my supervisors and maintaining an excellent working relationship with co-workers and clients. It is my understanding that your company is recognized for not only rewarding success, but giving employees opportunity to grow as well. I plan to take advantage of the training you offer so I can be more of an asset. Your company web site also lists yearly goals, which is a good motivator as well. After work, I enjoy playing tennis, so my measure of success is to win the match.

我用不同的方式定義成功。在工作上，成功是達到主管所設定的目標並和同事客戶維持良好的工作關係。就我了解貴公司是公認的會給員工成功獎勵並給予員工成長的機會。我計畫好好利用您提供的訓練讓自己成為公司有用的資產。您公司的網頁列出年度計畫也可以激勵我自己。下班後，我喜歡打網球，所以我定義的成功就是贏得球賽。

▶ 評解

這個回答有加註在工作外的成功定義，藉由健康的休閒娛樂向面試官表明自身身心健全。

單字　🎧 MP3 081

❶ **rewarding** [rɪ`wɔrdɪŋ] *adj.* 有益的；有報酬的

❷ **advantage** [əd`væntɪdʒ] *n.* 有利條件，優點，優勢

❸ **asset** [`æsɛt] *n.* 財產，資產

❹ **motivator** [`motɪvetɚ] *n.* 激發因素，動力

❺ **measure** [`mɛʒɚ] *n.v.* 測量；權衡

用句型取勝

as+形容詞或副詞 + as ... 和…一樣

要注意

1..這裡的形容詞／副詞用原級。

例句：

- I always work as hard as I can to reach the sales target.
  我總是努力工作以達成業務目標。
- I can say that my Japanese is as good as English.
  我可以說我的日文跟英文一樣好。

take advantage of~ 利用～

要注意

1. take advantage of 後可加事物或人。加事物是指正面地利用。加人是指負面地利用某人。
2. take advantage of 後加事物＝ make the most of something。

例句：

- I take full advantage of every new opportunity.
  我充分利用每一個新機會。
- I don't like the way my previous colleague takes advantages of those young interns.
  我不喜歡我之前的同事那樣利用年輕的實習生。
- I regret so much that I didn't take advantage of the opportunity to study abroad.
  =I regret so much that I didn't make the most of the opportunity to study abroad.
  我很後悔沒有利用那個機會出國念書。

- I took full advantage of my strength to win the competition.
  =I made the most of my strength to win the competition.
  我充分利用我的優勢贏了那場比賽。

💡 換個說法令人眼睛一亮

(1) For me success is the outcome of my hard work and dedication which I showed while working through my/company goals.
對我來說成功是我為達成工作（公司）目標而努力工作和奉獻的成果。

= My success is defined as my hard work and dedication for reaching my/company goals.
= When I achieved my/company goals after hard work and dedication, I consider myself successful.

(2) Your company web site also lists yearly goals, which is a good motivator as well.
您公司的網頁列出年度計畫也可以激勵我自己。

= The yearly goals listed on your company web site motivate me as well.
= I am motivated by the yearly goals listed on your company web site.

(3) I plan to take advantage of the training you offer so I can be more of an asset.
我計畫好好利用您提供的訓練讓自己成為公司有用的資產。

= I plan to go through the training program you offer to improve myself and make more contribution to you.
= I believe participating in your training program can make myself a valuable asset of the company.

2-6 未來目標

03 Would you rather work for money or job satisfaction?

Which would you prefer: excellent pay or job satisfaction?

你工作主要是為了薪水還是工作所帶來的滿足感？

▶ 題解

很明顯的，回答這樣的問題答案一定不會是為了錢，即使沒有人不喜歡高額的薪水。在面試時必須把自己的理想層次拉高，工作所帶來的滿足感的重要性絕對大於薪水。因此回答時不要談到多少的薪水會讓自己犧牲工作所帶來的滿足感。

▶ 短回答 ── 基本版 🎧 MP3 082

Some people may say that they work for money, while others work for a sense of accomplishment. For me, if it is to have job satisfaction, I will enjoy doing something significant, not dealing with the 9-5, long commutes and possible bad managers.

有些人可能會說他們工作是為了賺錢，而其他人是為了成就感而工作。對我來說，如果是為了有工作的滿意度，我會享受做一些有意義的事，而不是每天面對朝九晚五，長途通勤和可能出現的壞經理。

▶ 短回答 ── 進階版

I would always want my pay to be proportionate to the work I produce, and that would play a role in my job satisfaction. However, I would prefer to be happy with the work I do, so that I can come home and enjoy that feeling of contentment.

我總是希望我的薪水與我的工作產出是成正比的，這也會影響我的工作滿意度。不過，我更偏好做我喜歡的工作，這樣我就可以在每天下班後享受知足的感覺。

▶ 評解

兩個回答都説明了工作滿意度可以讓一個人樂於工作。

▶ 長回答 🎧 MP3 083

In this materialistic world, there are lots of people who believe that salary is the most important consideration when choosing a job or a career. But I believe that job satisfaction is the most important aspect above all else. Different people value different priorities in life. Some prefer financial well-being, while others including me go for more ethical values such as happiness, job security and a stress free environment. My personal conviction on this issue is that job satisfaction over money should be the main consideration in any career. It goes without saying that money is an "engine" of everything, but sometimes it may not be enough to provide job satisfaction to the employees.

在這個唯物主義的的世界裡，有很多人相信，選擇一個工作或職業時，工資是最重要的考慮因素。但我相信，工作滿意度是高於其他一切的最重要的面向。不同的人珍惜生命中不同的優先順序。有些人喜歡財務優渥，而其他人包括我會追求更多的道德價值，如快樂，工作保障和無壓力的環境。在這個問題上我個人的信念是工作滿意度應該超越過錢而為任何職業的主要考慮因素。不用説，金錢就是一切的「發動機」，但有時也未必足以提供員工工作滿意度。

▶ 評解

這樣的回答敘述可以説服面試官你誠摯地追求工作所帶來的滿足感。

🍎 單字 🎧 MP3 084

❶ **materialistic** [məˌtırıəl`ıstık] *adj.* 唯物論的；唯物主義的

❷ **ethical** [`εθık!] *adj.* 倫理的，道德的

❸ **security** [sı`kjʊrətı] *n.* 安全，安全感

❹ **conviction** [kən`vıkʃən] *n.* 確信，信念

❺ **issue** [`ıʃʊ] *n.* 問題；爭論；爭議

✍ 用句型取勝

prefer~ 偏好～

👉 **要注意**

1. prefer+ 名詞／動名詞／不定詞。
2. prefer A to B 在 = A 和 B 中更喜歡 A

例句：

- I prefer to work in a team, instead of working independently.
  = I prefer working in a team, instead of working independently.
  = I prefer working in a team to working independently.
  我較喜歡團隊工作而非獨立工作。
- In my free time, I'd prefer to just stay at home and relax.
  = In my free time, I'd prefer just staying at home and relax.
  在我空閒時，我喜歡待在家放鬆自己。

It goes without saying that~ 不用說～，不言而喻～

👉 **要注意**

1. that 後要加完整子句。
2. It goes without saying that~ = Needless to say, ~

例句：

- It goes without saying that money cannot buy everything.
  Needless to say, money cannot buy everything.
  不用說，金錢無法買到一切。
- It goes without saying that it's what I should do.
  =Needless to say, it's what I should do.
  不用說，這是我應該做的。

換個說法令人眼睛一亮

(1) Some people may say that they work for money, while others work for a sense of accomplishment.

有些人可能會說他們工作是為了賺錢，而其他人是為了成就感而工作。

= For some people, the purpose of work is making money, but others work for a sense of accomplishment.
= Some people work because they want to make money, while others work to have a sense of accomplishment.

(2) In this materialistic world, there are lots of people who believe that salary is the most important consideration when choosing a job or a career.

在這個唯物主義的世界裡，有很多人相信，選擇一個工作或職業時，工資是最重要的考慮因素。

= In this materialistic world, it's commonly believed that salary is the most important consideration when choosing a job or a career.
= In this materialistic world, many people only consider salary when choosing a job or a career.

(3) Different people value different priorities in life.

不同的人珍惜生命中不同的優先順序。

= Different people value different things in life.
= Different people have different priorities in life.

Part

2

99％會問的面試題

2-6 未來目標

04 Q What are your short term goals and long range objectives?

Tell us about your short-term and long-term goals.

你的短期和長期目標為何？

▶ 題 解

面試官想藉由這樣的問題了解應徵者是否會對工作投入，是否有企圖心。回答時要注意你的短期和長期目標必須相關。例如你的短期目標是在科技業工作，長期目標就不可能成為餐廳的高階主管。同時你的目標也必須和目標職位相關。可以鎖定一些適合大多數工作，較無特定性的目標。

▶ 短回答 — 基本版 🎧 MP3 085

As a college graduate, my short-term goal is to start building a presence in the industry, working for a company I respect and doing a job that I enjoy. My long term goals are to earn new responsibilities within the company; ultimately reaching higher positions and helping the company succeed in the long term.

作為一名大學畢業生，我的短期目標是要開始在行業中有自我的存在，為一個我尊重的公司工作並做我喜歡的工作。我的長遠目標是贏得公司內部更多的責任；最終達到更高的職位，並幫助該公司在長期的成功。

▶ 短回答 — 進階版

My short term goal is to improve my problem solving and interpersonal skills by working in a team. My long term goal is to create a unique and reputable image for me in any industry I work in, so that I can use my skills and experience towards helping my team members to improve themselves.

我的短期目標是在一個團隊中工作，以提高自己的問題解決能力和人際技巧。我的長遠目標是在我工作的行業裡創造一個獨特的，有信譽的自我形象，這樣我就可以用我的技能和經驗來幫助我的團隊成員提升自己。

▶ 評解

這兩個回答都是較無特定性的目標，適合大多數的工作。

▶ 長回答　🎧 MP3 086

My short term goal is to learn and acquire all the skills needed to perform excellent work in marketing. I want to find a position where I can contribute what I've learned through education and to gain real life experience. My long term goal is to get into a management position and take more responsibilities because I eventually want to become a marketing manager. I want to work with vendors and partners while managing a small group of workers. So I hope to be in a management position within seven years or so and I will do a diligent job by volunteering for extra work to gain more experience.

我的短期目標是學習和掌握所有能出色執行行銷所需的工作技能。我想找到一個可以貢獻在校所學並得到工作經驗的職位。我的長遠目標是要進入一個管理職位，並承擔更多的責任，因為我最終想成為一名行銷經理。我想要與供應商和合夥人合作管理一小群人。所以，我希望能在七年內左右得到一個管理職位，我會勤奮的工作，自願做額外的工作來獲得更多的經驗。

▶ 評解

短期和長期目標有關連性，且和目標職位（行銷工作）相關。回答中也説明自己的企圖心和願意為公司付出。

🍎 單字　🎧 MP3 087

❶ **perform** [pəˋfɔrm] *v.* 履行；執行；完成；做

❷ **responsibility** [rɪˌspɑnsəˋbɪlətɪ] *n.* 責任

❸ **eventually** [ɪˋvɛntʃʊəlɪ] *adv.* 最後，終於

❹ **vendor** [`vɛndɚ] *n.* 小販；叫賣者；供應商
❺ **partner** [`pɑrtnɚ] *n.* 合夥人，共同出資人

2 用句型取勝

where 當關係副詞的句型

要注意

1. 在此句中的 where 可不是疑問代名詞的「哪裡」，而是英語語法裡的「關係副詞」。用來修飾表示「地方」的名詞，而它是從「in which」、「on which」、「at which」所變化而來。

例句：

· I think no matter where I work or how old I get, there's always something new to learn about.
我認為不論我在哪裡工作，年紀多大，總有新東西要學習。

· The ABC company is the place where I worked for over ten years and I made many life-long friends.
ABC公司是我工作超過十年並交了很多一輩子朋友的地方。

while 所引導的時間副詞子句

要注意

1. when 和 while 用法的差異是：when 子句的動詞通常為過去（現在）簡單式，而 while 子句的動詞往往是過去（現在）進行式。
2. while 來引導時間副詞子句時通常表示同時在進行的兩個動作，在這樣的況下，兩個子句的動詞必須皆為進行式。

例句：

· I always take detailed notes while I was having a meeting.
我開會時都會做詳細的筆記。

· I was eager to learn new things while working on a new project.
當我在執行新的專案時，我求知若渴。

換個說法令人眼睛一亮

(1) My short term goal is to improve my problem solving and interpersonal skills by working in a team.

我的短期目標是在一個團隊中工作，以提高自己的問題解決能力和人際技巧。

= My short term goal is to have a chance of working in a team and therefore my problem solving and interpersonal skills can be improved.

= My short term objective is to improve my problem solving and interpersonal skills through teamwork.

(2) I want to find a position where I can contribute what I've learned through education and to gain real life experience.

我想找到一個可以貢獻在校所學並得到工作經驗的職位。

= I want to be in a position which offers me real like experience and fully utilizes what I have learnt through education.

= I hope I can be offered a job in which my knowledge and skills learnt from school are appreciated and I will be granted practical work experience.

(3) My long term goal is to get into a management position and take more responsibilities because I eventually want to become a marketing manager.

我的長遠目標是要進入一個管理職位，並承擔更多的責任，因為我最終想成為一名行銷經理。

= Due to the fact that I eventually want to be a marketing manager, my long term objective is to be granted a management position and take more responsibilities.

= With the hope of eventually being a marketing manager, my long range goal is to take more responsibilities in a management position.

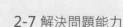

2-7 解決問題能力

01 How do you cope with conflict in the work place?

What do you do when you are faced with a conflict at work?

你如何處理工作場合中的衝突？

▶ 題 解

工作上與人的衝突在所難免。這個問題可看出應徵者如何處理衝突，如何跟同事或主管相處，如何處理難以取悅的客戶，如何面對人際上的壓力等。回答時儘量說明你如何面對衝突與解決它。

▶ 短回答 — 基本版 🎧 MP3 088

I always anticipate conflict and take steps to resolve this at the earliest possible stage, as I know that most of the conflicts can be resolved by just reaching out the people involved and communicating tactfully.

我總是對衝突有心理準備並按部就班在最可能的早期階段解決衝突。因為我知道大部分的衝突可以藉由找到相關人員並機智地與其溝通來解決。

▶ 短回答 — 進階版

Before proposing a solution to workplace conflict, I collect all relevant facts surrounding the conflict. According to my experiences, conflicts are often resolved if I devoted myself to determining root causes, while disregarding trivial or irrelevant facts.

在提出解決工作場合衝突的方法之前，我蒐集與此衝突所有相關的事實。根據我的經驗，如果我致力於找出根本原因，另一方面不理會瑣碎不重要的細節與不相關事實，衝突就會迎刃而解。

▶ 評 解

兩個回答都著重在說明如何面對與解決衝突。

▶ 長回答 🎧 MP3 089

I've experienced some situations wherein a disagreement led to conflict which had to be resolved. I have noticed that the main reason behind the occurrence of a conflict is the failure to see the situation's both sides. Hence, I had to ask the person to present his perspective before me and at the same time I ask him to permit me to explain my perspective fully. That is the point where I would make an effort to work with the person for the sake of finding out if there are any chances for a compromise to be reached.

我經歷過一些衝突都是因意見不一而引起。我注意到衝突發生的主要原因是沒有同時考慮到事件的雙方立場。因此，我必須詢問另一方的看法意見並要求對方同意我向他詳細解釋我的觀點。這就是我對衝突另一方所做的努力，為了要找出是否有機會達成妥協和解。

▶ 評 解

回答詳細說明如何找出衝突發商主要原因並試著解決它。

 🎧 MP3 090

❶ **disagreement** [ˌdɪsə`grimənt] *n.* 意見不一
❷ **conflict** [`kɑnflɪkt] *n.* 衝突；爭執
❸ **perspective** [pɚ`spɛktɪv] *n.* 看法，觀點
❹ **permit** [pɚ`mɪt] *v.* 允許，許可
❺ **compromise** [`kɑmprəˌmaɪz] *v.* 妥協，和解

Part

2

99％會問的面試題

用句型取勝

devote oneself to + N/ V-ing 奉獻心力努力去做某事

要注意

1. 可換成 be devoted to + N/ Ving，相當於 apply oneself to N/ Ving。除了反身代名詞外，一般名詞如時間、金錢、生命等也可做受詞，to 是介係詞，後接名詞或動名詞。

例句：

· I've devoted myself to research and development for the past three years. 我在過去三年致力於研發工作。
· Most of my spare time was devoted to animal welfare work.
  我大部分的空閒時間都花在動物福利工作。

lead to~ 導致～

要注意

1. lead to= result in= cause= bring as a result to。
2. to 後接名詞或動名詞。

例句：

· In formal meetings, I always avoid the wording that is likely to lead to ambiguity.
  =In formal meetings, I always avoid the wording that is likely to result in ambiguity.
  在正式會議中，我總是避免會導致模擬兩可的字詞。
· I truly believe that business success does not automatically lead to financial success.
  = I truly believe that business success does not automatically cause financial success.
  = I truly believe that business success does not automatically brings as a result to financial success.
  我真的相信經商成功不一定會賺錢。

換個說法令人眼睛一亮

(1) According to my experiences, conflicts are often resolved if sufficient time is devoted to determining root causes, while disregarding trivial or irrelevant facts.

如果有花足夠時間來找出根本原因，另一方面不理會瑣碎不重要的細節與不相關事實，衝突就會迎刃而解。

= I often resolve conflicts by devoting enough time to find out root causes and disregard trivial or irrelevant facts.

= According to my experiences, conflicts are resolved when root causes are determined and trivial or irrelevant facts are disregarded.

(2) I have noticed that the main reason behind the occurrence of a conflict is the failure to see the situation's both sides.

我注意到衝突發生的主要原因是沒有同時考慮到事件的雙方立場。

= I realized that conflict mainly results from failing to see the situation's both sides.

= I have noticed that conflict occurs when we fail to see the situation's both sides.

(3) That is the point where I would make an effort to work with the person for the sake of finding out if there are any chances for a compromise to be reached.

這就是我對衝突另一方所做的努力，為了要找出是否有機會達成妥協和解。

= This is the effort I made to work with person in order to find out if there are any chances for a compromise to be reached.

= I tried to work with the person for the purpose of finding out the possibility of reaching a compromise.

Part

2

99％會問的面試題

137

02 Q What major problems have you encountered at work?

Did you ever have any problem that bothered you a lot at work?
你曾經在工作上遭遇甚麼大問題嗎？

▶ 題 解

藉由這個問題應徵者可以加強說明自己的工作經驗。對這樣的問題一定要有所準備，如果你回答「沒有」，就會給面試官一個「此人並沒有足夠工作經驗」的印象。回答時要著重於說明自己是如何解決這個問題，而非花太多時間說明問題本身。

▶ 短回答 —— 基本版 🎧 MP3 091

When I found that one of my colleagues was saying things that weren't true behind my back, I went to him directly and talked it through. It turned out that he had misunderstood what I had said, and I was able to set the record straight with him, and my supervisor.

當我發現我的一個同事在我的背後說不是事實的事，我直接去找他，並一起談論這件事。原來，他誤解了我說的話，我因此能對他和我的上司澄清是非。

▶ 短回答 —— 進階版

Once I found a major flaw in the work of one senior member in my department, which could have been very costly to the company if it had been overlooked. I went directly to him, and called it to his attention so he could fix it before it affected the final outcome.

有一次，我發現在我的部門的一名資深成員在工作上有重大缺陷，這個缺陷如果被忽略可能會造成公司很大的損失。我就直接去找他，使他正視這個問題並在它影響到最終的結果前可以改進。

評 解

兩個回答都陳述了正面積極的問題解決辦法，並有良好的成果。

長回答 MP3 092

I had a customer complaining while I was working at Sports Direct. She had brought her two little boys' football teams T-shirts, and paid for their names and numbers to be printed on the back of the shirts. But some information was printed wrong. She wanted her money back and she was going to go elsewhere to get them done. I offered her a refund for the T-shirts that had the mistake on, or she could get the T-shirts re-printed but for 20% off the original price. She was happy and chose the 20% off deal. The customer came back again for more T-shirts to be printed after that.

我在Sports Direct（體育用品店）工作時有一個客戶抱怨。她帶來了她兩個小兒子足球隊球衣，付錢要求把他們的姓名和球員號碼印在衣服背面。但有些被印錯了。她想要退款，並到其他地方重印。我讓她選擇要退費，或是以原價的八折重印。她很高興，並選擇了八折的優惠。之後這位顧客又帶來更多的 T 恤要求打印。

評 解

處理客戶抱怨是應徵業務類工作必要的工作技能，用實際例子說明處理方法增加說服力。

 單 字 MP3 093

❶ **complain** [kəm`plen] *v.* 抱怨，發牢騷
❷ **brought** [brɔt] *v.* bring 的過去式與過去分詞
❸ **elsewhere** [`ɛls͵hwɛr] *adv.* 在別處；往別處
❹ **refund** [rɪ`fʌnd] *n.* 退還，歸還；償還
❺ **original** [ə`rɪdʒən!] *adj.* 最初的，本來的；原始的

Part

2

99％會問的面試題

用句型取勝

turn out~ 結果是

要注意

1. turn out that +子句。
2. turn out to be+名詞= become +名詞。
3. turn out +形容詞。

例句:

- The event we organized turned out to be a great success.
  = It turned out that the event we organized is a great success.
  我們策畫的這個活動結果很成功。
- I ensure my team members that things will turn out all right.
  我跟我的團隊成員保證事情都會好轉的。

set the record straight 澄清是非；糾正誤解

要注意

1. To set the record straight, S+V......。
2. 也可用 S+V...... in order to set the record straight 取代。

例句:

- To set the record straight, I must say now that I never supported the idea.
  =I must say now that I never supported the idea in order to set the record straight.
  為了糾正誤解，我現在必須說我從未支持這個意見。
- As a manager, I always search for the truth and set the record straight to avoid the slanders.
  作為一個主管，我總是追求真理，澄清是非以杜絕毀謗。

換個說法令人眼睛一亮

⑴ Once I found a major flaw in the work of one senior member in my department, which could have been very costly to the company if it had been overlooked.

有一次，我發現在我的部門的一名資深成員在工作上有重大缺陷，這個缺陷如果被忽略可能會造成公司很大的成本。

= Once I found that the work of one senior member in my department has a major flaw which can't be overlooked otherwise it could have been very costly to the company.

= Once I found a major flaw in the work of one senior member in my department, which could have cost the company huge amount of money if we had overlooked the issue.

⑵ I offered her a refund for the T-shirts that had the mistake on, or she could get the T-shirts re-printed but for 20% off the original price.

我讓她選擇要退費，或是原價的八折重印。

= I offered her a refund for the T-shirts that had the mistake on, or she could just pay 20% off the original price to re-reprint the T-shirts.

= I offer her either a refund for the T-shirts that had the mistake on or a 20% discount on reprinting the T-shirts.

⑶ The customer came back again for more T-shirts to be printed after that.

之後這位顧客又帶來更多的 T 恤進行打印。

= After that the customer brought back more T-shirts to be printed.

= Later on the customer asked us to print more T-shirts.

Part

2

99％會問的面試題

2-7 解決問題能力

Q 03 Did you ever have a heavy workload?

Describe a time when your workload was heavy.
你曾經有繁重工作量嗎？

▶ 題 解

面試官會問這個問題通常意味著應徵的這個職位工作量和要承擔的壓力是比較大的。回答時舉一個實際的例子，說明自己是有能力負荷大的工作量並抗壓把事情做好。如果沒有類似工作經驗，可以舉在校功課繁重的例子。

▶ 短回答 — 基本版 🎧 MP3 094

I used to work in a busy fashion store and there was a staff shortage. I had to work long hours to help keep the shop covered during its busiest period. At that time I viewed it as a challenge and was pleased that I was able to work hard and help.

我曾經在一個繁忙的時裝店工作，有工作人員短缺的問題。我不得不長時間工作，以幫助店家在其最繁忙的時段能正常營運。當時我把它視為一個挑戰，我很高興我能努力工作並提供幫助。

▶ 短回答 — 進階版

When I was working on a software implementation team at ABC Company, we took over another company and had to transit many clients to a new product in a short period of time. It required a lot of planning, time, hard work, and effort, but I was able to complete the project in a timely manner.

當我在 ABC 公司的一個軟體執行團隊工作，我們接手了另一家公司，不得不在短時間內把許多客戶過渡到新產品。這需要很多的規劃、時間、勤奮和努力，但我能夠及時完成這個專案。

▶ 評解

回答不僅描述工作繁重的情況，也強調自己努力工作把事情做好。

▶ 長回答 🎧 MP3 095

While working at my previous job in an advertising graphics department, I had already delivered a signed off piece to a client, who then contacted me urgently needing to change the graphic as it contained an error they had previously missed. They needed the revised graphic for printing in two days' time, and I had other clients that required attention. <u>Under the circumstances, I managed to use my time effectively in order to be able to make this last minute change to keep my client happy, and still complete my other works on time.</u>

當我之前在廣告製圖部門工作時，我已經送了一個簽字完稿的作品到客戶端，這個客戶之後再聯繫我並迫切需要改變圖形，因為它包含了一個他們之前沒檢查出的錯誤。他們需要在兩天的時間內將修改後的圖形打印，而我還有其他客戶需要處理。在那樣的情況下，我有效地利用和管理我的時間，以便能夠在最後的時間做修正讓我的客戶高興，而且還準時完成我的其他作品。

▶ 評解

回答強調能夠有效管理時間，這是應付繁重工作的必要技能。

🍎 單字 🎧 MP3 096

❶ **graphics** [`græfɪks] *n.* 製圖法
❷ **urgently** [`ɝdʒəntlɪ] *adv.* 緊急地，急迫地
❸ **contain** [kən`ten] *v.* 包含；容納
❹ **error** [`ɛrə] *n.* 錯誤，失誤，差錯
❺ **circumstance** [`sɝkəmˌstæns] *n.* 情況，環境；情勢

用句型取勝

used to +原型動詞，用來表示現在不存在的以前習慣

✍ 要注意

1. sb + be V + used + to +原型動詞，則表示某人習慣做某事，意思不同，要區分清楚。差別在加了一個 Be 動詞。

例句：

- I used to work ten hours a day.
  我曾經一天工作十小時。
- I used to do three projects at the same time and complete all of them in time.
  我曾經同時做三個專案並及時完成它們。

under the circumstances 在這樣的情況下

✍ 要注意

1. circumstance 這個字在當「情況」時，要用複數，而且搭配的介係詞是 under。
   circumstances 指的是外在種種條件和因素。
2. situation 和 circumstance 這兩個字都被翻譯為「情況」，但它們的意思並不一樣，實際用法上也不一樣。
   situation 要搭配的介係詞是 in 。situation 指的是一個已經形成的局面，而人陷在這個局面裡。

例句：

- Nobody can help me under the circumstances, but I still completed the job in a professional manner.
  在那樣的情況下沒有人可以幫我，但我還是很專業地完成了計畫。
- I was extremely tired under the circumstances, but I decided to work overtime in order to complete the job in time.
  我非常地累但我決定加班工作以及時完成工作。

換個說法令人眼睛一亮

(1) At that time I viewed it as a challenge and was pleased that I was able to work hard and help.

當時我把它視為一個挑戰，我很高興我能努力工作並提供幫助。

= At that time I considered it as a challenge and being able to work hard and provide help made me happy.

= I took the challenge and worked hard to provide help, which made me happy.

---

(2) It required a lot of planning, time, hard work, and effort, but I was able to complete the project in a timely manner.

這需要很多的規劃、時間、勤奮和努力，但我能夠及時完成這個專案。

= I spent lots of time on planning, paid effort, and work hard. At the end, I completed the project in time.

= The project was completed in time with my planning, hard work and effort.

---

(3) They needed the revised graphic for printing in two days' time, and I had other clients that required attention.

他們需要在兩天的時間內將修改後的圖形打印，而我還有其他客戶需要處理。

= They requested the graphic revised in two days' time, and I needed to serve other clients at the same time.

= I had to make sure that the graphic was revised and sent for printing in two days, and meanwhile I needed to serve other clients.

Part

2

99％會問的面試題

2-8 執行能力

01 How do you go about making important decisions at work?

What's your strategy of making difficult decisions at work?

在工作上你如何作重要的決定？

▶ 題解

這類的問題在應徵管理階層職務時是很常見的。當被問到這個問題時，應徵者應該把握機會說服面試官你有批判思考、分析、與創造的能力，或者因你良好管理技巧做出正確決定後為公司帶來利益，或者你正努力培養這些能力。

▶ 短回答 — 基本版 🎧 MP3 097

When I'm faced with an important decision, I would ask the advice of others. I try to consider everything. But ultimately I'm the one who decides. The higher I go in the management, the more responsibility I have and the more decisions I have to make by myself.

當我面對一個重要決定時，我會詢問別人的意見。我試著考慮所有因素。但最終我會是做決定的人。當我在越高的管理職位上時，我必須負的責任就越多，也必須靠自己做更多的決定。

▶ 短回答 — 進階版

For me, important decisions are made by knowledge, information, wisdom, and experience. I'll gather all the information I can find and then apply my experience while analyzing the information. With this combination, I'm confident I'll make the correct important decisions.

對我來說，做重要的決定時必須倚賴知識、資訊、智慧，和經驗。我會蒐集所有我可以找到的資訊，然後就我的經驗分析此資訊。在這樣的組合之下，我有信心我可以做出正確的重要決定。

▶ 評 解

進階版回答較優因有說明其批判思考與分析的能力。

▶ 長回答　🎧 MP3 098

I think all decisions are important, and having as much information about the decision as I can is one of the most important aspects. After examining all the facts, I would think about the outcome and consequences of each action. After weighing the pros and cons, I would come to the best decision. However, I'm aware that some decisions are not as black and white. In this situation, I would rely on my experience, or even work with my team members to come up with the best decision.

我認為所有的決定都是重要的，儘可能擁有最多關於這個決定的資訊是非常重要的。在檢視完所有的事實之後，我會思考每一個採取動作的結果與後果。衡量過優缺點後，我會做一個最好的決定。然而我知道有些決定不是那麼黑白分明。在這樣的狀況下，我會仰賴我的經驗，甚至和我的團隊成員一起做出最好的決定。

▶ 評 解

此回答詳細說明做決定的過程與方法並告知面試官有良好的判斷思考力。

🍎 單 字　🎧 MP3 099

❶ **aspect** [`æspɛkt] *n.* 方面，觀點
❷ **examine** [ɪg`zæmɪn] *v.* 檢查；細查
❸ **consequence** [`kɑnsəˌkwɛns] *n.* 結果，後果
❹ **weigh** [we] *v.* 考慮；權衡
❺ **aware** [ə`wɛr] *adj.* 知道的，察覺的

用句型取勝

be aware that ~ 意識到、察覺到～

要注意

1. that 後要加子句。

2. 也可用 be aware of 表示，但 of 後要加名詞或動名詞。be aware of 注意到了…是固定用法，介係詞不能改變的。就像 be tired of（厭倦），have great effect on（影響很大），depend on（依賴）。這些介係詞都是固定的，要特別記一下

例句：

- I am well aware that this is a tough job.
  = I am well aware of this tough job.
  我深知這是一個棘手的工作。

- At that time, I haven't been aware of having done something wrong.
  = At that time, I haven't been aware that I have done something wrong.
  在那時候，我還沒意識到我做錯事情。

rely on 倚賴～

要注意

1. count on 指望；rely on 倚賴於；depend on 取決於。這三個片語意思相近，但文法上要注意 depend on 主語不能用人，只能是 it。count on 指望；rely on 倚賴於主語可以是人。

例句：

- I told myself that I can't rely on my parents anymore when I graduate from college.
  = 大學畢業時我就告訴我自己我不能再依賴我的父母。

- My weakness is sometimes I rely too much on my supervisor's judgment.
  = 我的缺點是有時候我太倚賴我主管的判斷。

換個說法令人眼睛一亮

(1) For me, important decisions are made by knowledge, information, wisdom, and experience.
對我來說，做重要的決定時必須倚賴知識、資訊、智慧，和經驗。

= I think when I have sufficient knowledge, information, wisdom, and experience, I can make correct decisions.
= Knowledge, information, wisdom, and experience are important factors when we are making important decisions.

(2) I'll gather all the information I can find and then apply my experience while analyzing the information.
我會蒐集所有我可以找到的資訊，然後就我的經驗分析此資訊。

= I'll try my best to gather all the information and analyze it using my experience.
= I'll gather as much information as I can and apply my experience when I analyze the information.

(3) I think all decisions are important, and having as much information about the decision as I can is one of the most important aspects.
我認為所有的決定都是重要的，儘可能擁有最多關於這個決定的資訊是非常重要的。

= Both the decisions themselves and having as much information about the decisions as possible are very important.
= When making each important decision, what matters is to have as much information about the decision as possible.

2-8 執行能力

Please tell me your experience in teamwork.

Please give some examples of teamwork.
請告訴我你在團隊工作方面的經驗。

▶ 題 解

這是一個很典型的面試題目。現今社會不論何種工作都需要團隊合作，想當然耳雇主會希望找到擅長團隊合作的人。回答時要表達你在團隊合作的經驗裡達成了甚麼正面的結果。也可表達你對團隊合作的熱情，如何在團隊中學習。

▶ 短回答 — 基本版 🎧 MP3 100

I was part of a team responsible for evaluating and selecting a new vendor for our office equipment and supplies. The inter-departmental team reviewed options, compared pricing and service, chose a vendor, and implemented the transition to the new vendor.

我參與的團隊負責評估和選擇我們的辦公設備及耗材新的供應商。這個跨部門小組審查選項，比較價格和服務，選擇供應商，並和新的供應商執行買賣。

▶ 短回答 — 進階版

In my last position, I was part of a software implementation team. We all worked together to plan and manage the implementation schedule, to provide customer training, and ensure a smooth transition for our customers. <u>Our team always completed our projects ahead of schedule with very positive reviews from our clients.</u>

在我的上一個工作，我是一個軟體執行團隊的一部分。我們共同努力規劃和管理實施時間表，以提供客戶培訓，確保我們的客戶順利交易。我們團隊總是在時程前完

成我們的專案並從我們的客戶那得到非常正面的評價。

▶ 評 解

進階班回答較優因其表明了團隊合作達成的良好績效。

▶ 長回答 🎧 MP3 101

In high school, I enjoyed playing soccer and performing with the marching band. Each required a different kind of team play, but the experience of learning to be a member of a group was invaluable. I continued to grow as team member while on my debate team and through my marketing class where we had numerous team assignments. I prefer teamwork. Different team members contribute different perspectives and the synergy between team members can produce creative and productive results. I believe that I have a lot to contribute to a team environment, and am comfortable in both leadership and player roles.

在高中時，我喜歡踢足球與軍樂隊表演。兩者都需要不同類型的團隊合作技能，但學習成為一個團隊成員的經驗是非常寶貴的。我在我參加的辯論隊和有很多小組作業的行銷課裡持續成長。我更喜歡團隊合作。不同的團隊成員貢獻不同的觀點且團隊成員之間的協力合作能產生有創造力和生產力的結果。我相信我對一個團隊會有很多貢獻，我也樂於擔任領導和團員的角色。

▶ 評 解

這個回答適用於較缺乏工作經驗的應屆畢業生。可以用社團和上課經驗來説明團隊合作的學習過程。

🍎 單字 🎧 MP3 102

❶ **debate** [dɪˋbet] *n.* 辯論，討論，爭論
❷ **numerous** [ˋnjumərəs] *adj.* 許多的，很多的
❸ **assignment** [əˋsaɪnmənt] *n.* 作業，功課
❹ **perspective** [pəˋspɛktɪv] *n.* 看法，觀點
❺ **synergy** [ˋsɪnədʒɪ] *n.* 共同作用，合力，協力

151

用句型取勝

ahead of 指時間或空間的「在…之前」

☞ 要注意

1. ahead of 也可表示「比…（高）」。
   Ex: He is ahead of me in English language skills.（他英語文能力比我強。）
2. 用於 ahead of time, 意為「提前」或「提早」。

例句：

- A punctual person like me always finishes everything ahead of time.
  像我這樣守時的人總是事先把事情做好。
- Our team always tried to get ahead of others in everything.
  我們團隊總是試圖處處領先他人。

continue+to V~ 繼續（做）～事

☞ 要注意

1. 也可用 continue+to+ 原形動詞表示繼續（做）～事。
   也可以用 continue + Ving。
2. continue+N. 表示繼續～事物。

例句：

- Our team continues to meet every week.
  = Our team continues the weekly meetings.
  = Our team continues meeting every week.
  我們團隊繼續每週碰面。
- We all know that it's useless to continue such a barren argument.
  我們都知道繼續這無聊的爭辯是沒用的。

換個說法令人眼睛一亮

(1) I was part of team responsible for evaluating and selecting a new vendor for our office equipment and supplies.

我參與的團隊負責評估和選擇我們的辦公設備及耗材新的供應商。

= The team I took part in was responsible for evaluating and selecting a new vendor for our office equipment and supplies.

= I participated in a team that was in charge of evaluating and selecting a new vendor for our office equipment and supplies.

(2) Our team always completed our projects ahead of schedule with very positive reviews from our clients.

我們團隊總是在時程前完成我們的專案並從我們的客戶那得到非常正面的評價。

= Our team always completed our project prior to the deadline and received very positive feedback from our clients.

= Not only did our team complete our projects ahead of schedule but also received very positive feedback from our customers.

(3) I continued to grow as team member while on my debate team and through my marketing class where we had numerous team assignments.

我在我參加的辯論隊和有很多小組作業的行銷課裡持續成長。

= I continue learning to be a good team member with the debate team and through my marketing class that gave us lots of team assignments.

= Being part of the debate team and the marketing class with numerous team assignments made me continuously grow as a team member.

Part

2

99％會問的面試題

153

03 Please describe the pace at which your work.

What's your pace while working?
請形容你的工作速度。

▶ 題 解

這樣的問題要小心回答。記得工作速度快不一定就好，工作速度太慢也不是雇主希望看到的。很多雇主寧願雇用用穩健步伐工作的人。回答時選擇說明自己用從容平穩的速度工作，但通常在期限前完成工作且工作的品質是好的。

▶ 短回答 ─ 基本版 🎧 MP3 103

I am well known for finishing my work ahead of deadlines without having to rush. I think of myself as diligent about my job. That means not only getting things done on time, but doing them right.

大家都知道我不用倉促行事就可在期限前完成工作。我覺得自己對工作是勤奮的。這不僅意味著把事情按時完成，也把事情做好。

▶ 短回答 ─ 進階版

Well, if something isn't done well, it doesn't matter if it's on schedule. At my last job we had a big holiday project that had to be done on time for the Christmas. I requested more resources. With a few temporary hires, we made it, and quality didn't suffer.

嗯，如果事情做不好，是否有如期完成就不是那麼重要了。在我的上一份工作，我們有一個大型的假日專案，為了聖誕節必須按時完成。我要求更多的資源。有了一些臨時員工，我們做到了，而且品質也沒有受到影響。

評 解

兩個回答都強調按時把工作完成並把事情做好。

▶ **長回答** 🎧 MP3 104

Planning is like my training, so I can work at a pace that reaches the goal while not burning me or others out. The people who work for me and I found that if we find a right pace and stick to it, we can do a little more than what is required. Constant impossible deadlines mean constant turnover. I used to have a boss that constantly pushed people to work faster, and then complained when there were mistakes. We were always replacing people that quit with new hires. I talked with her about it, and she toned it down a little. Later on she went from near bankruptcy to pretty decent success.

規劃就像是我的訓練，這樣我就可以在一個速度下工作不僅達到目標，也不會讓自己和其他人筋疲力竭。我和為我工作的人發現，如果我們發現一個對的步伐，堅持下去，我們能做的比需要更多一點。一直給一個不可能做到的最後期限意味著人員不斷更替。我曾經有一個老闆會不斷地催促人工作速度加快，然後有失誤時就抱怨。我們總是在雇用新人來代替那些離職的人。我就此與她談，她低調了一點。之後她從瀕臨破產到擁有相當不錯的成就。

▶ **評 解**

回答中說明速度快並不一定是好的，有時還會導致失誤，重點是找到一個適合的步伐來把工作做好。

 單 字 🎧 MP3 105

❶ pace [pes] *n.* 步速；速度；進度

❷ stick [stɪk] *v.* 停留；堅持；固守

❸ turnover [ˋtɝnˌovɚ] *n.* 人員更替數；人員更換率

❹ replace [rɪˋples] *v.* 取代

❺ bankruptcy [ˋbæŋkrəptsɪ] *n.* 破產，倒閉

用句型取勝

be known for~ 因～而著名

👆 要注意

1. S+ be known for 後所接內容表示某人或某物的特點或特長。
2. S+ be known as 後接名詞，此名詞表示一個人的身分、職業。
3. S+ be known to +N 誰所了解或知道
4. S+ be known to +V 人人都知道某人做了甚麼事
5. known 前可加 well 或 best 來形容，表示「非常著名」。

例句：

· My previous manager is well known for fair dealing.
我之前的主管因平等待人而非常著名。

· I am known for my unconventional views.
=I am known as a person with unconventional views.
我以我的新觀點著稱。

replace A with B 用 B 取代 A

👆 要注意

1. replace A with B = substitute B for A。

例句：

· We replaced those employees with poor performance with new hires.
= We substituted new hires for those employees with poor performance.
我們雇用新人來取代那些表現不好的職員。

· My previous company replaced manual operation with online operating system.
= My previous company substituted online operating system for manual operation.
我之前的公司用線上作業系統來取代人工操作。

換個說法令人眼睛一亮

⑴ I am well known for finishing my work ahead of deadlines without having to rush.

大家都知道我不用倉促行事就可在期限前完成工作。

= Everybody knows that I can finish my work prior to deadlines without rushing myself.

= I always finish my work ahead of deadlines while not rushing myself, which is known very well by others.

⑵ The people who work for me and I found that if we find a right pace and stick to it, we can do a little more than what is required.

我和為我工作的人發現，如果我們發現一個步伐，堅持下去，我們能做的比需要更多一點。

= My staff and I found that if we stick to a right pace, we can do a little more than what is required.

= My staff and I found that we can do more than expected if we stick to a right pace.

⑶ Constant impossible deadlines mean constant turnover.

一直給一個不可能做到的最後期限意味著人員不斷更替。

= Constantly giving impossible deadlines leads to a high turnover rate.

= A high turnover rate usually comes from constant impossible deadlines.

2-8 執行能力

04 How would you describe your work style?

What is your style of work?
你的工作風格如何？

▶ 題 解

這是一個大哉問，因工作風格包含很多面向。面試官想測試你是否有能力針對一個複雜的問題清楚，重點式地表達想法。回答時僅說自己是一個勤奮工作的人並不是一個好答案，而是要更加深入說明，有實例作證更好。

▶ 短回答 — 基本版　🎧 MP3 106

I am very careful. I keep records of my work all the time so that I can check the performance every time and avoid repeating work. And even more, I check for mistakes and make corrective actions as necessary.

我很小心。我一直記錄我所有的工作，這樣我可以每次檢查我的表現並避免重複工作。我甚至檢查錯誤並在必要時糾正行動。

▶ 短回答 — 進階版

Individually, I am always on the top of the best performance. However, to achieve the position I have now, I worked very closely with my colleagues and cooperated well with my team members. That's given me many advantages in dealing with tasks.

我個人總是有最好的工作表現。不過，要達到我現在這個職位，我與我的同事非常密切地工作和我的團隊成員們合作無間。這給了我在處理任務時很多優勢。

▶ 評 解

團隊合作與檢查紀錄的習慣就是比只說勤奮工作較為深入的實例。

▶ 長回答 🎧 MP3 107

My workplace style is adaptive. In general I try to keep a fast pace, focus on the schedule in order to complete one project and move onto another. Yet I try to be efficient and I am a bit of a perfectionist, so if the project requires me to slow down in order ensure that the final result is error free, I will do so. I work well on my own but I am happy to work within a team. I take my role in any project seriously, so I am always dedicated and driven.

我的工作風格是適應力強的。在一般狀況下我儘量保持快節奏，注重時間表為了完成一個專案並進行到下一個。但我儘量保持效率且有點完美主義，所以如果該專案需要我慢下來以確保最終的結果是沒有錯誤的，我就會這樣做。我獨立工作時表現好，但我也很高興能在一個團隊中工作。我把我在任何專案中所負責的角色嚴肅看待，所以我一直對工作奉獻與受到驅策的。

▶ 評 解

常回答的內容提到多項正面的工作風格，更具說服力。

🍎 單 字 🎧 MP3 108

❶ **adaptive** [ə`dæptɪv] *adj.* 適應力強的
❷ **perfectionist** [pɚ`fɛkʃənɪst] *n.* 追求完美的人
❸ **seriously** [`sɪrɪəslɪ] *adv.* 嚴肅地
❹ **dedicated** [`dɛdə͵ketɪd] *adj.* 專注的；奉獻的
❺ **driven** [`drɪvən] *adj.* 受到驅策的

用句型取勝

in general 通常，一般而言；大體上

👉 要注意

1. in general = general speaking
2. 與 in general 相關的片語有：
   as ... go(es) 就…來說
   as far as 遠到…，直到…
   by and large= on the whole 總的來說，一般來說
   in general 通常，一般而言；大體上
   in short 簡而言之
   in terms of ... 從…立場；就…而言
   on the part of 就…而言；代表…；由…做出的
   when it comes to 一談到…；就…而論
   with respect to 就…而言；在…方面

例句：

- In general, I finish work ahead of schedule.
  一般而言，我會在進度超前的情況下完成工作。
- My work performance is good in general.
  我的工作表現通常都很好。

yet 的兩種用法

👉 要注意

1. yet 是連接詞，和 but 意思相近。
2. 在完成時態（perfect tense）的否定句中表示「仍然（未）」。

例句：

- I can't always work fast, yet I make sure there is no error in my work.
  我不是總是能以快速度工作，但我確保我的工作沒有錯誤。

· I have not yet got the chance to review the sales report.
我還沒有機會看過那個銷售報告。

💡 換個說法令人眼睛一亮

(1) I keep records of my work all the time so that I can check the performance every time and avoid repeating work.
我一直記錄我所有的工作，這樣我可以每次檢查我的表現並避免重複工作。

= I check the performance every time and avoid repeating work by recording my work all the time.
= Keeping records of my work all the time helps me check the performance every time and avoid repeating work.

(2) In general I try to keep a fast pace, focus on the schedule in order to complete one project and move onto another.
在一般狀況下我儘量保持快節奏，注重時間表為了完成一個專案並進行到下一個。

= Generally speaking, I work fast, keeping my eyes on the schedule in order to complete one project and move onto another.
= In general, I complete projects one by one by keeping a fast pace and focusing on the schedule.

(3) I work well on my own but I am happy to work within a team.
我獨立工作時表現好，但我也很高興能在一個團隊中工作。

= I am good at both independent work and team work.
= I enjoy and work well in both independent work and team work.

What will you do to adjust yourself to the new job in the first 60 days?

What can we expect from you in the first 60 days?

你會如何在前兩個月讓自己適應新工作？

▶ 題解

面試官會問這個問題是因為想找出能儘快對公司有所貢獻的新人。回答重點是要提到自己學習速度快並會要求自己在前兩個月就能有生產力。自己會如何快速學習並掌握與新工作有關的知識和技能。願意接受挑戰與儘快融入新環境。

▶ 短回答 — 基本版 🎧 MP3 109

I prefer to write down objectives for learning to stay on track. For example, you have emphasized how important the online purchasing system to this job, so I would include the goal of mastering that system during the first two weeks at the top of my list.

我喜歡寫下學習目標以跟上腳步。舉例來說，你已經強調了網上採購系統對這個工作非常重要，所以我會將掌握該系統列為我頭兩個星期目標清單的第一位。

▶ 短回答 — 進階版

I will compile a list of questions that couldn't be answered through printed resources as I go through my daily routine. Then, I would address these questions to my supervisor or her designee at appropriate times to protect my boss from untimely interruptions.

在我每天的例行工作中，我會匯編無法由印刷資料中獲得解答的問題。然後，我會在適當的時間向我的主管或她指定的人提及這些問題，以保護我的老闆不受到不合時宜的干擾。

評 解

兩個回答都説明了重點：如何快速學習新工作所需的知識和技能。

▶ 長回答 🎧 MP3 110

I will reach out to all the colleagues in my department and intersecting departments to learn as much as possible about the roles that various individuals play within the operation. <u>I will devour the policies and procedures for the unit that you have referred to</u>. During the evenings, I'll continue reading everything I can find about the company and industry to get an accurate fix on the state of the firm within the marketplace. Our professional association offers some online tutorials on advanced Excel so I will work on those during my off hours.

我會向在我的部門和其他部門裡所有的同事盡可能學習不同個人在營運中所扮演的角色。我會大量地讀你提及的關於該單位的政策和程序。在晚上，我會繼續閱讀關於公司和產業的一切，以獲得對市場內公司的狀態精確的修正。我們的職業工會提供進階 Excel 的線上個別輔導課程，所以我將在我的下班時間學習。

▶ 評 解

回答中表明強烈的學習動機與將採用多元的學習管道。

 單字 🎧 MP3 111

❶ **intersecting** [ˌɪntɚˋsɛkt] *adj.* 相交的，交叉的
❷ **devour** [dɪˋvaʊr] *v.* 貪婪地看（或聽，讀等）
❸ **refer** [rɪˋfɝ] *v.* 論及，談到，提及
❹ **association** [əˌsosɪˋeʃən] *n.* 協會，公會，社團
❺ **tutorial** [tjuˋtorɪəl] *n.* 個別指導課程

Part

2

99％會問的面試題

用句型取勝

protect ... from sth （保護）使…免於

👉 要注意

1. protect ... from sth = protect ... against doing.
2. prevent ... from doing sth = stop ... from doing sth 阻止…做…。

例句：

· I tried not to seem critical or judgmental while giving advice that would protect him from ridicule.
  = I tried not to seem critical or judgmental while giving advice that would prevent/ stop him from being ridiculed.
  我在給他提供意見時盡量避免顯得挑剔或妄下判斷，讓他免受奚落。
· I understand that most people protect themselves from injury to their self - esteem.
  = I understand that most people prevent others from hurting their self-esteem.
  我了解大多數人會保護自己自尊心不受傷害。

refer to 談到、提到

👉 要注意

1. refer 一定要加 to。
2. refer to 也有表示「查閱」、「與…有關」、「涉及」、「關於」、「指的是」的意思。

例句：

· As a department manager, I usually refer to my planning for the future in the monthly meetings.
  作為一個部門主管我通常在每月會議中談到對未來的規劃。
· We technicians usually refer to the operation manual for answers.
  我們技術人員通常會查閱操作手冊找尋答案。

換個說法令人眼睛一亮

(1) I will compile a list of questions that couldn't be answered through printed resources as I go through my daily routine.

在我每天的例行工作中，我會匯編無法由印刷資料中獲得解答的問題。

= I will compile a list of questions for which I can't find answers from printed resources during my daily routine work.

= A list of questions that couldn't be answered through printed resources will be compiled as I go through my daily routine.

(2) I will reach out to all the colleagues in my department and intersecting departments to learn as much as possible about the roles that various individuals play within the operation.

我會向在我的部門和其他部門裡所有的同事盡可能學習不同個人在營運中所扮演的角色。

= I will try my best to learn the roles that various individuals play within the operation from all the colleagues in my department and intersecting departments.

= I will do my best to understand what roles individuals play in the firm from people in my department and intersecting departments.

(3) Our professional association offers some online tutorials on advanced Excel so I will work on those during my off hours.

我們的職業工會提供進階 Excel 的線上個別輔導課程，所以我將在我的下班時間學習。

= During my free time, I will learn advanced Excel through online tutorials offered by our professional association.

= During my off hours, I will take advantage of some online tutorials offered by our professional association to learn advanced Excel.

2-8 執行能力

06 Give me an example of using your initiative in your previous job?

Can you describe a time when you have taken initiative?

給我一個你在之前工作採取主動的例子？

▶ 題解

雇主都希望找到在工作上主動積極的人，而非被動地第一個口令一個動作。回答時要以實例說明你如何採取主動，而採取主動做的工作又為公司帶來甚麼好處。也可說明你的新想法和新作為改善了公司的某一部分。

▶ 短回答 — 基本版 🎧 MP3 112

On one occasion, we were informed that we could send vacation requests via email. We had template forms for other purposes but not for vacation, so I created a template and started to use it. Everyone else also started to use it and eventually, it became our shop standard.

有一次，我們被告知我們可以透過電子郵件發送休假請求。我們有作其他用途的制式格式，但不適合休假，所以我創建了一個格式並開始使用它。其他人也都開始使用它，最終，它成了我們公司的標準。

▶ 短回答 — 進階版

I don't generally wait to be told to do something, I try to think of things I can do to benefit the situation. For instance, when I was told to build the membership guide, I realized the previous person who did it had left no records of how to use the template and how to download the data. I then created a process instruction sheet so that it was down in writing.

我通常不會等待著被告知要做些什麼，我試圖想我可以做甚麼事以造福現狀。例如，當我被告知要建立會員指南，我意識到以前做這個工作的人沒有留下如何使用制式格式以及下載資料的記錄。然後，我建立了一個使用程序說明書，所以它就有書面資料了。

▶ 評 解

兩個回答都以實例說明主動積極的工作態度。

▶ 長回答 🎧 MP3 113

On my job, I had several complicated processes that I would have to do on a regular basis. In addition to just doing those processes, I documented each process step by step, and created a shared directory where other members of my team could access the information. No one asked me to do this, and it was not required. Ten years later, people still come by with one of those documents to ask me questions, and they tell me how valuable the information has been for them and how much they appreciate my taking the time to do that.

在我的工作，我有幾個複雜的程序我必須定期做。除了只是做那些程序，我還記錄了每一步程序，建立一個和團隊中的其他成員共享的指南。沒有人要求我這樣做，它不是必需的。十年後，人們仍然會用這些文件來問我問題，他們告訴我這些資訊對他們而言是多麼有價值，他們非常感謝我抽出時間來做到這一點。

▶ 評 解

回答中說明主動建立的指南為公司帶來長期的益處。

🍎 單 字 🎧 MP3 114

❶ **process** [`prɑsɛs] *n.* 步驟；程序；工序；製作法
❷ **document** [`dɑkjəmənt] *v.* 紀錄
❸ **directory** [də`rɛktərɪ] *n.* 指南，使用手冊
❹ **access** [`æksɛs] *v.* 接近，進入；接近的機會，進入的權利；使用
❺ **appreciate** [ə`priʃɪˌet] *v.* 感謝，感激

用句型取勝

via 經過；通過；憑藉

👉 要注意

1. 很多人不知 via 和 through 在用法上的區別。through 有三種詞性「介係詞」，「副詞」和「形容詞」；而 via 只有一種詞性「介係詞」。這兩個詞要區別對待的時候通常都是它們都被用做「介係詞」的時候。

2. through 做介係詞的時候，有如下意思：(1)穿越：從一邊進，從相對的或另一邊出(2)在…之中或之間(3)經過(4)透過：用…途徑或媒介。而 via 作為介係詞只有兩種意思：(1)經過(2)通過，憑藉。總結起來。用 via 的地方都可以用 through。因為 via 的兩個意思都被 through 包括了。但是用 through 的地方不一定能用 via。因為 through 的意思比 via 要廣泛。而且還有多種詞性。一般 through 較常用。via 相對而言用的比較少。

例句：

· I usually send my staff notices via internal email system.
我通常透過公司內部電腦郵件系統給員工發公告通知。

· In my previous job, I need to send daily reports via email to my boss.
我之前的工作必須每天藉由電子郵件向我的老闆報告。

for~purposes 為了～目的

👉 要注意

1. 介係詞要用 for。for ~ purposes = for the purpose of ~

例句：

· I went to the USA after graduation for research purposes.
= I went to the USA after graduation for the purpose of research.
我為了研究在畢業後去了美國。

· We give special offers for the purpose of introducing the new product to the market.
為了介紹新產品到市場，我們提供特別報價。

換個說法令人眼睛一亮

⑴ I don't generally wait to be told to do something, I try to think of things I can do to benefit the situation.

我通常不等待被告知要做些什麼，我試圖想我可以做甚麼事以造福現狀。

= Instead of waiting to be told to do something, I usually think of things I can do to benefit the situation.

= I don't wait to be informed of what to do, instead, I think of what I can do to benefit the situation.

⑵ I documented each process step by step, and created a shared directory where other members of my team could access the information.

我記錄了每一步程序，建立一個和團隊中的其他成員共享的指南。

= I put the procedure into writing as well as created a shared directory and therefore other members of my team could access the information in it.

= I made my team members be able to access the information by documenting each process step by step and then creating a shared directory.

⑶ They tell me how valuable the information has been for them and how much they appreciate my taking the time to do that.

他們告訴我這些資訊對他們而言是多麼有價值，他們非常感謝我抽出時間來做到這一點。

= They tell me the information has been very valuable for them and they thank me for taking the time to do that.

= They tell me they consider the information as very valuable and my taking time to do that has been greatly appreciated.

01 What's your management style?

How would you describe your management style?

你的管理風格為何？

▶ 題解

這個問題在應徵管理職位時是很基本的問題。面試官想要知道你如何管理領導員工，以及你每天如何處理與管理有關的工作。然而，管理有很多不同方式，針對不同部門或公司屬性也會有不同的管理風格。建議在面試前根據目標職位做相關研究找出最適合的管理方式。

▶ 短回答 — 基本版 🎧 MP3 115

I'm that kind of manager who varies my style depending on the type of situation or the nature of the employee. Sometimes constant checks and pressure application is required and sometimes giving space is a better option.

我是那種會視情況和員工特質而改變管理風格的主管。有時候頻繁檢查和施壓是必須的，而有時候給員工一點個人空間是較好的選擇。

▶ 短回答 — 進階版

My management style is a participative one. I believe that an organization can best survive if there is minimal rate of attrition in the company. Therefore, I am a manager who is more employee-centric rather than being a profit lover/seeker.

我的管理格是屬於分擔型的。我相信一個組織如果有很低的摩擦耗損率能最好地生存下來。因此我是一個比較以員工為重而非一味追求獲利的主管。

▶ 評解

兩個回答都清楚陳述個人管理風格。

▶ 長回答 🎧 MP3 116

My management style varies depending on the employee. I've found that people are different so a one-size fits all style doesn't work. However, I do apply some general rules such as focusing on hiring smart people with great problem solving skills and good communication; taking the time to explain the business value of the work the employees are assigned to ensure motivation; and most importantly, having compassion for each person - show the person I value them, show the person I care when things are hard, and invest my time in the person.

我的管理風格會依據員工而改變。我了解每個人都不同因此「一個尺寸適合所有風格」是行不通的。然而我還是有採用一些通則例如聚焦在錄用聰明且有很好問題解決與溝通能力的人；花時間向員工解釋工作的商業價值以提高動機。最重要地，對每個人都有憐憫之心－表現出我重視這個人（員工），當工作很困難時表現出我的關心，並花時間和員工相處。

▶ 評解

回答中講述的管理通則適合大多數的管理職位。

📖 單字 🎧 MP3 117

❶ **vary** [ˋvɛrɪ] *v.* 使不同；變更；修改
❷ **apply** [əˋplaɪ] *v.* 應用；實施
❸ **solve** [sɑlv] *v.* 解決
❹ **compassion** [kəmˋpæʃən] *n.* 憐憫；同情
❺ **invest** [ɪnˋvɛst] *v.* 投資

用句型取勝

this kind of ~　這種種類的～

👉 要注意

1. kind of 用於表示種類，尤其用於 a kind of, this kind of ,that kind of, what kind of, every kind of 等結構。

例句：

- What kind of manager Mr. Wang is?
  王先生是哪一種主管？
- I promise I will not make this kind of promise again.
  我承諾我不會再犯這種錯誤。

depend on~ 取決於～

👉 要注意

1. depend 當取決於～時，只用作不及物動詞，通常與介係詞 on, upon 連用。
2. depend on [upon]＋某人或某物。
3. depend on [upon]＋子句。

例句：

- Our success depends on everyone's hard work.
  = Our success depends on whether everyone works hard or not.
  我們的成功取決於每個人的努力。
- I believe the opportunities available will depend on my previous work experience and qualifications.
  我相信能否有機會將取決於我的工作經歷和學歷。

💡 **換個說法令人眼睛一亮**

(1) I'm that kind of manager who varies my style depending on the type of situation or the nature of the employee.
我是那種會視情況和員工本質而改變管理風格的主管。

= My managing style varies according to the type of situation or the nature of the employee.
= My managing style differs when I am in different types of situations and meeting different employees.

(2) I am a manager who is more employee-centric rather than being a profit lover/ seeker.
我是一個比較以員工為重而非一味追求獲利的主管。

= Being a manager, I care more about employees rather than profits.
= I am not a profit-centric manager; rather, I care employees the most.

(3) I do apply some general rules such as focusing on hiring smart people with great problem solving skills and good communication.
我還是有採用一些通則例如聚焦在錄用聰明且有很好問題解決與溝通能力的人。

= One of the general rules I apply is hiring smart people with great problem solving skills and good communication.
= I do apply some general rules. For example, I hire smart people who have great problem solving and good communication skills.

2-9 管理能力

02 Describe how you managed a problem employee?

Did you ever have a problem employee, and how did you manage him/her?

你如何管理一個有問題的員工？

▶ 題解

當應徵管理階層職位時，你必須展現你是能夠管理各種類型的員工的。管理動機強表現好的員工是每個主管都會的，但雇主會希望能找到能改善員工不良表現的主管。回答時可以舉例說明你如何面對一個有問題的員工，並用何方法使其改善。

▶ 短回答 — 基本版 🎧 MP3 118

I would figure out what might be causing the problem and ask the employee to tell me how he perceives the issues. I also ask myself questions like: Does he need more training so he's not reliant on his coworkers?

我會找出什麼是造成問題的可能原因，並要求員工告訴我他如何看待這個問題。我也問自己這樣的問題：他是否需要更多的訓練，然後他可以不依賴他的同事？

▶ 短回答 — 進階版

I would talk to the person, mention his good qualities first, and move into the topics of concern. My main hope is to handle the issue without frustrating him, but giving him a direction of improvement and allowing him to take it from there.

我會和此人談，並先提到他好的特質，然後進入所關心的話題。我主要是希望能夠處理問題，但不挫敗他，而是給他改善的方向，並讓他從那裡開始做起。

▶ 評解

兩個問題陳述如何和員工談，並幫助其改善。

▶ 長回答 🎧 MP3 119

If I've identified factors contributing to the problem, I'd make suggestions about how the person might do things differently. For instance, if he has a time management issue, I would suggest that he begin planning projects backwards and set interim deadlines for himself to better structure his work. If he has a different idea than I do about how he should be spending his time, use this chance to get aligned so that we're both on the same page about expectations. After this conversation, in many cases, the employee will make the improvements needed. But if the problem persists, I talk about it again, but this time escalating the seriousness of the conversation.

如果我已找出造成問題的因素，我會建議此人做事情不同的方法。舉例來說，如果他有時間管理的問題，我建議他倒回去規劃專案，並為他自己設置過渡期限，以便更好地建構自己的工作。如果他對如何使用時間和我有不同的想法，利用這個機會達到密切合作，這樣我們會對期望有共識。在這次談話後，在許多情況下員工都會做出必要的改進。但如果問題仍然存在，我會再講一遍，但這次加強談話的嚴肅性。

▶ 評解

用實際的例子說明增加說服力。

🍎 單字 🎧 MP3 120

❶ **interim** [ˈɪntərɪm] *adj.* 間歇的，過渡期間的

❷ **structure** [ˈstrʌktʃɚ] *v.* 構造；組織；建造

❸ **aligned** [əˈlaɪnd] *adj.* 使結盟；使密切合作

❹ **persist** [pɚˈsɪst] *v.* 持續；存留

❺ **escalate** [ˈɛskəˌlet] *v.* 使逐步上升（增強或擴大）

用句型取勝

contribute to ～ 促成～，導致～

👆 要注意

1. contribute to = attribute to。
2. contribute 前加結果，後加原因（原因+contribute+結果）。
3. attribute 主詞常是人，動詞後加結果，to 後加原因（人＋attribute+結果＋to+原因）。

例句：

· Failing to concentrate contributes to his inefficiency at work.
= I attribute his inefficiency at work to failing to concentrate.
他工作沒效率歸因於無法專心。

· Talking to him in person contributed to my understanding of what his problems are.
= I attributed my understanding what his problems are to talking to him in person.
親自跟他談促成我能了解他的問題所在。

S+suggest~ 某人建議～

👆 要注意

1. 有「建議」的意思。advise、propose 也有此意，請比較它們用法的異同：(1)都可接名詞。(2)都可接動名詞。(3)都可接 that，that 後子句用 should+動詞原形，should 可以省略。

例句：

· I suggested/proposed/advised her to give up the unpractical idea.
=I suggested/proposed/advised her giving up the unpractical idea.
=I suggested/proposed/advised that she (should) give up the unpractical idea.
我建議她放棄這個不切實際的想法。

- I suggested them a way to tackle the problem.
  我建議他們怎樣處理這問題的方法。

💡 換個說法令人眼睛一亮

(1) I would figure out what might be causing the problem and ask the employee to tell me how he perceives the issues.
我會找出什麼是造成問題的可能原因，並要求員工告訴我他如何看待這個問題。

= I would identify the factors causing the problem and ask for the employee's opinions on this issue.
= I would find out what leads to the problem and the employee's perception of this issue.

(2) I would talk to the person, and mention his good qualities first, and move into the topics of concern.
我會和此人談，並先提到他好的特質，然後進入所關心的話題。

= I would have a conversation with the person, mentioning his good qualities, followed by the topics of concern.
= During the conversation with the person, I mention his good qualities first and then go on to the topics of concern.

(3) After this conversation, in many cases, the employee will make the improvements needed.
在這次談話後，在許多情況下員工都會做出必要的改進。

= Most of the employees will improve themselves after the conversation.
= Having a conversation with the employee often makes him/her make the needed improvements.

2-10 社交能力

01 How do you effectively communicate with others?

Tell us how you demonstrate good communications skills.

你如何有效率地和別人溝通？

▶ 題解

毫無疑問地，所有的雇主都希望雇用能與人有效率溝通的員工。因為沒有一個工作是不必與其他人溝通的。回答要描述你用甚麼方法和他人有效溝通，可以附加一些很正面的個人特質，例如良好的傾聽者，體貼的特質等。

▶ 短回答 — 基本版 🎧 MP3 121

I acknowledge another person's thoughts and feelings. Recognizing what someone else has to say, and how he/ she is feeling, is important for two-way communication between the sender and receiver. I recognize those thoughts and feelings without imposing personal analysis or judgment.

我承認其他人的想法和感受。認可別人想要說的話，和他們的感受，對訊息發送者和接收者之間的雙向溝通是非常重要。我會認真理解這些想法和感受，且絕不強加個人的分析和判斷。

▶ 短回答 — 進階版

I consider listening as an important element of communication, particularly in confrontations or difficult communicative situations. Focus on paying attention to body language that sets the speaker at ease. This in itself helps offset defenses and creates a comfortable communication environment.

我認為傾聽是溝通的一個重要組成部分，特別是在衝突或難以溝通的情況。著眼於讓説話者放鬆的肢體語言。這本身就有助於抵銷抗辯，並創建舒適的溝通環境。

▶ 評 解

兩個回答都描述了採用何種方法達到與他人良好溝通。

▶ 長回答 🎧 MP3 122

Effective communication is vital in our personal and professional lives. Misunderstandings can cost money, time and ruin relationships. Consequently, I ask questions when I need help understanding, then summarize what I am hearing. If I need more information, I'll ask for it in a manner that allows the other participants to clarify. For example, instead of directly asking, "So you don't like Mrs. Simmons?", I ask in a manner that does not corner the individual, such as, "If we hire Mrs. Simmons, how will that affect your job performance?" Then offer a summary of the responses and conversation.

有效的溝通對我們個人生活和職業生涯是至關重要的。誤解會花費金錢、時間並破壞人際關係。因此，當我需要幫助來理解某事，我會提出問題然後就我了解到的做一個總結。如果我需要更多的信息，我詢問的方式會讓其他參與者清楚明白。而不是直接問，例如，「所以你不喜歡西蒙斯太太？」，而是用另一種不使人陷入困境的方式問，例如，「如果我們僱用西蒙斯夫人，這將如何影響你的工作表現」然後提供反應和談話的摘要。

▶ 評 解

回答中指出生活上的實例來説明如何有效溝通不造成誤解。

♟ 單字 🎧 MP3 123

❶ **misunderstanding** [ˋmɪsʌndəˋstændɪŋ] *n.* 誤解
❷ **ruin** [ˋrʊɪn] *v.* 毀滅；崩潰；毀壞
❸ **summarize** [ˋsʌməˌraɪz] *v.* 總結，概述，概括
❹ **manner** [ˋmænə] *n.* 方式，方法
❺ **directly** [dəˋrɛktlɪ] *adv.* 直接地

Part

2

99％會問的面試題

用句型取勝

consider A as B 把 A 看做 B

👉 要注意

1.. consider 表示「認為」、「把……看作」，下面三個句型值得注意（有時三者可互換）：
　　(1)consider＋that＋子句
　　(2)consider A＋as＋名詞或形容詞
　　(3)consider A＋(to be)＋名詞或形容詞

例句：

· I consider myself as honest and hardworking.
　=I consider myself as an honest and hardworking man.
　=I consider that I am honest and hardworking.
　=I consider that I am an honest and hardworking man.
　我認為我自己是一位誠實且努力工作的人。

· I consider myself to be a considerate manager who cares the feelings of other people. 我認為自己是一個體貼的主管，會關心其他人的感受。

pay attention to~ 注意～

👉 要注意

1. pay attention to的英文意思是：place importance on。

例句：

· As far as I am concerned, a good organizer pays attention to detail.
　我認為一個好的組織者會注意到細節問題。

· When I am about to announce something, I would say to my team members: Pay attention to what I am going to say.
　當我要宣布事情時，我會對我團隊成員說：注意我將要說的話。

換個說法令人眼睛一亮

(1) I recognize those thoughts and feelings without imposing personal analysis or judgment.

我會認真理解這些想法和感受，且絕不強加個人的分析和判斷。

= Instead of imposing personal analysis or judgment, I recognize those thoughts and feelings.

= I don't impose personal analysis or judgment. Instead, I recognize those thoughts and feelings.

---

(2) I consider listening as an important element of communication, particularly in confrontations or difficult communicative situations.

我認為傾聽是溝通的一個重要組成部分，特別是在衝突或難以溝通的情況。

= In confrontations or difficult communicative situations, listening is an important element of good communication.

= Listening is an important key to successful communication, especially in confrontations or difficult communicative situations.

---

(3) Misunderstandings can cost money, time and ruin relationships.

誤解會花費金錢、時間並破壞人際關係。

= Misunderstanding costs time and money and has negative effects on relationships.

= It takes time and money to resolve misunderstanding and misunderstanding also ruins relationships.

2-10 社交能力

02 A co-worker is rude to customers, what would you do?

How would you react when a co-worker is rude to customers?

當你的同事對客戶無禮時，你會怎麼做？

▶ 題 解

不論你是應徵甚麼職級，甚麼類型的工作，面試官都想要確認你是有人際溝通技巧，可以和同事、主管、客戶和諧相處的人。「當你的同事對客戶無禮時，你會怎麼做？」回答這樣的問題時要陳述你會用正面和諧的方法處理這個問題。

▶ 短回答 ── 基本版　🎧 MP3 124

I'd try to get friendly with him, and see if there was something going on that was making him unhappy. Maybe he would just want to talk, and his attitude would improve.

我會用友善的態度對他，看看是否有一些事情使他不高興。也許他只是想與人談談，他的態度就會有所改善。

▶ 短回答 ── 進階版

If it only happened when the supervisor was gone, I would definitely call it to his attention. I wouldn't want to be a snitch, but a store's reputation depends largely on its customer service, and rude sales associates can create a negative impact on that reputation.

如果這件事只有發生在主管走後，我一定會讓他注意這件事。我不會想成為一個打小報告的人，但賣場的聲譽在很大程度上取決於它的客戶服務，無禮的銷售人員會為這個聲譽造成負面影響。

▶ 評 解

回答重點在用友善的態度來幫同事自我改善。

▶ 長回答 🎧 MP3 125

I would like to meet with him privately for a few minutes. During the meeting, I'd calmly say that there have been some problems during client meetings that I would like to bring to his attention, discuss, and jointly resolve. I focus on his negative behaviors such as specific rude remarks and interruptions that are not good for the firm's relationship with clients. However, I'd speak to my boss about the situation if he refuses to meet with me to discuss the problem; denies there is a problem; or refuses or is unable to change his behavior.

我想和他私下談幾分鐘。談話中,我會平靜地說,在客戶會議裡出現一些問題,我想提請他注意,討論,共同解決這些問題。我重點會放在他的負面行為例如特定粗魯的話,干擾客戶等不利於公司與客戶關係的行為。然而我會告知我的老闆這樣的狀況如果他拒絕與我見面討論問題;否認有問題存在;或拒絕或無法改變他的行為。

▶ 評 解

回答重點在於「私下談」、「平靜」、「共同解決」。

🍎 單字 🎧 MP3 126

❶ **privately** [ˋpraɪvɪtlɪ] *adv.* 私下地;不公開地
❷ **calmly** [ˋkɑmlɪ] *adv.* 冷靜地,沉著地
❸ **jointly** [ˋdʒɔɪntlɪ] *adv.* 共同地
❹ **rude** [rud] *adj.* 粗野的,粗魯的,無禮的
❺ **interruption** [ˌɪntəˋrʌpʃən] *n.* 打擾,干擾

Part 2 —— 99％會問的面試題

✍ 用句型取勝

call sth to sb's attention 使某人留心，注意某事

👉 要注意

1. call sth to sb's attention =call sb's attention to sth
   = make sb pay attention to sth。
2. 上述的兩個片語裡的動詞 call 可用 bring 替代。
3. call sb's attention to sth = draw/ catch sb's attention to sth。

例句：

- I call/ bring the right way of promoting products to the new sales person's attention.
  = I call/ bring/ draw/ catch the new sales person's attention to the right way of promoting products.
  =I make the new sales person pay attention to the right way of promoting products.
  我叫新的業務留心推銷商品的正確方法。
- The manager called/ brought John who has been isolated in the office to my attention.
  = The manager called/ brought/ drew/ caught my attention to John who has been isolated in the office.
  =The manager made me pay attention to John who has been isolated in the office.
  經理讓我多留心在辦公室裡被孤立的 John。

a negative impact on sth/ sb 對某事或某人的負面影響

👉 要注意

1. impact 可用 effect 或 influence 代替，都為名詞，但注意 effect 與 influence 的冠詞要用 an。

例句：

· Being too critical has a negative impact on individuals' social relationships. 太過吹毛求疵的或愛挑剔對個人的人際關係有不良影響。
· Poor customer service has a negative impact on a restaurant's operation. 服務態度不佳對餐廳的營運有負面影響。

💡 換個說法令人眼睛一亮

(1) I'd try to get friendly with him, and see if there was something going on that was making him unhappy.
我會用友善的態度對他，看看是否有一些事情使他不高興。

= I'd talk to him in a friendly manner and try to understand if he is upset over something.
= I would be friendly to him and ask him whether he is upset about something.

(2) I would like to meet with him privately for a few minutes.
我想和他私下談幾分鐘。

= What I like to do is to talk to him in private for a few minutes.
= I think I will have a short meeting with him in private.

(3) I focus on his negative behaviors such as specific rude remarks and interruptions that are not good for the firm's relationship with clients.
我重點會放在他的負面行為例如特定粗魯的話，干擾客戶等不利於公司與客戶關係的行為。

= My focus will be on his negative behaviors such as specific rude remarks and interruptions that might ruin the firm's relationship with clients.
= I emphasize his negative behaviors such as specific rude remarks and interruptions that have negative effects on the firm's relationship with clients.

2-10 社交能力

03 Q Have you worked with someone you didn't like? If so, how did you handle it?

How did you get along with someone you didn't like at work?

你曾經和你不喜歡的人共事過嗎？如果有，你如何面對處理？

▶ 題 解

這也是有關人際關係與社交的問題。工作上難免遇到不喜歡的人，但常常無法避免必須與他／她共事。回答時避免情緒化的字眼，要告知面試官你會以正面理性的態度與此人共事。不用特意表明你喜歡所有在工作上遇到的人，那會讓人對你所說的話抱持懷疑。

▶ 短回答 ─ 基本版　🎧 MP3 127

Yes, I've worked with someone whom I found difficult to like as a person. However, when I focused on the skills she brought to the job and her ability to solve problems, slowly my attitude towards her changed. We were never friends, but we did work well together.

是的，我曾經和一個我很難喜歡的人共事過。然而，當我專注於她帶到工作的技能與她解決問題的能力，慢慢地我對她改變了態度。我們從來不是朋友，但我們真的很好地一起工作。

▶ 短回答 ─ 進階版

When I work with someone annoying, I don't think about how the person acts, I think about how I react. It's more productive to focus on my own behavior because I can control it. I enhance my ability to handle stress, which means the annoying person isn't that annoying anymore.

當我與討厭的人共事時,我不去想這個人的行為如何,我會思考我該怎麼反應。專注於我自己的行為更有效率因為我可以控制它。我提升自己處理壓力的能力,這意味著討厭的人不再那麼討厭了。

▶ 評 解

兩個回答都說明自己用理性的態度面對。

▶ 長回答　🎧 MP3 128

My way to get to like someone I don't like is to spend more time with him/her, for instance, working together on a project that requires coordination. By working together, I can understand the person better and perhaps even develop some empathy. I may discover there are reasons for his/her actions: stress at home, pressure from the boss, or maybe (s)he tries to do what I ask for and fails. In short, spending more time with my foe grants me the opportunity to have more positive experiences. However, if it's someone who violates my sense of what's moral, I will just get away without hesitation.

我去喜歡我不喜歡的人的方式是花更多的時間與他/她相處,例如,在需要協調的專案裏一同合作。透過合作,我能更加理解這個人,甚至發展一些同理心。我可能會發現他/她的行為背後的理由:家裡的壓力,來自老闆的壓力,也許他(她)嘗試做我要求的事但失敗了。總之,花更多的時間與我的敵人相處給予我機會去擁有更多的正面經驗。但是,如果此人侵犯了我的道德感,我會毫不猶豫脫身。

▶ 評 解

用正面積極的態度多花時間與此人相處,進一步了解他/她,消除不必要的偏見。

🍎 單字　🎧 MP3 129

❶ **coordination** [koˋɔrdn͵eʃən] *n.* 協調
❷ **empathy** [ˋɛmpəθɪ] *n.* 同理心;同情
❸ **discover** [dɪsˋkʌvɚ] *v.* 發現
❹ **violate** [ˋvaɪə͵let] *v.* 違犯;違背,違反
❺ **moral** [ˋmɔrəl] *n.* 道德;品行;風紀

用句型取勝

grant sb sth　同意／給予某人某事

要注意

1. 注意這個片語沒有介係詞，有些人會說 grant to sb with sth，是錯誤的。
2. grant 當「給予」時，可用 provide 替代。grant sb sth = provide sb with sth = provide sth to sb。
3. 也可用被動形式表示。Sb is granted sth。
4. take ~ for granted 表「把~視為理所當然」。

例句：

- Being a manager, I don't grant anybody the privilege of doing something.
  最為一個主管，我不賦予某人做某事的特權。
- I was very lucky to be granted the opportunity to get promoted.
  我很幸運能被給予升遷的機會。

without hesitation 毫不猶豫地

要注意

1. 可放在句首或句尾，形容毫不猶豫地做某事。
2. sb+V without hesitation = sb be not hesitated to V = sb don't hesitate to V。

例句：

- I accepted my colleague's invitation to dinner without hesitation.
  = Without hesitation, I accepted my colleague's invitation to dinner.
  我毫不猶豫答應我同事一起吃晚餐的邀請。
- Please contact me without hesitation if you need me.
  = Don't be hesitated to contact me if you need me.
  = Don't hesitate to contact me if you need me.
  如果你需要我，不要猶豫請和我聯絡。

換個說法令人眼睛一亮

(1) I've worked with someone whom I found difficult to like as a person.

我曾經和一個我很難喜歡的人共事過。

= I've worked with someone I found annoying.
= I used to have a colleague I don't like.

---

(2) However, when I focused on the skills she brought to the job and her ability to solve problems, slowly my attitude towards her changed.

然而，當我專注於她帶到工作的技能與她解決問題的能力，慢慢地我對她改變了態度。

= However, when I only think of her professional skills and problem solving abilities, I started to have a different attitude towards her.
= However, when I focused on her professional skills and problem solving abilities, gradually my attitude towards her changed.

---

(3) It's more productive to focus on my own behavior because I can control it.

專注於我自己的行為更有效率因為我可以控制它。

= Focusing on my own behavior is more productive because I can control it.
= Emphasizing my own behavior is more productive because that's something I can control.

2-11 創造能力

01 Give me an example of your creativity.

Are you a creative person?
請給我關於你的創造力的一個例子。

▶ 題 解

創造力是現代職場較欠缺的。藉由這個問題面試官想找出富有創造力的員工。回答重點在展現你可以跳脫傳統思考，展現新思維，有創意思考的能力，能用新方法解決舊有問題等。能有實際例子佐證更佳。

▶ 短回答 —— 基本版　🎧 MP3 130

My creativity comes when I come up with innovating new ideas which are useful to the environment. Everyone has the creativity but it comes into picture when people are vexed up with their difficulties. For me creativity is making "the impossible into possible."

我的創造力是當我想出對環境有用的創新新思路。每個人都有創造力，當人們為了困難煩惱時，就會產生創造力。對我來說，創意是使「不可能變成可能」。

▶ 短回答 —— 進階版

Creativity is an art which happens to be unique and its depth of uniqueness varies from person to person. I am creative because I can do the same things differently. Interestingly, surprisingly in a much better way than anyone imagined. I love doing it.

創意是一門藝術，恰好是獨特的，獨特性的深度因人而異。我有創意因為我可以用不同的方法做同樣的事情。有趣的是，令人驚訝的比任何人想得到的方法都還好。我喜歡這樣做。

評 解

兩個回答都展現了創意的基本要素：新思維，獨特性。

長回答 🎧 MP3 131

During my college days my favorite pastime was watching my favorite TV series like *Friends*. But it was hard to find them on the Internet. So, I decided to make a blog containing my favorites TV series along with my review regarding those. I made the blog, linked it to many sites and as time passed it became famous. After my graduation I made another tech blog where I used Google advance search tool to gather all top news from all tech sites and linked it to my blog. And ever since then I've gained enormous knowledge as well as become more creative.

在我的大學時代我最喜歡的消遣是看我最喜歡的電視劇例如《六人行》。但很難在網路上找到這些電視劇。所以，我決定寫一個部落格裏面有我最愛的電視劇與我對它們的評論。我做的部落格可以連結到許多網站，隨著時間過去它名聲大噪。我畢業後我做了另一個技術部落格，我用 google 進階搜尋工具來收集所有技術網站的最新新聞然後連結到我的部落格。從那之後，我獲得了龐大的知識，以及變得更有創意。

評 解

用實際例子說明自己如何做一件有創意的事，並帶來正面的結果。

🍎**單字** 🎧 MP3 132

❶ **pastime** [ˋpæsˏtaɪm] *n.* 消遣；娛樂
❷ **contain** [kənˋten] *v.* 包含；容納
❸ **link** [lɪŋk] *v.* 連接，結合；聯繫
❹ **enormous** [ɪˋnɔrməs] *adj.* 巨大的，龐大的
❺ **creative** [krɪˋetɪv] *adj.* 創造的；創造性的；有創造力（或想像力）的

用句型取勝

come up with ~（針對問題等）想出；提供

要注意

1. come up with 也有「趕上」、「準備好（錢等）」的意思。

例句：

- My colleagues often asked me how I came up with such a fantastic idea.
  我同事常問我我是如何想出這麼棒的點子。
- As a programmer, my main job is to come up with a solution to the system problems.
  作為一個程式設計師，我的主要工作是想出解決系統問題的方法。

ever since then 從那之後

要注意

1. ever since then 要注意 since 結構的用法，後面的主要句子要用完成式。ever since then 也可省略 ever (since then)，後面的主要句子一樣要用完成式。
2. from then on 也表示「從那之後」，但後面的主要句子不一定要用完成式，通常用過去簡單式就可。

例句：

- (Ever) since then, I've learnt a way to think and act creatively.
  = From then on, I learned a way to think and act creatively.
  從那之後，我就學習到一種創意思考與行動的方法。
- (Ever) since then, I've tried to look at the bright side of things and abandoned the conventional way of thinking.
  = From then on, I tried to look at the bright side of things and abandoned the conventional way of thinking.
  從那之後，我就試著看事情的光明面並捨棄傳統思考方式。

換個說法令人眼睛一亮

(1) Everyone has the creativity but it comes into picture when people are vexed up with their difficulties.

每個人都有創造力，當人們為了困難煩惱時，就會產生創造力。

= Everyone can be creative, especially when they are puzzled over their difficulties.

= For most people, creativity comes when they are vexed up with their difficulties.

---

(2) During my college days my favorite pastime was watching my favorite TV series like *Friends*.

在我的大學時代我最喜歡的消遣是看我最喜歡的電視劇例如《六人行》。

= During my college days I loved to watch my favorite TV series like *Friends* in my free time.

= When I was a college student, my hobby was watching my favorite TV series like *Friends*.

---

(3) After my graduation I made another tech blog where I used Google advance search tool to gather all top news from all tech sites and linked it to my blog.

我畢業後我做了另一個技術部落格，我用 google 進階搜尋工具來收集所有技術網站的最新新聞然後連結到我的部落格。

= After graduating I created another tech blog in which I used Google advance search tool to gather all top news from all tech sites and linked it to my blog.

= After graduating I made another tech blog where I gathered all top news from all tech sites by Google advance search tool and then I linked it to my blog.

01 Describe a situation in which you lead a team.

Describe a situation where you have to show leadership.

請形容你如何領導一個團隊。

▶ 題解

這是有關領導力的問題。某些工作會牽涉到人員領導與管理。這樣的職缺會希望找到一個能計畫、組織、與領導別人工作的人,並能夠激勵他人完成工作。這個問題可讓面試官了解你是否有能力領導其他人完成工作達到公司的目標。

▶ 短回答 — 基本版 🎧 MP3 133

Due to the company-wide lay-offs, people remaining were overworked and more mistakes were being made. As the department manager, I listen to their needs, apply patience, and try to help them increase work efficiency. I did a good job to get performance back on track.

因為公司全面的裁員,留下來的人必須超時工作,也因此錯誤百出。作為部門經理,我傾聽他們的需求,有耐心,並幫助他們增加工作效率。我做得不錯,讓員工工作表現重回正軌。

▶ 短回答 — 進階版

As a team leader, I communicate the strategic vision with clarity; translate the vision into concrete direction and plans; identify and communicate priorities, short term objectives, timelines, performance measures; clear responsibilities and performance agreements; provide quality judgment and advice.

作為一個團隊領導者，我明確溝通策略願景，將願景轉化為具體的方向和計劃；識別和溝通重點、短期目標、時限、表現評量；讓職責和績效協議明確化；提供優質的判斷和建議。

▶ 評解

基本版說明了如何領導解決部門問題，進階版明列優質領導策略。

▶ 長回答　🎧 MP3 134

I was given the responsibility of head waitress and successfully held this position for over two years. Being a head waitress in a busy city center restaurant, I was required to adopt a supervisory role and it was necessary to arrange many different tasks at once. This involved giving instructions to members of staff, but I also made the time to listen, which improved communication within the team. By communicating effectively, I helped generate team morale and this motivated me and other waitresses. Through good organization and communication, I ensured efficient functioning of the restaurant.

我被賦予服務生領班的職責並成功做了超過兩年。作為一個在市中心繁忙餐廳的領班，我必須擔任一個管理的角色並且必須在同時間安排許多不同的任務。這包含了指導下屬並花時間聆聽，聆聽改善了團隊溝通。藉由有效溝通，我帶來團隊士氣並激勵了我和其他服務生。藉由好的體制和溝通，我確保了餐廳有效率的運作。

▶ 評解

這個回答詳細說明如何領導下屬確保公司有效率的運作。

 單字　🎧 MP3 135

❶ **adopt** [ə`dɑpt] *v.* 採取；採納
❷ **involve** [ɪn`vɑlv] *v.* 需要，包含，意味著
❸ **instructions** [ɪn`strʌkʃən] *n.* 教誨；教導
❹ **generate** [`dʒɛnə͵ret] *v.* 造成，引起
❺ **morale** [mə`ræl] *n.* 士氣，鬥志

用句型取勝

sb is required to do sth 某人被要求做某事

要注意

1. ask, request, demand 和 require這四個動詞皆有「要求，請求」的意思。ask, request 和 require 都可以接受詞 + to do something，但 demand 則沒有這項用法。
2. 這四個動詞都可接 that 所引導的名詞子句。

例句：

· In my previous job, I was required (requested, asked) to work on weekends from time to time.
在我之前的工作，我有時會被要求在週末工作。

· Being a sales manager, I was usually required to increase the overall sales by a certain percentage.
作為一個業務主管，我通常會被要求提高特定比例的銷售額。

· The director required that we (should) work all night.
主任要求我們通宵工作。

By +Ving ......, S+V ...... 藉由做～事，某人……

要注意

1. By 後要加動名詞。

例句：

· By arriving twenty minutes earlier, I can be more prepared for this interview.
藉由早到 20 分鐘，我可以更充分準備這次面試。

· By holding weekly meetings, the manager ensures efficient functioning of the department.
藉由每週一次的會議，經理確保了部門有效率的運作。

換個說法令人眼睛一亮

(1) I was given the responsibility of head waitress and successfully held this position for over two years.

我被賦予服務生領班的職責並成功做了超過兩年。

= I have been the head waitress for over two years and my job performance has been good.

= I have successfully held the position of head waitress for over two years.

---

(2) I was required to adopt a supervisory role and it was necessary to arrange many different tasks at once.

我必須採取一個管理的角色並且必須在同時間安排許多不同的任務。

= My job required me to take a supervisory role and arrange many different tasks at once.

= In order to do the job well, I took a supervisory role and arranged many different tasks at once.

---

(3) By communicating effectively, I helped generate team morale and this motivated me and other waitresses.

藉由有效溝通，我帶來團隊士氣並激勵了我和其他服務生。

= The effective communication I developed generated team morale, which motivated me and other waitresses.

= I helped generate team morale by communicating effectively and the team morale motivated me and other waitresses.

Part

2

99％會問的面試題

2-12 領導能力

How would you attract someone to listen to you and to follow you?

How do you make your leadership work?

你如何讓人聽從你？

▶ 題解

這個問題在應徵管理類職務是相當重要的。一個好的主管必須能夠讓下屬聽從你，面試官於是想藉由這個問題找到有這樣特質的人。回答時可以從很多方向著手，例如做員工好榜樣，讓員工喜歡自己，貼近員工內心等等。

▶ 短回答 ── 基本版　🎧 MP3 136

I am able to work with all types of personalities. I can identify right topics for conversation. <u>Once a connection is made, it is easier for me to make the employees follow my example and orders, because they naturally like me.</u>

我能夠與所有類型的人共事。我能為談話識別正確的主題。一旦人與人之間的聯結建立，這樣更容易讓我的員工以我為榜樣並聽從我的命令，因為他們從本質上喜歡我。

▶ 短回答 ── 進階版

I simply make people feel like I am their partner. I also compliment other people a lot. If I see a reason for saying something good about someone, I say it. <u>Acting like this, people generally like me and have a tendency to follow my leadership.</u>

我只是讓人覺得我是他們的合作夥伴。我也多加讚美他人。如果我看到可以稱讚人的理由，我就會稱讚他。這樣的做法，通常都讓人們喜歡我，並傾向於服從我的領導。

▶ 評解

回答中陳述的主管特質都是會令人服從他／她的領導。

▶ 長回答　🎧 MP3 137

I made myself a natural leader, a great role model people want to follow and listen to. I made myself attractive, not with my look, but with my thoughts and actions. I am able to get close to the heart of every single employee. What's more important, I am fully confident about my own vision. I easily connect with the others, doesn't matter if we talk about people from outside of the company, business partners, politicians, or simply anyone who can be beneficial for the organization. These characteristics make people listen to me and follow me.

我讓我自己是一個天生的領導者，一個讓人想聽從我的榜樣。我讓我自己有吸引力，不是因為我的外貌，而是我的思想和行動。我能接近每一個員工的內心深處。更重要的是，我對我自己的洞察力有信心。我很容易與他人連結，不論我們談論的是來自公司外部的人，業務合作夥伴，政治人物，或者只要是有利於組織的任何人。這些特點讓人們聽我的話，跟隨我。

▶ 評解

除了題解中提到的好的領導特質外，此回答也說明自己可以和不同的商業對象建立連結。

 單字　🎧 MP3 138

❶ **natural** [ˋnætʃərəl] *adj.* 天生的；天賦的
❷ **attractive** [əˋtræktɪv] *adj.* 有吸引力的
❸ **vision** [ˋvɪʒən] *n.* 洞察力，眼光
❹ **connect** [kəˋnɛkt] *v.* 聯繫；結合
❺ **politician** [ˌpɑləˋtɪʃən] *n.* 從事政治者，政治家

Part 2

99％會問的面試題

用句型取勝

make/ have + O + V

☞ 要注意

1. 使役動詞 make 與 have 後面接的受詞所做之動作若是主動的，意為「叫受詞去…」，則用原形動詞。。

2. 使役動詞 get 後面接的受詞所做之動作若是主動的，意為「叫受詞去…」，則用不定詞。

3. 使役動詞 make、have、get 所接受詞後面的動作，若是意為「讓受詞被…」，則需用過去分詞。

例句：

- I made my employees follow my suggestions.
  我使我的員工聽從我的建議。
- I make my team members compliment each other.
  我讓我團隊成員彼此稱讚對方。

have a tendency to do sth 有做某事的傾向

☞ 要注意

1. have a tendency 的用法較have the tendency 多。

2. have a tendency to do sth = tend to do sth。

例句：

- I don't think it's good to have a tendency to correct everything people say, or criticize everything people do wrong.
  = I think tending to correct everything people say or criticize everything people do wrong is not good.
  我認為有糾正人們說的每一件事或批評人們做錯的每一件事的傾向是不好的。

· People have a tendency to follow my leadership when they consider me as a great model.
當他們視我為好榜樣時，人們會有服從我的領導的傾向。

換個說法令人眼睛一亮

(1) I am able to work with all types of personalities.
我能夠與所有類型的人共事。

= I am able to work with different people with different personalities.
= I have the capability of working with all types of personalities.

---

(2) I made myself a natural leader, a great role model people want to follow and listen to.
我讓我自己是一個天生的領導者，一個讓人想聽從我的榜樣。

= People want to follow and listen to me because I work as a natural leader and a great role model.
= Being a natural leader and a great role model, I make people follow and listen to me.

---

(3) I made myself attractive, not with my look, but with my thoughts and actions.
我讓我自己有吸引力，不是因為我的外貌，而是我的思想和行動。

= My thoughts and actions made me attractive, not my look.
= People are attracted to me because of my thoughts and actions rather than my look.

2-12 領導能力

03 As a supervisor, how do you motivate yourself?

Being a manager, what do you do to motivate yourself?

作為一個主管，你如何激勵自己？

▶ 題 解

領導者要負擔的責任比一般職員來得重與多，不可避免的會遇到困難或無可抗力的因素帶來的無力感。因此一個優秀的主管不但要有能力激勵下屬，也必須能激勵自己度過難關。這個面試問題就可以一窺應徵者是否有這樣的能力。回答時要強調你個人對達成目標的熱情會激勵自己處理各種難題。

▶ 短回答 — 基本版　🎧 MP3 139

I have never had problems with personal motivation. Being a leader and carrying all the responsibility on my shoulders, I certainly meet difficult situations in job. However, I understand that setbacks are essential steps on the way to final success. This is my personal philosophy.

我從未缺少個人動機。作為一個領導者，擔所有的責任在我肩上，在工作上我一定會碰到困難。然而我了解，挫折是邁向最終成功的關鍵步驟。這是我個人的理念。

▶ 短回答 — 進階版

I always have a list of my goals on the table. These include both company goals and personal goals. When I find myself in a difficult situation, or being without motivation, <u>I always take the list and spend some time thinking about the goals I want to achieve.</u> It always makes me motivated to push forward, even if the way is extremely difficult.

我一直將我的目標清單放在桌上。這些包括公司目標和個人目標。當我發現自己遭遇困難，或缺乏動機時，我就會拿起這列表，花一些時間思考我想要達到的目標。它總是讓我積極地向前進，即使方式是極其困難的。

⊙ 評 解

兩個回答中都闡述挫折困難都不減個人動機，反而會激勵自己。

⊙ 長回答 🎧 MP3 140

There's always something inside me that keeps pushing to expand myself by working harder, smarter, stronger, and more efficiently. If there's an extra mile to go, the strength inside me draws out the willingness and ability to go the extra mile. Besides, being a manager, my employees motivate me. I love helping and making them happy. It brings such satisfaction to see the smile on someone's face after I've just helped them in some ways. I am also motivated by achieving where others have failed, mostly by achieving my set goals and targets within the allotted time.

總有一種內在的東西推動我拓展自己更努力地、更聰明地、更堅強地、更有效率地工作。如果需要加倍的努力，我內心的力量會引出意願和能力去加倍努力。此外，作為一個管理者，我的員工激勵我。我喜歡幫助他們，並讓他們開心。幫助他們之後我在他們臉上看見笑容，這個笑容帶給我莫大的滿足感。達到別人所無法達到的也會激勵我，主要藉由在規定時間內達到我設定的目標。

⊙ 評 解

回答中說明激勵自己的因素，這樣的動機讓自己更努力更有效率地工作。

🍎 單字 🎧 MP3 141

❶ **expand** [ɪk`spænd] *v.* 擴張；發展；增長
❷ **satisfaction** [ˌsætɪs`fækʃən] *n.* 滿意，滿足；稱心
❸ **achieve** [ə`tʃiv] *v.* 完成，實現
❹ **target** [`tɑrgɪt] *n.* （欲達到的）目標，指標
❺ **allotted** [ə`lɔtɪd] *adj.* 專款的，撥出的；指定的

用句型取勝

sb spend time +Ving 某人花時間做某件事

要注意

1. spend 用於花費「時間、金錢」，主詞只能是「人」，其後若有第二個動詞，則只能用「動名詞」形式。

2. spend句型用法：

   人 + spend + 時間／$ + V-ing

   人 + spend + $ + on + 物品

3. take 也用於花費「時間」，主詞有三種可能情形，其後若有第二個動詞，則只能用「不定詞」形式。

4. take 句型用法：

   It + takes + 人 + 時間 + to + 原形動詞

   V-ing（動名詞當主詞）+ takes + 人 + 時間

   人 + take + 時間 + to + 原形動詞

例句：

- I spend quite some time talking with my staff to understand their needs.

  = It takes me quite some time to talk with my staff to understand their needs.

  我花蠻多時間和我的員工交談了解他們的需求。

- Every day after work I spend some time reviewing my monthly goals.

  = Reviewing my monthly goals takes me some time every day after work.

  每天下班後我都花一些時間檢視每月目標。

go the extra mile 加倍努力（要想成功 就多付出一點）

例句：

· I tell my staff: To do your duty is not enough. You must go the extra mile.
我告訴我的員工：只做好份內的事是不夠的，你必須加倍努力。

· I appreciate the staff who is willing to go the extra mile.
我欣賞願意加倍努力的員工。

換個說法令人眼睛一亮

⑴ I have never had problems with personal motivation.
我從未缺少個人動機。

= I am never lack of personal motivation.
= I am always self-motivated.

⑵ Being a leader and carrying all the responsibility on my shoulders, I certainly meet difficult situations in job.
作為一個領導者，擔所有的責任在我肩上，在工作上我一定會碰到困難。

= As a leader in charge of many things, meeting difficult situations in job is unavoidable.
= Being a leader and carrying all the responsibility on my shoulders, I always expect for difficult situations at work.

⑶ It brings such satisfaction to see the smile on someone's face after I've just helped them in some way.
幫助他們之後我在他們臉上看見笑容，這個笑容帶給我莫大的滿足感。

= After helping them in some ways, I saw the smile on their face, which gives me great satisfaction.
= The smile appeared on people's face after I helped them brings me great satisfaction.

Part

2

99％會問的面試題

205

2-12 領導能力

04 As a supervisor, how do you motivate others?

How do you motivate staff?

作為一個主管，你如何激勵他人？

▶題 解

一個好的主管的重要特質之一就是能激勵員工把工作做好。回答時可根據你的個人信念和經驗。唯一要注意的是不要只說你如何獎勵那些工作表現好的員工，而是強調你如何在員工的工作過程中激勵他們。換言之，重要的不是結果，而是過程。

▶短回答 —— 基本版　🎧 MP3 142

I congratulate staff on life events such as new babies, inquire about their vacation trips, and ask about how both personal and company events turn out. I care enough to stay tuned into these kinds of employee life events and activities.

我恭賀員工人生中的大事例如嬰兒出世，詢問他們的度假旅遊，也關心他們的個人或公司活動結果如何。我對他們夠關心，持續關注類似的員工生活和活動。

▶短回答 —— 進階版

My way to motivate others is to communicate responsibly and effectively any information employees need to perform their jobs most effectively. For instance, I meet with employees following management staff meetings to update their information about changing due dates, customer feedback, product improvements, training opportunities, and so on.

我激勵別人的方式是負責任與有效地傳遞員工可以幫助他們更有效率工作的任何訊

息。舉例來說，我會在管理人員會議後和員工開會，傳達他們有關到期日改變，客戶回饋，產品改進和培訓機會等訊息。

▶ 評 解

溫暖的關心和有效溝通都會是激勵員工的好方法。

▶ 長回答 🎧 MP3 143

I tell my staff that it is okay to disagree with me, allowing the implementation of new ideas, even if these ideas are different from mine. I provide positive reinforcement, rewards, and recognition to reinforce the standards and practices I believe my staff members are capable of achieving. Furthermore, my expectation about the performance standards is clearly stated to all employees and I express my sincere belief that they can meet or exceed these standards. Meanwhile I provide frequent feedback that reinforces what people do well and corrects the approaches that need improvement. By doing so, I create a motivating work environment to enhance staffs' self-esteem. People feel like they are more competent, more appreciated, and more contributing.

我告訴我的員工不同意我是可以的，我允許履行新理念，即使這些想法與我的不同。我提供正面鼓勵、獎勵和表彰，以加強我相信我的工作人員都能夠達到的標準和做法。此外，我對所有員工明確說明我對績效標準的期望，並表示我衷心相信他們能達到或超過這些標準。同時我提供頻繁的回饋，從而強調人們做得好的地方和糾正需要改進的方法。透過這樣做，我建立了一個激勵人心的工作環境，以提高員工的自尊。人們覺得自己更能幹，更受到賞識，並有更多貢獻。

▶ 評 解

當員工的自尊被充分尊重時，他們就會激勵自己努力工作。

▶ 單 字 🎧 MP3 144

❶ **implementation** [ˌɪmpləmɛnˋteʃən] *n.* 履行；完成
❷ **reinforcement** [ˌriɪnˋforsmənt] *n.* 加強，加固，強化

❸ **state** [stet] *v.* 陳述；聲明；說明
❹ **self-esteem** [ˌsɛlf əsˋtim] *n.* 自尊
❺ **competent** [ˋkɑmpətənt] *adj.* 有能力的，能幹的；能勝任的，稱職的

用句型取勝

disagree with
和……不同、和某人見解不同、或不同意某個主意、說法

要注意

1. disagree with 後面可加人或事物。

   disagree with sb on sth 和某人在某件事上見解不同。

2. disagree about/on/over 不是「不同意某些事或某人的意見、說法等」，而是「就某些事和某人有不同意見或說法」。

例句：

· I disagree with John on many things, but we remained as good colleagues and good friends.
  我和 John 在很多事上見解不同，但我們還是好同事好朋友。

· I and my previous boss disagreed about/on/over the cost-benefit analysis.
  我和我之前的老闆就成本效益分析上有不同的意見想法。

even if 即使～

要注意

1. even if（即使）是假設語氣，不能用來描述已經發生的事實。
2. even though（雖然）則是接實際已經發生的事。

例句：

· I never scold, even if my staff made mistakes.
  我從不斥責，即使我的員工犯錯。

- I always tell myself that don't fail to do good even if it is small.
  我總是告訴我自己不因善小而不為。

換個說法令人眼睛一亮

(1) My way to motivate others is to communicate responsibly and effectively any information employees need to perform their jobs most effectively.
我激勵別人的方式是負責任與有效地傳遞員工可以幫助他們更有效率工作的任何訊息。

= I motivate others by communicating responsibly and effectively any information employees need to best perform their jobs.
= I believe employees become motivated when the supervisor communicates responsibly and effectively any information they need to best perform their jobs.

(2) My expectation about the performance standards is clearly stated to all employees and I express my sincere belief that they can meet or exceed these standards.
我對所有員工明確說明我對績效標準的的期望，並表示我衷心相信他們能達到或超過這些標準。

= I make it clear to all employees about my expectation of the performance standards and I express my sincere belief that they can meet or exceed these standards.
= I clearly inform all employees about my expectation of the performance standards and let them know that I sincerely believe their capability of meeting or exceeding these standards.

2-13 個人事務

01 What was the toughest decision you ever had to make?

Can you share your toughest decision in life?

你做過最困難的決定為何？

▶ 題 解

在職場上做決定（決策）是不可避免的。這個問題想了解求職者的決策過程。要回答好這個問題首先要準備一個好的例子，然後解釋為何做這個決定是困難的，你如何做一個明智的決擇，而這個決定又可以帶來甚麼正面的結果。

▶ 短回答 —— 基本版 MP3 145

The toughest decision was to choose between diploma in Economics and seeking a career. I chose seeking a career because practical knowledge is more important than theoretical knowledge for a better career.

在取得經濟學學位和找工作之間做選擇是非常困難的決定。我選擇就業因為有好的工作實務知識比理論知識重要。

▶ 短回答 —— 進階版

The toughest decision I had made was to choose Information Technology as my major. It was difficult as everyone said there is no future for IT sector in recession. But I believe strongly that if I have professional knowledge and confidence in myself, I can survive and prove myself.

我做過最困難的決定是選擇資訊工程作為我的主修，因為每個人都說在經濟蕭條時資訊業是沒有未來的。但我堅決相信如果我有專業知識與對自己有自信，我還是可以生存並證明我自己。

▶ 評解

基本版回答是可以接受的，進階版較優處是有解釋為何做這個決定是困難的與如何做明智的決定。

▶ 長回答 🎧 MP3 146

The toughest decision of my life was to choose between searching a job and preparing for MBA entrance exams. Having an engineering degree in computer science from a well-known university, I was expected to start working in the high-tech industry and make good money. However, with strong motivation for gaining professional knowledge in business administration, <u>I decided to spend time on preparing for MBA program application</u>. This decision later was proven to be a right one because it helped me to grow both professionally and personally. With both degrees in engineering and business fields, I was offered a supervisory job in last than five years of working.

我做過人生中最困難的決定是在找工作與準備 MBA 入學考試之間做選擇。擁有名校的電腦工程學位，我被期待在高科技產業工作並賺大錢。然而我有很強的動機想獲得在企管的專業知識，我決定花時間準備 MBA 申請。這個決定後來證明是對的因為它幫助我個人與專業的成長。同時擁有工程與企管學位讓我在我五年內就做到管理職位。

▶ 評解

這樣的回答完整說明了為何做這個決定是困難的，如何做一個明智的決擇，而這個決定又可以帶來甚麼正面的結果。

🍎 單字 🎧 MP3 147

❶ **entrance exam** [ˈɛntrəns] [ɪɡˈzæm] *n.* 入學考試

❷ **engineering** [ˌɛndʒəˈnɪrɪŋ] *n.* 工程

❸ **motivation** [ˌmotəˈveʃən] *n.* 動機

❹ **business administration** [ˈbɪznɪs] [ədˌmɪnəˈstreʃən] *n.* 企管

❺ **application** [ˌæpləˈkeʃən] *n.* 申請

用句型取勝

choose between A and B　在 A 和 B 之間做選擇

要注意

1. A 和 B 之間要用 and 而非 or。
2. 如果在三者以上之間做選擇用 among。
3. choose between A and B = make a choice between A and B
4. 注意 choose 為不規則動詞，三態為 choose, chose, chosen。

例句：

- I had to choose between giving up my job and hiring a nanny.
  = I had to make a choice between giving up my job and hiring a nanny.
  我必須在放棄工作與雇用保母之間做選擇。
- It's hard to choose between the two candidates. They both have very good education and work experiences.
  很難在這兩個候選人間做選擇。他們都有很好的學歷和工作經驗。

spend time on~ 花時間在～上

要注意

1. spend 若意思是「花費」時，主詞必須是「人」，可用於花費時間或人。
2. 花費時間也可用 take，但主詞要改成「事物」。
3. on 後加名詞或動名詞。on 也可以省略。

例句：

- I spent a whole month (on) doing market research.
  = Doing market research took me a whole month.
  我花一整個月做市場調查。
- You will be surprised if I tell you how much time I spend on socializing with my clients.
  你會感到驚訝如果我告訴你我花多少時間在與客戶交際。

換個說法令人眼睛一亮

(1) The toughest decision was to choose between diploma in Economics and seeking a career.

在取得經濟學學位和找工作之間做選擇是非常困難的決定。

= It was difficult to decide whether I want to pursue a diploma in Economics or seek a career.

= Deciding on pursuing a diploma in Economics or seeking a career was not easy at all.

---

(2) Having an engineering degree in computer science from a well-known university, I was expected to start working in the high-tech industry and make good money.

擁有名校的電腦工程學位，我被期待在高科技產業工作並賺大錢。

= With an engineering degree in computer science from a well-known university, people expect me to work in the high-tech industry and make good money.

= Graduating from a well-known university with a major in engineering, I was expected to start working in the high-tech industry and make good money.

---

(3) With strong motivation for gaining professional knowledge in business administration, I decided to spend time on preparing for MBA program application.

有很強的動機想獲得在企管的專業知識，我決定花時間準備 MBA 申請。

= I chose to spend time on preparing for MBA program application due to my strong motivation for gaining professional knowledge in business administration.

= The reason I decided to spend time on preparing for MBA program application is that I wanted to gain professional knowledge in business administration.

2-13 個人事務

02 What type of work environment do you prefer?

Can you describe your ideal work environment?

你喜歡怎麼樣的工作環境？

▶ 題 解

面試官會想了解應徵者所喜愛的工作環境是否和現實中公司相吻合，所以回答的重點是你所敘述的工作環境必須是符合你應徵工作的公司。回答時要注意不要描述不切實際的理想狀況。也可說明自己對不同工作環境適應力強，靈活有彈性。

▶ 短回答 —— 基本版 🎧 MP3 148

Ideally, I would like to work in an environment with individuals working independently towards team goals or individual goals. Minor elements like dress codes and cubicles are not what I am cncerned about. Most important to me is an atmosphere that fosters attention to quality, honesty, and integrity.

理想情況下，我喜歡在一個每個人各自為團隊與個人目標努力工作的環境裡工作。較細微的因素例如服裝規定與辦公室小隔間不是我在意的。對我來說最重要的是一個促進重視品質，誠實與正直的工作氛圍。

▶ 短回答 —— 進階版

My ideal work environment is the one that is adaptive. When necessary, it easily handles fast paced work, and is ready for any challenges it undertakes, but also slows down when work is slow, recognizing the natural shifts in business and responding accordingly.

我理想的工作環境是一個是能自我適應的。在必要時，可輕鬆處理快節奏的工作，

並準備承擔它的任何挑戰，但當工作節奏變慢時也可放慢速度，認識到企業的自然變化並能隨之應變。

▶ 評 解

兩個回答都描述非常正面的工作環境且符合現實。

▶ 長回答 🎧 MP3 149

My ideal working environment is the one where there's a good sense of team spirit. A strong work ethic is obviously important but the human side is also important. I enjoy working with people who have a decent sense of humour and who, while they might take their work very seriously, don't necessarily take themselves overly seriously! I like people who are down to earth but who have a dynamic and progressive approach to their work. I really enjoy working as part of a highly committed and professional team.

我理想的工作環境是一個富有團隊精神的地方。具有良好職業道德顯然是重要的，但人性的一面也很重要。我喜歡富有幽默感的人，他們工作很認真，但不會太過於嚴肅！我喜歡腳踏實地的人，但擁有一個充滿活力和進取的工作態度。我真的很喜歡在一個高度投入和專業團隊裡工作。

▶ 評 解

回答中所敘述的工作環境是大部分公司所肯定與追求的，所以這樣的答案萬無一失。

🍎 單字 🎧 MP3 150

❶ **spirit** [`spɪrɪt] *n.* 精神，心靈
❷ **ethic** [`ɛθɪk] *n.* 倫理；道德
❸ **dynamic** [daɪ`næmɪk] *adj.* 有活力的；有生氣的
❹ **progressive** [prə`grɛsɪv] *adj.* 進取的
❺ **approach** [ə`protʃ] *n.* 方法，門徑；態度

✐ 用句型取勝

sb +beV+ concerned+ about ~ 某人關心~

👉 要注意

1. concerned這裡作形容詞，解表示「關心」，可和 about 或 for 連用。
2. sb + beV + concerned + about ~ 某人關心~ = Sb +has/ have+ concern + about~。
3. concern 作名詞，和 of 連用，是指「（事情）關乎（某某）」。

例句：

· Most of the treasurers including me are concerned about the company's corporate image as the image has great impact on the company's stock prices.
大部分的財務主管包括我都關心公司的企業形象因為形象對公司股價有很大的影響。

· I appreciate those managers who are concerned about their employees.
我欣賞那些會關心員工的主管。

· This matter is the concern of every one of us.
這是關乎我們每一個人的事。

sb+take+something+seriously 某人認真看待／嚴肅看待某事

👉 要注意

1. 注意在這裡 seriously 要用副詞。

例句：

· Sometimes my colleague is mean and rude, but I try not to take what he said too seriously.
有時候我同事很卑鄙且無理，但我試著不要太在意他說的話。

- When the manager assigns you a job task, you have to take it seriously.

當經理指派一個工作任務給你，你必須認真對待它。

換個說法令人眼睛一亮

(1) Ideally, I would like to work in an environment with individuals working independently towards team goals or individual goals.

理想情況下，我喜歡在一個每個人各自為團隊與個人目標努力工作的環境裡工作。

= I always dream of working in an environment where everybody works independently to reach team or individual goals.

= For me, the best work environment is the one where everybody works hard in order to fulfill team or individual goals.

Part

2

99％會問的面試題

(2) Most important to me is an atmosphere that fosters attention to quality, honesty, and integrity.

對我來說最重要的是一個促進重視品質，誠實與正直的工作氛圍。

= What I care the most is an atmosphere that fosters attention to quality, honesty, and integrity.

= An atmosphere that brings attention to quality, honesty, and integrity is very important to me.

(3) I really enjoy working as part of a highly committed and professional team.

我真的很喜歡在一個高度投入和專業團隊裡工作。

= Working in a highly committed and professional team really gives me a sense of satisfaction.

= I truly enjoy working with highly committed and professional team members.

2-13 個人事務

03 Q What are your hobbies?

What do you enjoy doing in your spare time?

你的興趣是甚麼？

▶ 題 解

這樣的問題想要了解求職者整體身心健康狀況。因此回答必須是有益身心健康的嗜好以展現你的健康、活力、與紓解壓力的能力。另外志工服務也是對求職有益的嗜好，因志工服務代表良好的人格特質，也可帶來潛在的客戶。

▶ 短回答 ── 基本版 🎧 MP3 151

I like to read books, listen to music, and browse the Internet in my spare time. Reading books inspires my mind, listening to music keeps me relaxed whenever I got tensed, and browsing Internet keeps my knowledge updated.

我喜歡在空閒時閱讀書籍，聽音樂，和上網。閱讀書籍啟發我的心靈，聽音樂讓我在壓力大時放鬆我自己，而上網讓我隨時更新我的知識。

▶ 短回答 ── 進階版

In my spare time I like to go golfing since it relaxes me after a long week of work. I've also been involved in fundraising efforts for cancer research ever since my grandmother died of breast cancer. I'm hoping that the research can save the lives of others.

在我休閒時我喜歡打高爾夫球因為它讓我能在一週的工作後放鬆自己。自從我祖母因乳癌過世後我也參與為癌症研究募款的活動，我希望這個研究可以拯救其他人的生命。

⊙評解

兩種回答都展現有益身心健康與紓壓的嗜好。進階版的志工服務更優。

⊙長回答 🎧 MP3 152

I am a real sports fan, both watching and playing. I enjoy the excitement that sports such as baseball, basketball, and tennis have to offer. I especially enjoy team sports. Knowing that a group of people are working so closely together to achieve a specific goal is inspiring to me in many ways. I know that many of your clients are high-profile sports clubs and companies, and I think that because of my dedication to sports of all kinds, I could definitely bring a unique perspective and insight to the company.

我是一個真正的運動迷，喜歡看球也喜歡打球。我喜歡球類例如棒球、籃球、和網球所帶來的興奮感。知道一群人努力合作完成某一個目標在很多方面都能激勵我。我知道貴公司的很多客戶都是高級運動俱樂部和公司，我認為我對各種球類的投入一定能為公司帶來獨特的見解和洞察力。

⊙評解

這樣的回答很優因為有把個人興趣連結到工作所需與對公司的貢獻。

🍎單字 🎧 MP3 153

❶ **achieve** [ə`tʃiv] *v.* 完成，實現
❷ **inspire** [ɪn`spaɪr] *v.* 鼓舞，激勵
❸ **dedication** [ˌdɛdə`keʃən] *n.* 奉獻；投入
❹ **perspective** [pɚ`spɛktɪv] *n.* 洞察力
❺ **insight** [`ɪnˌsaɪt] *n.* 洞察力，眼光

Part

2

99％會問的面試題

用句型取勝

enjoy+Ving 喜歡做～

👉 要注意

1. enjoy後接的動詞必須是動名詞。也可接名詞。

例句：

- I enjoy classical music very much.
  我非常喜歡古典樂。
- I enjoy having a picnic with my family and friends on holidays.
  我喜歡在假日和家人朋友一起野餐。

sb's dedication to~ 某人致力於或奉獻於～

👉 要注意

1. sb's dedication to~ = sb is dedicated to~，表致力於〔某事〕。其中 to 是介係詞，後面應該接名詞，所以若要動作，就得使用動名詞Ving。
2. dedicated to someone 是另一常用的片語，意思大不相同，表「獻給…」。

例句：

- This award is dedicated to those who are rated as the best customer service representatives by our clients.
  這個獎是獻給那些被我們客戶評為最佳客服代表的人。
- Her dedication to her work was admirable.
  她對工作的奉獻可欽可佩。
- My dedication to teaching gained the respect of my colleagues.
  我對教學的奉獻贏得同事們的尊敬。

💡 換個說法令人眼睛一亮

⑴ In my spare time I like to go golfing since it relaxes me after a long week of work.
在我休閒時我喜歡打高爾夫球因為它讓我能在一週的工作後放鬆自己。

= Playing golf is my hobby that relaxes me after a long week of work.
= After a long week of work, I relax myself by play golfing.

⑵ I've also been involved in fundraising efforts for cancer research ever since my grandmother died of breast cancer.
自從我祖母因乳癌過世後我也參與為癌症研究募款的活動。

= My involvement in fundraising efforts for cancer research derived from my grandmother dying of breast cancer.
= Right after my grandmother died of breast cancer; I started making efforts to raise money for cancer research.

⑶ Knowing that a group of people are working so closely together to achieve a specific goal is inspiring to me in many ways.
知道一群人努力合作完成某一個目標在很多方面都能激勵我。

= I was inspired in many ways by knowing that a group of people are working so closely together to achieve a specific goal.
= Being in a team working for the same goal inspires me in many ways.

2-13 個人事務

04 Are you willing to relocate or travel?

What do you think of travelling or relocation required in the new job?

你願意轉換工作地點（城市）或出差嗎？

▶ 題 解

當面試官問這個問題時通常他也期待肯定的答覆。如果你也喜歡出差，或者對移居到另一個城市表示歡迎，就熱切地給一個肯定的答案。但如果你因某些因素（如已結婚有小孩要照顧）無法經常出差或搬家，也不要直接拒絕，可以持較開放的口吻來回答。

▶ 短回答 ── 基本版　🎧 MP3 154

I would like to relocate because being in one place for a long time doesn't help us. I believe relocating has many benefits such as learning new things, new cultures, new languages and coming across different kinds of people.

我很樂意轉換工作地點（城市）因為在同一個地方工作太久對我們並沒有幫助。我相信轉換工作地點有很多好處例如學習新事物、新文化、新語言，並可遇見很多不同的人。

▶ 短回答 ── 進階版

Relocation is always been a good way to success as it always shows me a new way of life, offer me an opportunity to share my knowledge and gain knowledge from others. It always teaches me to be innovative and get adoptable with changes easily.

轉換工作地點（城市）一直是邁向成功的好方法因為它提供一個新的生活方式，一

個分享我的知識的機會，並向他人學習。轉換工作地點總是教導我創新並快速適應改變。

▶ 評解

兩個回答都熱切地回應願意出差或轉換工作地點（城市），並表明強烈學習動機。

▶ 長回答 🎧 MP3 155

I am more than willing to travel. I understand the importance of going above and beyond the call of duty to satisfy customer requests. Furthermore, Merrill Lynch's customer-focus belief means that travel is expected in some circumstances. I am willing to make this commitment to do whatever it takes to develop that long-term relationship with a small business or client. It is only through this relationship that loyalty can be maintained and financial gains and growth can occur for both the client and Merrill Lynch. It is my understanding from other financial consultants that I have worked before.

我非常樂意出差。我了解付出超越職責要求來滿足客戶的重要性。再者，美林證券以客為尊的信念也代表著出差在很多情況是必須的。我很樂意做這樣的承諾，盡我所有努力和小型企業和客戶建立長期關係。只有透過這樣的關係忠誠度才能被維持且美林證券和其客戶都能有財務收益與增長。這是我之前在其他財務顧問公司工作所學習到的。

▶ 評解

這樣的回答很優，顯示出你對目標職位的產業別很了解。

🍎 單字 🎧 MP3 156

❶ willing [`wɪlɪŋ] *adj.* 願意的，樂意的
❷ circumstance [`sɝkəmˌstæns] *n.* 情況，環境；情勢 [P]
❸ commitment [kə`mɪtmənt] *n.* 託付，交託；委任 [U]
❹ loyalty [`lɔɪəltɪ] *n.* 忠誠；忠心 [U]
❺ consultant [kən`sʌltənt] *n.* 顧問

✍ 用句型取勝

in some circumstances 在某些情況下

👉 要注意

1. 可放在句首、句中、或句尾。

例句：

- In some circumstances it may be necessary for me to visit individual clients in person.
  = It may be necessary for me to visit individual clients in person, in some circumstances.
  在某些情況下我可能需要親自拜訪個別客戶。

- If you find a new job, it is likely to be on the very same level you've been on, not a higher level, but in some circumstances it may be better for you.
  如果你找到了新工作，這個工作可能和你之前的工作差不多，而非更高的職位，但在某些情況下這可能對你更好。

do whatever it takes to ~ 不計代價、窮盡一切努力來~

👉 要注意

1. do 在這裡是最普遍使用的動詞，但有時也可用 try 或 give。
2. 以換句型來說，你可以將 to... 的部份，當成句子的主要動詞，而將 whatever it takes 當成補充，意思還是一樣。這種用法經常出現在口頭說話時。

例句：

- I will do whatever it takes to make my clients satisfied with my services.
  = I will make my clients satisfied with my services, whatever it takes.
  我會盡我所有努力來讓我的客戶滿意我的服務。

- I will do whatever it takes to cut down costs and increase revenue.

= I will cut down costs and increase revenue, whatever it takes.
我將盡所有努力來降低成本與提高收益。

換個說法令人眼睛一亮

(1) I would like to relocate because being in one place for a long time doesn't help us.
我很樂意轉換工作地點，因為在同一個地方工作太久對我們並沒有幫助。

= I would like to relocate because it's not helpful to be in one place for a long time.
= I don't think it's good to be in one place for too long and therefore I am positive about relocation.

(2) I am willing to make this commitment to do whatever it takes to develop that long-term relationship with a small business or client.
我很樂意做這樣的承諾，盡我可能和小型企業和客戶建立長期關係。

= I am committed to do everything that aims to develop a long-term relationship with a small business or client.
= You have my commitment to do whatever needed to develop a long-term relationship with a small business or client.

(3) It is only through this relationship that loyalty can be maintained and financial gains and growth can occur for both the client and Merrill Lynch.
只有透過這樣的關係忠誠度才能被維持且美林證券和其客戶都能有財務收益與增長。

= Loyalty can be maintained only through this relationship and both the client and Merrill Lynch can have financial gains and growth.
= This relationship can lead to loyalty and the financial gains and growth of both the client and Merrill Lynch.

2-13 個人事務

05 What are you passionate about?

What do you have passion for?

你熱愛甚麼？

▶ 題解

這個問題給應徵者一個很好的機會説明甚麼是你生命中重要的東西與你願意獻身或致力於何事物。不一定只能説與工作有關的答案，但要確定你熱愛的事物部會對工作有害。好的答案是提到對工作有益的人格特質如樂於助人，熱愛生活，或有益身心的娛樂嗜好。

▶ 短回答 — 基本版 🎧 MP3 157

I always want to make a difference. <u>When I'm involved with a project at work, I want to do my best to achieve success.</u> I feel the same way about what I do in my personal life.

我總是希望能有所作為。當我專注於工作上的專案，我要盡我所能取得成功。我對我個人的生活也是一樣的態度。

▶ 短回答 — 進階版

One of my greatest passions is helping others. When I was younger, I've enjoyed helping mom with household repairs. As I grew older, that habit grew and I desired to help others. I like helping people find solutions that meet their specific needs.

我對幫助他人有最大的熱情。當我小時候，我很喜歡幫媽媽做家庭維修。隨著我長大，這個習慣也跟著我，所以我渴望幫助他人。我喜歡幫助人們找到滿足其特定需求的解決方案。

評 解

熱愛有所作為與樂於助人都是在職場會加分的特質。

▶ 長回答 🎧 MP3 158

I've been waiting for a question like this! <u>I am passionate about love, expression, everything to do with emotions!</u> I am passionate about my future, about shaping my life and living to the fullest. I am passionate about my identity as a person, as a musician, as a boyfriend, son and brother. I am passionate about explanations and the reasons why we are here. I am passionate about music, and how it can take me away from my pain. I am passionate about exploring my inner depths, so that I can love all of me.

我一直在等待著這樣的問題！我熱愛愛情、表達、一切和情感有關的事物！我熱愛我的未來，熱愛塑造我的生命和把生活發揮到淋漓盡致。我熱愛我作為一個人的身份，作為一個音樂人、作為男友，兒子，和哥哥。我熱愛有關我們為什麼在這的所有解釋和理由。我熱愛音樂，以及它是如何帶我離開我的痛苦。我熱愛探索我的內心深處，讓我可以愛我的所有。

 評 解

這樣的回答讓人感覺你是一個正面積極且熱愛生命的人。

🍎 **單 字** 🎧 MP3 159

❶ **passionate** [ˋpæʃənɪt] *adj* . 熱情的；熱烈的，激昂的
❷ **expression** [ɪkˋsprɛʃən] *n*. 表達；表示
❸ **identity** [aɪˋdɛntətɪ] *n*. 身分；本身；本體
❹ **explanation** [ˌɛkspləˋneʃən] *n*. 說明，解釋
❺ **inner** [ˋɪnɚ] *adj*. 精神的，內心的

用句型取勝

be involved with/ in 熱中 專注

要注意

1. be involved with/ in 還有「參與、加入、捲入」的意思。
2. sb beV involved with/ in sth = sth involve sb。
3. I am involved with/ in sth = I involve myself with/ in sth。

例句：

- I was so involved in my work that I also worked on weekends.
  = I involved myself in my work, so that I also worked on weekends.
  我非常專注於我的工作，所以我週末時也在工作。
- I was reluctant to involve myself in the private fight.
  = I was reluctant to be involved in the private fight.
  我討厭捲入私鬥。

sb be passionate about ~ 對～有熱情

要注意

1. 這個片語要用 passion 的形容詞 passionate 。
2. sb be passionate about~ = sb have/ has passion for~。注意兩個片與介係詞的不同。
3. passion 可當可數或不可數名詞。故 sb have/ has passion for~ = sb have/ has a passion for~ = sb have/ has passions for~

例句：

- I am a woman who is passionate about life and work.
  = I am a woman who has passion for life and work.
  我是一個熱愛生活也熱愛工作的女性。

‧ I always choose a job that I can be passionate about.
= I always choose a job that I can have passions for.
我永遠選擇我對它充滿熱情的工作。

💡 換個說法令人眼睛一亮

⑴ As I grew older, that habit grew and I desired to help others.
隨著我長大，這個習慣也跟著我，所以我渴望幫助他人。

= That habit grew as I grew older and I enjoy helping others.
= I still keep the habit as I grew older and I love helping others.

⑵ I am passionate about love, expression, everything to do with emotions!
我熱愛愛情、表達、一切和情感有關的事物！

= I am passionate about everything related to emotions like love and expression.
= I am passionate about emotions such as love and expression.

⑶ I am passionate about music, and how it can take me away from my pain.
我熱愛音樂，以及它是如何帶我離開我的痛苦。

= I have passion for music and how it can take me away from my pain.
= I am passionate about music that keeps me away from feeling pain.

Part

2

99％會問的面試題

2-14 敏感問題

How much salary do you expect?

How much do you expect to get paid?
你期待的薪水是多少？

▶ 題 解

這是一個敏感的問題，但很多面試官會問。類似「依公司規定」這樣的答案是較好的選擇。但如果你要説出一個具體的數字，這個數字必須是符合現實的。也就是説，你必須在面試前針對類似工作，或類似資格條件要求的工作進行一番研究以了解薪水行情。

▶ 短回答 — 基本版 🎧 MP3 160

As a freshman in the work place, my preferences are job satisfaction and career development instead of the salary itself. As money is the basic need for anyone to survive, I except a salary according to company norms and my work.

作為一個職場新鮮人，我的優先權是工作的滿意度與職涯發展而非薪水本身。但錢還是每個人生存所需，我期待您根據公司規定和我的工作給我薪水。

▶ 短回答 — 進階版

The esteemed organization like yours has the salary structure for each position, and therefore I believe you will give me a reasonable salary based on my skills and experience. I am eager to get an opportunity to work for you and grow and learn as I work.

貴公司受人敬重，每個職位都有它的薪資結構，所以我相信您會依據我的技能和經驗給我合理的薪資。我很渴望能有機會為貴公司工作並成長與學習。

▶ 評 解

基本版回答強調正面的工作態度──追求工作滿意度與職涯發展。進階版回答強調強烈動機為目標公司工作。

▶ 長回答　🎧 MP3 161

My research and experience tell me that a reasonable salary for this position would fall somewhere between NTDXXX and NTDXXX. However, there are many things to consider, like the people I will be working with, career development and progression, and of course the job itself and the overall work environment. As a result, I'm quite open and flexible on salary as the opportunity to add value and to be valued is more important to me. I'd appreciate it if you would like to tell me how you value this position and what your budget is for this role.

就我的了解與經驗告訴我這個職位的合理薪資大約介於台幣～到～之間。然而還有很多事要考慮例如與我一起共事的人，職涯發展，當然還有工作本身和整體工作環境。因此，我對薪資採開放與有彈性的態度因為能為公司帶來價值和被賞識對我來說更重要。我會很感激如果您願意告訴我你如何衡量這個職位與您對這個角色的預算為何。

▶ 評 解

此回答先表明自己對類似工作薪資有一定了解，但還是強調薪資不是最主要考慮的因素，而是能為公司貢獻與被賞識。

🍎 單字　🎧 MP3 162

❶ **reasonable** [`riznəb!] *adj.* 合理的，正當的；適當的
❷ **consider** [kən`sɪdɚ] *v.* 考慮，細想
❸ **progression** [prə`grɛʃən] *n.* 發展；改進
❹ **appreciate** [ə`priʃɪˌet] *v.* 欣賞，賞識
❺ **budget** [`bʌdʒɪt] *n.* 預算

用句型取勝

> **instead of ... 不是…**

要注意

1. instead of 當介係詞，表「不是…」，後方需搭配「名詞」或「動名詞」(Ving)。可和 rather than 互換。instead of 和 rather than 放句首時，記得打逗號。
2. rather than 也可當「連接詞」，表「不是…」，連接形態和詞性對等的字詞，如兩個名詞、兩個動詞或兩個副詞。rather than 也可和 instead of 一樣當「介係詞」使用，後方搭配「名詞」或「動名詞」(Ving)。
3. rather than 連接兩個主詞時，動詞需和「第一個主詞」一致。

例句：

- What I really care is the overall work environment instead of the salary itself.
  我真正在意的是整體工作環境而非薪水本身。
- Kevin rather than I is in charge of the project.
  負責這個專案的是 Kevin 而不是我。

> **beV+eager+to 熱切的、渴望的去做某事**

要注意

1. 表示渴望做某事，後接不定詞。
2. 表示渴望得到某物，後接介係詞 for、after、about 等。

例句：

- I am eager to have a business trip in America.
  我很渴望能去美國出差。
- The general manager prefers those employees who are eager for knowledge.
  總經理喜歡求知心切的員工。

💡 換個說法令人眼睛一亮

⑴ As a freshman in the work place, my preferences are job satisfaction and career development instead of the salary itself.

作為一個職場新鮮人，我的優先權是工作的滿意度與職涯發展而非薪水本身。

= As a freshman in the work place, my first priority is not salary. I care more about job satisfaction and career development.
= Being a freshman in the work place, I care more about job satisfaction and career development rather than the salary.

⑵ The esteemed organization like yours has the salary structure for each position, and therefore I believe you will give me a reasonable salary based on my skills and experience.

貴公司受人敬重，每個職位都有它的薪資結構，所以我相信您會依據我的技能和經驗給我合理的薪資。

= The salary structure for each position in an esteemed company like yours will ensure me a reasonable salary based on my skills and experience.
= I believe a reasonable salary based on employees' skills and experience is guaranteed by the salary structure for each position in an esteemed organization like yours.

⑶ My research and experience tell me that a reasonable salary for this position would fall somewhere between NTDXXX and NTDXXX.

就我的了解與經驗告訴我這個職位的合理薪資大約介於台幣~到~之間。

= According to my research and experience, a reasonable salary for this position would fall somewhere between NTDXXX and NTDXXX.
= I think a reasonable salary for this position would fall somewhere between NTDXXX and NTDXXX, based on my research and experience.

If hired, how long do you plan on working here?

How long do you expect yourself to work here if we hire you?

如果錄取了，你預計在這裡工作多久？

▶題 解

這是較敏感的問題，但很多面試官會問。回答前提是「誠實」。如果你知道兩年內你會搬到另一城市，就直接說「在那之前我會希望在這裡穩定工作。」如果你希望長期在這間公司耕耘，附帶說明這個職位這個公司有那些優勢使你希望這會是一份長期的工作。

▶短回答 — 基本版 🎧 MP3 163

I have always been looking to establish and settle my career in a company where I will be challenged to take more responsibilities and my good work will be appreciated. Here if I find those opportunities then I would definitely work for a long time.

我一直希望能在一個能讓我面對挑戰、負起更多責任且欣賞我工作能力的公司建立和穩定發展我的職業。如果在這裡我可以有這機會，我肯定會長期在這工作。

▶短回答 — 進階版

As far as I am concerned, the company offers some excellent opportunities for employees and has the capacity of providing a better career for employees like me. Thus as long as I can contribute to you, I will be available for working here for long.

就我而言，貴公司提供很好的機會給員工且有能力提供像我這樣的員工好的工作。因此只要我可以為貴公司奉獻，我願意在這裡長期工作。

▶ 評 解

兩個回答都表達強烈的動機為公司奉獻,進階版就說明了求職者有先了解目標公司與職位。

▶ 長回答 🎧 MP3 164

I can see a long tenure with this company. I know there are a range of opportunities across the spectrum of my profession with this firm. I've heard good things about your training and study support programs, which is perfect for my own studies. I always dream of working for a company that is willing to invest on employee training. If I can achieve a promotion, and get the broad experience I need to progress in the industry, I'll be here for a long period of time and work my best to make significant contributions to you.

我可以在貴公司看到一個長遠的終身職業。我知道在貴公司有我專業範圍內的各種機會。我聽說您們的培訓和研究支持計畫非常好,這對我自己的研究是很有助益的。我一直夢想在一個願意投資在員工訓練的公司工作。我如果可以有升遷機會,並且獲得在這個產業要進步所需要的廣泛知識,我會在這裡長期工作並我所能提供顯著貢獻給公司。

▶ 評 解

這個回答不僅說明這個公司有那些優勢讓人想要在這長期工作,也透露強烈的學習與積極在工作上有所表現的動機。

 單 字 🎧 MP3 165

❶ **tenure** [ˋtɛnjʊr] *n.* 終身職位
❷ **spectrum** [ˋspɛktrəm] *n.* 系列;範圍
❸ **broad** [brɔd] *adj.* 廣泛的
❹ **progress** [prəˋgrɛs] *v.* 進步
❺ **significant** [sɪgˋnɪfəkənt] *adj.* 顯著的

✍ 用句型取勝

> **as far as sb. / sth. + be concerned**
> 對…來說，就…而言，關於…方面

👉 要注意

1. be 動詞要用現在簡單式。
2. as far as I am concerned = as for me=in my opinion=from my point of view，通常都放在句首，但也可放句尾。

例句：

- As far as I am concerned/ As for me/ In my opinion/ from my point of view, your company is the best in the industry.
  對我來説，您們公司是這個行業中最好的。
- The training I have received fits me for the job, as far as I am concerned.
  就我而言，我所受的訓練使我能勝任這個工作。

> **as long as S + V, S + V...** 只要

👉 要注意

1. 用在未來時態上，**as long as** 引導的副詞子句是條件句，故應採現在式，主要子句採未來式。也就是 As long as S + 現在式 V, S + will + V...。
2. as long as = so long as。

例句：

- I believe that as long as I make efforts, I will get the chance to be promoted.
  = I believe that so long as I make efforts, I will get the chance to be promoted.
  我相信只要努力，我就會有升遷的機會。

換個說法令人眼睛一亮

(1) I have always been looking to establish and settle my career in a company where I will be challenged to take more responsibilities and my good work will be appreciated.

我一直希望能在一個能讓我面對挑戰負起更多責任且欣賞我工作能力的公司建立和穩定發展我的職涯。

= I always want to settle down with an employer who challenges me to take more responsibilities and appreciate my talent.

= An employer who challenges me to take more responsibilities and appreciate my talent is the one I am willing to work with for a long period of time.

(2) I've heard good things about your training and study support programs, which is perfect for my own studies.

我聽說您們的培訓和研究支持計畫非常好，這對我自己的研究是很有助益的。

= Your training and study support programs have good reputation and are very good to my own studies.

= Your training and study support programs are popular and perfect for my studies.

(3) I always dream of working for a company that is willing to invest on employee training.

我一直夢想在一個願意投資在員工訓練的公司工作。

= A company that is willing to invest on employee training is the one I always dream of working for.

= My dream employer is the one who is willing to invest no employee training.

03 Q What do you expect from a supervisor?

Can you describe an ideal supervisor in your mind?

你對主管有什麼期待？

▶ 題解

這個問題的用意在了解求職者是否對公司的管理制度有合理的期待，這也是一個陷阱題，當被問到這個問題時，很多人會不由自主地抱怨之前的主管，這絕對不是面試官想要聽到的答案。回答重點是強調之前主管的優點（不論你有多不喜歡她／他）。

▶ 短回答 —— 基本版　🎧 MP3 166

In my last job, I liked the fact that management did not show favoritism and <u>they understand employees' needs as well as their strengths. Of course, these things take time to know, but I would hope my supervisor will try to know me in that way.</u>

在我之前的工作中，主管們並不會偏袒任何人並理解員工的需求和優勢。當然，這些事需要時間去了解的，但我會希望我的主管會用這種方式試著了解我。

▶ 短回答 —— 進階版

My pervious supervisor is an ideal one because I was able to go to him without hesitation if I have an issue or idea and feel comfortable to express my thoughts. He is also open-minded and always lets me know if there is anything I could do to improve myself.

我之前的主管就很完美，因為當我遇到問題或有想法時我能夠毫不猶豫地並愉悅地向他表達我的想法。他也是心胸開闊的人並總會讓我知道我還有那些需要改進的地方。

評解

兩個回答都強調喜愛之前的主管，這也說明了求職者在之前的工作是適應良好的。

長回答 MP3 167

My last supervisor had a lot of qualities I appreciated. She would often ask for my opinions and thoughts on the best course of action before I started on a project. She would also schedule regular check-ups with me to ensure we were on the same page, and every once in a while we would enjoy a conversation over coffee about my future projects and responsibilities. I respect her because she is always goal driven and encourages us to work hard for overall company success, and she values and acknowledges the contributions of employees. I hope that any supervisor I have shares those qualities.

我之前的主管有很多我欣賞的特質。她在我開始做一個專案時會用很好的方式詢問我的意見和想法。她也會定期檢查我的工作進度以確保雙方的進度相同。我們每隔一段時間就會一起喝個咖啡聊聊我未來要做的專案和責任。我尊敬她因為她總是目標導向並鼓勵我們為公司整體成就努力工作。她尊重並認同員工的貢獻。我希望我的任何主管都會有相同的特質。

評解

這個回答讓面試官覺得你和主管有良好互動且你的工作表現優良，對公司有貢獻。

單字 MP3 168

❶ **quality** [`kwɑlətɪ] *n.* 特質；品質

❷ **appreciate** [ə`priʃɪˌet] *v.* 欣賞，賞識

❸ **ensure** [ɪn`ʃʊr] *v.* 保證；確保

❹ **value** [prə`grɛs] *v.* 尊重；重視，珍視

❺ **acknowledge** [ək`nɑlɪdʒ] *v.* 承認；認同

用句型取勝

as well as 不但；而且

要注意

1. as well as 表「以及」的用法，相當於 and 之意，可用以連接對等的字。
2. as well as 連接主詞的用法 （表不但…而且…） = not only ~ but also~ = both ~ and ~。
3. As well as 連接主詞時，動詞以第一個主詞做變化。
4. not only ~ but also~ 連接主詞時，動詞以第二個主詞做變化。

例句：

- Tom as well as his colleagues is going to the seminar tonight.
  = Not only Tom but also his colleagues are going to the seminar tonight.
  = Both Tom and his colleagues are going to the seminar tonight.
  Tom 和他同事今晚要去研討會。
- The manager said to me that he likes my way of thinking as well as the creative ideas I presented.
  = The manager said to me that he likes not only my way of thinking but also the creative ideas I presented.
  = The manager said to me that he likes both my way of thinking and the creative ideas I presented.
  經理跟我説他喜歡我的思考方式和我提出的創意想法。

of course 一定；當然

要注意

1. of course=without doubt

例句：

- Of course, the old school tie has been a help for me to expand my business.

當然，校友關係對我擴展業務是有幫助的。

- Of course people don't always make right decisions, including me.
當然人們並不是總是做正確的決定，包括我。

換個說法令人眼睛一亮

(1) My pervious supervisor is an ideal one because I was able to go to him without hesitation if I have an issue or idea and feel comfortable to express my thoughts.

我之前的主管就很完美，因為當我遇到問題或有想法時，我能夠毫不猶豫並愉悅地向他表達我的想法。

= I like my previous supervisor very much because he never lets me feel pressured when I have an issue or idea and need to express my thoughts to him.

= My previous supervisor is the one I would feel very comfortable to express my thoughts to when I have an issue or idea, and therefore he is the best supervisor in my mind.

---

(2) He is also open-minded and always lets me know if there is anything I could do to improve myself.

他也是心胸開闊的人並總會讓我知道我還有那些需要改進的地方。

= He is also open-minded and always gives suggestions on things I can do to improve myself.

= He always keeps an open mind and advises me of anything I can do to improve myself.

---

(3) I respect her because she is always goal driven and encourages us to work hard for overall company success.

我尊敬她因為她總是目標導向並鼓勵我們為公司整體成就努力工作。

= I respect her as she is always goal oriented and motivates us to work towards the company's success.

= Her goal orientation won my respect and motivated us to work harder for overall company success.

2-14 敏感問題

04 When was the last time you were angry? What happened?

Tell me a situation in which you get angry.
你上次生氣是何時？發生了甚麼事？

▶ 題解

面試官會問這樣的問題主要是想知道應徵者是否會在工作場合失去控制。也就是說，「生氣」這個字眼指的是「失去控制」。面試官想要了解你如何處理會讓你生氣的情境。回答要避免有「失去控制」的字眼。應該要說明自己的高 EQ。

▶ 短回答 —— 基本版 🎧 MP3 169

Anger to me means loss of control. I do not lose control. When I get stressed, I step back, take a deep breath, thoughtfully think through the situation and then begin to formulate a plan of action.

生氣對我來說就是失去控制。我不會失去控制。當我有壓力時，我退一步，深呼吸，沉思地把整個情形想一遍，然後開始想應對方法。

▶ 短回答 —— 進階版

I was frustrated when I had a drunken customer in my last job. I didn't get angry. I know if I had gotten angry, it may have led to further violence. Instead I just called for my supervisor who came and removed the person. I carried on with my shift.

在我之前的工作，當我遇到酒醉的客人時我很沮喪。我並沒有生氣。我知道如果我生氣可能會導致更進一步的衝突，因此我請主管出面請此人離開，並繼續上班。

▶ 評 解

兩個回答都強調不會在工作場合生氣讓自己失控。且會有所應對方式。

▶ 長回答　🎧 MP3 170

I don't think anger is an appropriate workplace emotion. <u>I have dealt with situations that I found frustrating</u>; for example, I had a boss who was very aggressive in his management style. I felt I was constantly being criticized for things beyond my control. I sat down with him and talked about ways that we could improve our communication. <u>In the long run, after having that conversation, I found that I learned a lot of things from him.</u> If I let the anger controlled me, my bad emotions would have incapacitated me.

我不認為生氣是適當的工作場合情緒。我已經處理過讓我沮喪的工作情境。例如，我有一個老闆他的管理風格是非常有侵略性的。我覺得我一直因我無法控制的事被他苛求。我和他坐下來討論有何方法可改善我們之間的溝通。從長遠來看，有了這樣的晤談後，我覺得我從老闆那學到很多事。如果我讓憤怒控制了我，我的壞情緒可能會讓我失去行為能力。

▶ 評 解

由實際的例子說明如何面對與處裡令人沮喪或生氣的工作情境。

🍎 單字　🎧 MP3 171

❶ **emotion** [ɪˋmoʃən] *n.* 感情，情緒

❷ **frustrating** [ˋfrʌstretɪŋ] *adj.* 令人洩氣的，使人沮喪的

❸ **aggressive** [əˋgrɛsɪv] *adj.* 侵略的，侵犯的

❹ **constantly** [ˋkɑnstəntlɪ] *adv.* 不斷地；時常地

❺ **criticize** [ˋkrɪtɪˌsaɪz] *v.* 批評；批判；苛求；非難

用句型取勝

in the long run, ~ 長遠來看（終究），～

要注意

1. 通常放在句首，後加逗號，接一完整句子。
2. 也可放句尾或句中。

例句：

- In the long run, pursuing my studies abroad is good for me.
  = Pursuing my studies abroad is good for me in the long run.
  長遠來看，到國外求學對我是好的。
- I believe in the long run, it always pays to the diligent.
  = I believe it always pays to the diligent in the long run.
  我相信努力終究是值得的。

deal with~ 處理～

要注意

1. deal with=cope with=handle=treat=take actions about。

例句：

- In my previous job, I have piles of documents to deal with every day.
  = In my previous job, I have piles of documents to cope with every day.
  我的上一份工作每天都有很多疊文件需要處理。
- My work experience equipped me to deal with all kinds of people.
  = My work experience equipped me to handle all kinds of people.
  我的工作經驗使我能與各式各樣的人打交道。

換個說法令人眼睛一亮

⑴I know if I had gotten angry, it may have led to further violence.

我知道如果我生氣可能會導致更進一步的衝突。

= I know my anger may have led to further violence.
= I know there may have been further violence if I had gotten angry.

⑵I don't think anger is an appropriate workplace emotion.

我不認為生氣是適當的工作場合情緒。

= I don't think we should get angry in the workplace.
= Getting angry is not appropriate in the workplace.

⑶I had a boss who was very aggressive in his management style.

我有一個老闆他的管理風格是非常有侵略性的。

= I had a very aggressive boss.
= My boss is very aggressive in his management style.

2-14 敏感問題

05 What do people most often criticize about you?

Did you ever be criticized at work?

人們最常批評你甚麼？

▶ 題解

這樣的問題想要了解面試者是否有備受批評之處與如何接受批評。回答時要小心，不要給人你在工作上一直被批評的印象，但也不要暗示你認為你是完美的。回答時可以闡述一個和目標職位無太大關聯之被批評處。或你已針對你的缺點做改進。

▶ 短回答 — 基本版 🎧 MP3 172

People often said that I am sometimes too nice to people, and that I should be a little tougher. I am that way because I believe everyone deserves respect, even if they aren't being very nice to me.

人們常說我有時對人太好，而我有時應該強硬一點。我會這樣是因為我相信每個人都值得被尊重，即使他們並非對我很好。

▶ 短回答 — 進階版

Many years ago my supervisor told me that I was too critical of other people's work. I took that to heart, and made sure from that point forward that my analysis and suggestions are always supportive and helpful rather than critical.

我有一個上司在很多年前告訴我，我太挑剔別人的工作。我把他說的話放進心理，並確保從那時起，我對別人的分析和建議永遠是支持與幫助的，而不是批判性的。

▶ 評 解

基本版回答所說被批評之處無傷大雅，進階版有告知已針對被批評處做改進。

▶ 長回答　🎧 MP3 173

I face criticism with positive attitude as it offers me information on how to improve myself. I used to be an introvert. I was criticized for not voicing my opinions, ideas and suggestions in meetings. Our director always liked my proposals whenever I discussed with him before meetings, but in the meetings I seldom uttered these. I improved upon the point and tried my best to lay my opinions in the meetings. I therefore improved my confidence and communication skills. Meanwhile I am no longer introverted and now I can easily mix with people and exchange ideas.

我用積極的態度面對批評，因為它為我提供了關於如何改進自己的訊息。我曾經是一個內向的人。我被批評在會議裡沒有說出自己的意見，想法和建議。當我每次開會前跟我們主任討論時他一直很喜歡我的建議，但在會議上我很少說出這些。我立刻改進了這點，盡我所能把我的意見在會議中表達。我因此提高了我的自信和溝通能力。同時不再內向，而現在我可以很容易地融入他人並交換想法。

▶ 評 解

此回答優點在有強調用積極的態度面對批評並改善自己的缺點。

🍎 單字　🎧 MP3 174

❶ **introvert** [ˋɪntrəˌvɝt] *n.* 內向的人

❷ **voice** [vɔɪs] *v.* （用言語）表達，說出

❸ **proposal** [prəˋpozḷ] *n.* 建議，提議；計畫；提案

❹ **utter** [ˋʌtɚ] *v.* 發出（聲音等）；說，講；表達

❺ **exchange** [ɪksˋtʃendʒ] *v.* 交換；交流；交易

Part **2**

99％會問的面試題

247

用句型取勝

sb deserve sth~某人值得；應得，該得，應受（賞罰、幫助等）

👉 要注意

1. deserve 後接名詞或代名詞，通常只用做及物動詞，且不能用於進行時態。
2. deserve 後接不定詞，若該動詞表示主動意義，則用不定詞的主動式。若該動詞表示被動意義，則用不定詞的被動式，或者動詞的 -ing 形式。

例句：

· I think my qualifications are good and I deserve a better job.
我認為我的資格條件不錯，我應得一份更好的工作。

· I am not perfect and sometimes I do make mistakes. I deserve to be criticized.
= I am not perfect and sometimes I do make mistakes. I deserve being criticized.
我不完美，有時我也會犯錯。我應當被批評。

sb is criticized for~ 某人因～被批評

👉 要注意

1. for 後要加名詞或動名詞。
2. 也可以寫：sb1 is criticized by sb2 for ~某人因甚麼被另一人批評。
3. 上述的被動語句可改成主動。

例句：

· I was criticized by my boss for handing in the report late.
= My boss criticized me for handing in the report late.
我老闆批評我遲交報告。

· My colleague was criticized for sensationalizing the story.
我同事因大肆喧染此事而備受批評。

換個說法令人眼睛一亮

(1) I am that way because I believe everyone deserves respect, even if they aren't being very nice to me.
我會這樣是因為我相信每個人都值得被尊重，即使他們並非對我很好。

= I behave like this because I respect everybody even though they are not very nice to me.
= Everyone deserves respect, and therefore I am like this even if they don't treat me the same way.

(2) I face criticism with positive attitude as it offers me information on how to improve myself.
我用積極的態度面對批評，因為它為我提供了關於如何改進自己的訊息。

= I am positive about criticism because it helps me improve myself.
= I welcome criticism since it provides a motive to improve myself.

(3) I improved upon the point and tried my best to lay my opinions in the meetings.
我立刻改進了這點，盡我所能把我的意見在會議中表達。

= I improved it right away and did whatever I can to express myself in the meetings.
= I improve myself by trying to illustrate myself more in the meetings.

Part

2

99％會問的面試題

2-14 敏感問題

Q06 What has been the greatest disappointment in your life?

Can you tell me something that made you most disappointed?

你人生中最大的失望／遺憾為何？

▶ 題解

藉由這個問題面試官想了解你對人生中的遺憾如何面對或你是否是很容易氣餒的人。回答時可談論任何讓你失望或遺憾的事，這件事並不一定要是很嚴重的事，重點是你用積極樂觀的態度面對它。有時人生當時的「遺憾」，事後想起來或許會變成人生的收穫。

▶ 短回答 ── 基本版　🎧 MP3 175

My biggest disappointment is that my dad passed away just after I graduated from college and got my first job. He was a pioneer in the technology industry during his time, and he was so proud of me following in his footsteps.

我最大的遺憾是，我的父親在我大學畢業，剛得到第一份工作時就去世了。在他在職期間，對於我能克紹箕裘，他感到非常地驕傲。

▶ 短回答 ── 進階版

My biggest disappointment is that I wasn't able to follow my dream of being a professional dancer since I was injured as a teenager during a performance. But I realize now that if I had taken that direction, I would not have my advanced degrees and a career I love.

我最大的遺憾是我沒能實現成為專業舞者的夢想，因為我青少年時在一個表演中受傷。但我現在了解到，如果我走了那條路，我就不會有高學歷和我愛的職業生涯。

▶ 評解

進階版較優因其陳述了用樂觀的態度面對遺憾。

▶ 長回答 🎧 MP3 176

Of all the disappointments in my life, the greatest one was I wasn't able to go straight to graduate school out of college. However, I think the two years I spent working helped to focus me on what I really wanted to study, and ultimately made my graduate school experience much better. <u>Having a little extra time to figure things out,</u> I was much better prepared to make decisions about what I wanted to study and how that would prepare me for my career. I think I have made a right decision about my career and I have enjoyed what I am doing since then.

在我生命中所有的失望中最大的一個是我沒能在大學畢業後直接讀研究所。然而，我覺得我工作的這兩年幫助我找到真的想讀的，也因此使我在研究所的經驗變得更好。多了一點額外的時間來理出頭緒，讓我能針對想要攻讀的方向及學校的學習能對我的工作有怎樣的幫助這些部分有更充分的準備。我想我就我的職業生涯做了一個正確的決定，從那之後我一直都很喜愛我的工作。

▶ 評解

當時的遺憾反而對現在的職涯很有幫助。回答中正面積極的態度會令面試官讚賞。

🍎 單字 🎧 MP3 177

❶ **disappointment** [ˌdɪsəˋpɔɪntmənt] *n.* 失望；掃興，沮喪
❷ **straight** [stret] *adv.* 直接地，一直地
❸ **graduate school** [ˋgrædʒʊˌet] [skul] *n.* 研究所
❹ **ultimately** [ˋʌltəmɪtlɪ] *adv.* 最後；終極地
❺ **prepare** [prɪˋpɛr] *v.* 準備；使……準備好

用句型取勝

since 自從

👆 要注意

1. since 表「自從」，可作介係詞或副詞連接詞。若作介係詞，接一個時間名詞（last Friday, five years ago, 1999）作受詞，若作副詞連接詞，則引導過去式的副詞子句。被修飾的子句則用現在完成（進行）式，句型為：

現在完成式句型：S + have/ has V-pp + since + S + 過去V/ since + N
現在完成式（進行式）句型：S + have/ has been + V-ing + since + S + V/ since + N

例句：

· I have worked for that company since I graduated from college.
  = I have worked for that company since graduating from college.
  我大學畢業後就在那家公司工作。

· I have not had a chance to visit my previous colleagues since I left that job.
  = I have not had a chance to visit my previous colleagues since my resignation.
  我離職後一直沒有機會去探望我之前的同事。

figure out ~ 想出，理解~

👆 要注意

1. figure out 後可加名詞或子句。
2. 名詞或介係詞可放在 figure 和 out 的中間。

例句：

· Our team tried very hard to figure out how to deal with this issue.
  = Our team tried very hard to figure out a way to deal with this issue.

我們團隊非常努力要想出一個解決這個爭議的方法。

- I told my staff that it is something they should figure out themselves.

我告訴我的員工這件事他們必須自己想辦法。

💡 換個說法令人眼睛一亮

(1) My biggest disappointment is that I wasn't able to follow my dream of being a professional dancer since I was injured as a teenager during a performance.

我最大的遺憾是，我沒能實現成為專業舞者的夢想，因為我青少年時在一個表演中受傷。

= I wasn't able to follow my dream of being a professional dancer due to an injury in my teenage time, which is my biggest disappointment.

= I was so disappointed about my failing to be a professional dancer because of my injury earlier.

(2) I think the two years I spent working helped to focus me on what I really wanted to study, and ultimately made my graduate school experience much better.

我覺得我工作的這兩年幫助我找到於我真的想讀的，也因此使我在研究所的經驗變得更好。

= My two years of working experience helped me figure out my study interest and ultimately made my graduate school experience a better one.

= I could focus myself on my study interest and ultimately made my graduate school experience a better one as result of my two years of working experience.

2-14 敏感問題

07 Are you overqualified for this Job?

Do you think your qualifications are much better than we expected?

對這個工作而言，你的條件是否太好？

▶ 題 解

這樣的問題在面試中不算少見。回答時不要強調你優異的資格條件，這會讓面試官質疑你是否真的對這個職位有興趣。重點是要表明你想在這家公司工作的強烈動機或你可以對公司帶來甚麼？

▶ 短回答 — 基本版 🎧 MP3 178

This job is so attractive to me that I'm willing to sign a contract committing to stay for a minimum of 12 months. There's no obligation on your part. How else can I convince you that I'm the best person for this position?

這份工作對我來說是如此吸引人，我很願意簽訂合約承諾在這工作至少12個月。你這方無任何義務責任。我還能怎麼讓你相信我是最適合這個職位的人？

▶ 短回答 — 進階版

My children have grown and I am no longer concerned with title and salary. I like to keep myself busy. A reference check will show I do my work on time, and do it well as a team member. I'm sure we can agree on a salary that fits your budget.

我的小孩都長大了，我不再在乎職稱和薪水。我喜歡保持忙碌。詢問我的推薦人會顯示我按時做我的工作，並且是很好的團隊成員。我相信我們可以在符合您預算的薪水達成共識。

 評 解

兩個回答都表明動機，進階版回答也明白表明職稱和薪水不是首要考慮考慮目標。

▶ 長回答 🎧 MP3 179

As you note, I've worked at a higher level but this position now is exactly what I'm looking for. You offer opportunity to achieve the magic word: balance. I'm scouting for something challenging but a little less intense so I can spend more time with my family. Downsizings have left generational memory gaps in the workforce and knowledge doesn't always get passed on to the people coming up. I could be a mentor -- calm, stable, and reliable. For my last employer, I provided the history of a failed product launch to a new marketing manager, who then avoided making the same mistakes.

如你所知，我在更高的職位上工作過，但現在這個位置正是我要找的。您提供機會達到一個神奇的字：平衡。我在找尋具有挑戰性的工作，但工作不那麼繁重，所以我可以花更多的時間與我的家人相處。裁員已經導致勞動世代記憶空白，知識並不總是能傳遞到新人們。我可以做一個導師──冷靜，穩定，可靠。在我上一個工作，我告知一個新的行銷經理一個失敗的產品發表的故事，他就避免了犯同樣的錯誤。

▶ 評 解

此回答不僅表明動機，也主動說明能為公司做甚麼。

📖 單 字 🎧 MP3 180

❶ scout [skaʊt] v. 偵察；搜索
❷ downsizing [ˋdaʊnˌsaɪzɪŋ] n. 縮減人員開支
❸ generational [ˌdʒɛnəˋreʃən!] adj. 一代的
❹ mentor [ˋmɛntɚ] n. 導師
❺ launch [lɔntʃ] n. 發行

Part 2

99％會問的面試題

用句型取勝

so 形容詞/ 副詞 that 主詞 + 動詞　如此地…以至於…

要注意

1. 也可用「such 名詞 that 主詞+動詞」替代。

例句：

- I am so interested in this position that I will do whatever to prove that I am the right person for it.

  = This is such an interesting position that I will do whatever to prove that I am the right person for it.

  我對這職位是如此地感興趣以至於我會做任何事來證明我是這職位的適當人選。

- I have always worked so hard that I hardly have time to spend with my children.

  = I am such a hard working person that I hardly have time to spend with my children.

  我總是如此努力工作以至於我幾乎沒時間陪伴我的小孩。

convince sb of sth 說服某人某事

要注意

1. convince sb of sth 也可用「convince sb that +完整句子」替代。
2. convince 與 persuade 意思相近，但有些微不同：convince 是「讓某人信服某種說法或提議的真實性」，persuade 則是用來指「說服某人做某事」。
3. convince 與 persuade 用法不同。 persuade sb to V = convince sb of sth。要注意 convince 後面是不接不定詞。persuade 和 convince 後都可接that+完整句子。

例句：

- Let me convince you that I have the strong motivation to work for you.

讓我說服你我是有強烈動機為您工作的。

· I want to convince my supervisor of my dedication to this job.

我試圖讓我的主管相信我會致力於這項工作。

換個說法令人眼睛一亮

⑴ This job is so attractive to me that I'm willing to sign a contract committing to stay for a minimum of 12 months.

這份工作對我來說是如此吸引人，我很願意簽訂合約承諾在這工作至少12個月。

= This is such an attractive job to me that I'm willing to sign a contract committing to stay for a minimum of 12 months.

= This job is so attractive to me that I like to commit to stay for at least 12 months by signing a contract.

⑵ My children have grown and I am no longer concerned with title and salary.

我的小孩都長大了，我不再在乎職稱和薪水。

= My children have grown and title and salary are no longer what I am concerned for.

= My children have grown and I am not concerned about title and salary any more.

⑶ I'm scouting for something challenging but a little less intense so I can spend more time with my family.

我在找尋具有挑戰性的工作，但工作不那麼繁重，所以我可以花更多的時間與我的家人相處。

= I'm looking for a challenging, but less intense job which allows me to spend more time with my family.

= In order to spend more time with my family, I'm searching for something challenging but a little less intense.

Part 3

實際面試對答
The Interview Scenarios

Engineer

3-1

工程師

👥 角色

D: David, the hiring manager.面試者

H: Henry, the job applicant.求職者

💼 情景

Henry is applying for the senior computer programmer position at ABC company.

Henry 應徵 ABC 公司的資深電腦程式設計師一職。

💬 對話 🎧

D: First of all, can you give me a **brief** introduction about yourself?

首先，你可以先簡短介紹你自己嗎？

H: With my qualifications and experience, I feel I am hardworking, responsible and diligent in any project I undertake. Your organization could benefit from my analytical and **interpersonal** skills.

依我的資格和經驗，我覺得我對待從事的每一個專案都很努力、負責、勤勉。我的分析能力和與人相處的技巧，對貴單位必有價值。

D: Sounds good. I know from your resume that you worked as a computer programmer in your

聽起來不錯。我從你的履歷得知你之前是一名電腦程式設計師。你能告訴我你的工作內容嗎？

previous job. Can you tell me what you have done in that job?

H：To be specific, I do system analysis, trouble shooting and provide software support.

具體地說，我做系統分析，解決問題以及軟體供應方面的支援。

D：You have worked there for five years. What made you want to leave?

你已經在那裏工作了五年，是甚麼讓你想要離開？

H：I feel there is no opportunity for **advancement**. I am hoping to get an offer of a better position.

我覺得沒有升遷的機會。我希望能獲得一份更好的工作，如果機會來臨，我會抓住。

D：It's good to know that you <u>are motivated to</u> upgrade yourself to a higher position, but what make you think you would be a **success** in this position?

很高興知道你有動機想要提升自己到一個較高的職位，但你如何知道你能勝任這份工作？

H：My graduate school training combined with my years of professional experiences should qualify me for this particular job. I am sure I will be successful.

我在研究所的訓練，加上多年的專業經驗，使我適合這份工作。我相信我能成功。

📖 單字

❶ **brief** [brif] *adj.* 簡略的，簡短

相關詞 **prolonged** [prə`lɔŋd] *adj.* 延長的；拖延的

briefing [`brifɪŋ] *n.* 簡報

常用法 in brief 簡言之

例 In brief, I have made up my mind to quit my job.

簡言之，我已下定決心辭掉工作。

❷ **specific** [spɪ`sɪfɪk] *adj.* 特殊的，特定的

相關詞 **general** [`dʒɛnərəl] *adj.* 一般的，普遍的；非專業性的

particular [pə`tɪkjələ] *adj.* 特殊的；特定的；特別的

常用法 to be specific 具體地說

例 To be specific, the argument in his graduation thesis is logical.

具體地說，他畢業論文的論點符合邏輯。

❸ **interpersonal** [ˌɪntə`pɝsən!] *a.* 人際關係的

相關詞 **communication** [kəˌmjunə`keʃən] *n.* 傳達；交流；溝通

Interpersonal intelligence [ˌɪntə`pɝsən! ɪn`tɛlədʒəns] *n.* 人際溝通

智慧；人際智能

例 We need a person who has good interpersonal intelligence to do this job.

我們需要一個有好的人際溝通智慧的人來做這個工作。

❹ **advancement** [əd`vænsmənt] *n.* 晉升

相關詞 **promotion** [prə`moʃən] *n.* 提升，晉級

raise [rez] *n.* 加薪

例 The reason I am interested in this job is that it offered good opportunities for advancement.

我對這個工作感興趣的原因是它提供很好的升遷機會。

面試時別講錯

我在研究所的訓練，加上多年的專業經驗，使我適合這份工作。

（✗）I graduate school training and many yearsprofessional experiences, I am suitable for this job.

（○）My graduate school training combined with my years of professional experiences should qualify me for this particular job.

錯誤的句子是中文式英文，很多人都會犯這樣的錯誤。研究所英文說「graduate school」，有些人會說成「research school」。多年的專業經驗英文應說「many years of professional experiences」而非「many years professional experiences」。錯誤的句子裡沒有連接詞，可以改為「Because of my graduate school training and many years of experiences, I am suitable for this job.」。正確句子中的「combined with」就等於「and」，因此「A and B= A combined with B」。另「A qualify sb for B」指的是「A使某人有資格做B」。

Part

3

實際面試對答

延伸說法

(1) I have never involved in fundraising and therefore this job is quite challenging for me. However, this is also a chance for me to grow.
我從來沒有從事過募款，所以這個工作是蠻具挑戰性的。然而這也是一個成長機會。

(2) I am not afraid of making mistakes. I am only afraid that I can't learn anything from the mistake itself.
我不怕犯錯。我只怕我沒有從錯誤本身學習到東西。

Sales

3-2

業務人員

角色

S: Susan, the hiring manager. 面試官
W: Wendy, the job applicant. 面試者

情景

Wendy is applying for the sales position at SHISEIDO.
溫蒂正在應徵 SHISEIDO 的業務職位。

對話

S : Why are you applying for this sales job with us?

你為什麼會來應徵我們公司的業務工作?

W : I enjoy challenging myself and this would be a challenging job.

我喜歡挑戰我自己,而這份工作會很有挑戰性。

S : You were a salesperson at Ford, selling cars at your last job. But do you know that we sell beauty products?

你之前的工作是福特汽車的業務,負責賣車。你知道我們是賣美容產品的嗎?

W : Definitely I do. A person who can sell more than one product is considered as a good salesperson. In addition, selling a completely different product

我當然知道。能賣超過一個產品的人才算好業務。除此之外,銷售一個完全不同的產品是非常有挑戰性的,我把它視為是精進我業務技巧的好機會。

is very challenging , which I see as a good opportunity to sharpen my sales skills.

S：Well, you sure seem to have a lot of confidence. I like that in a prospective employee. If you don't mind me asking, how did you hear about this position?

嗯，你一定很有自信。我喜歡未來的員工有這樣的特質。如果你不介意我問，你是如何知道這個職缺的？

W： I went to a career fair last week in the civic center downtown. My network helps me and I got the chance to talk with your HR manager there. That's where I got the lead on this job.

上週我參加在市區市民中心舉辦的就業博覽會。我的人際網絡（人脈）幫了我，所以我有機會在那裏和你們的人事經理講到話。也因此我得到了這個工作的領先優勢。

S：I think you would be a huge asset to our company. I'd like to offer you the position. What do you think?

我認為你會是我們公司的大資產。我決定錄取你，你認為呢？

W：That's great, sir. I am pleased to accept it. You won't be sorry. I'll be setting good sales records in this company in my first year!

那太棒了，我很高興接受這份工作。你不會後悔的。在我工作的第一年我就會創造良好銷售紀錄！

Part

3

實際面試對答

🍎 單字

❶ sharpen [ˈʃɑrpṇ] *v.* 字面上是「變尖；變鋒利」。文中sharpen的衍生為「精進」

相關詞 enhance [ɪnˈhæns] *v.* 提高，增加（價值，品質，吸引力等）
　　improve [ɪmˈpruv] *v.* 改進，改善；增進

例 I always remind myself that a workman must sharpen his tools if he is to do his work well.
我總是提醒自己：工欲善其事，必先利其器。

❷ prospective [prəˈspɛktɪv] *adj.* 預期的，盼望中的；未來的；即將發生的

相關詞 proposed [prəˈpozd] *adj.* 被提議的；所推薦的
　　forthcoming [ˌforθˈkʌmɪŋ] *adj.* 即將到來的
　　likely [ˈlaɪklɪ] *adj.* 很可能的

例 In my previous sales position, a lot of money went on wining and dining prospective clients.
在我之前的業務工作裡，很多錢都花在宴請潛在客戶上。

❸ networking [ˈnɛtˌwɝkɪŋ] *n.* 建立關係網絡

相關詞 online social networking site 線上社交網站
　　speed networking 快速人脈網路（供商業人士快速認識別人的活動）

例 A very important part of my job is to exploit the opportunities of networking, otherwise I risk being left behind.
我工作很重要的一部分是抓住機會建立關係網絡，否則我會有落後的風險。

❹ asset [ˈæsɛt] *n.* 財產，資產

相關詞 fixed assets 固定資產；不動產
　　asset allocation 資產分配
　　liquid assets 流動資產

例 My previous boss used to tell me that my leadership qualities were the greatest assets of the company.
我之前的老闆曾經告訴我，我的領導才能是公司最大的資產。

面試時別講錯

我的人際網絡幫了我，所以我有機會在那裏和你們的人事經理講到話。

（✗）My relationship helps me and I have the chance there talk your HR manager.

（○）My networking helps me and I got the chance to talk with your HR manager there.

「人際網絡」英文正確說法為「networking」，很多人會照中文意思講成「relationship」。另外，中文句子會先說地點再說動作，例如「在那裏和你們的人事經理講到話」。但英文的句子要先說動詞，時間地點放後面。所以上句英文正確說法為「talk with your HR manager there」。「和~說話」中式英文常會忽略了要加「to」或「with」而講成「talk your HR manager」，要注意介係詞。

延伸說法

(1) My ambition and ability to work well under pressure help me become a good sales.
我的企圖心和抗壓力幫助我成為一個好的業務。

(2) I spend time understanding subordinates' needs, which helps me lead my department.
我會花時間了解下屬需求，這幫助我領導我的部門。

Part

3

實際面試對答

267

Administrative Assistant

3-3

外商行政助理

👥 角色

T: Tom, the hiring manager. 面試官
M: Mary, the job applicant. 面試者

💼 情景

Mary is applying for the administrative assistant position at a foreign company.
瑪莉正在應徵外商公司行政助理的職位。

💬 對話

T： What leadership qualities did you develop as an administrative assistant?

作為一個行政助理,你有怎樣的領導特質?

M： I demonstrate my leadership skills by motivating people and working together as a team.

我藉由激勵他人和與人團隊合作來展現我的領導技能。

T： Did you ever be **criticized** by your coworkers or supervisors? How do you usually handle criticism?

你有曾經被同事或主管批評過嗎?你通常如何處理別人的批評?

M： I think criticism is unavoidable. I just don't say anything;

我想批評是很難避免的。我通常不會説什麼,否則情況更糟,不

otherwise the situation could become worse. I do, however, accept **constructive** criticism and will try to improve myself.

過我會接受建設性的批評，然後試著改進自己。

T：As you know, we are an American company, and therefore we have high expectations for staff's English language proficiency. Do you think your English is good enough to **fulfill** every job tasks we assign to you?

如妳所知，我們是美商，所以對員工的英語文能力有很高的期待。你認為你的英文能力足夠應付我們指派給你的每個工作任務嗎？

M：Though my major is not applied English, I have been attending English language training classes at a language center on weekends for the past five years. Knowing that English is very important to my job, I keep practice and improving it.

雖然我的主修不是應用英語，我在過去五年都在週末上語言中心的英語訓練課程。我知道英文對我的工作非常重要，我持續練習與精進我的英文。

T：What makes you frustrated in a work situation?

在工作中，什麼事令你不高興？

M：Sometimes I find narrow-minded people are quite frustrating.

有時候我覺得心胸狹窄的人蠻令人洩氣的。

Part

3

實際面試對答

T：Are you a multi-tasked person? In other words, do you work well under stress or pressure?

你是一位可以同時承擔數項工作的人嗎？也就是說，你能承受工作上的壓力嗎？

M：Yes, I think so. The trait is needed in my current position and I know I can handle it well.

是的。這種特點就是我目前工作所需要的，我知道我能應付自如。

單字

❶ **criticism** [`krɪtə͵sɪzəm] *n.* 批評；苛求，挑剔

相關詞 **criticize** [`krɪtɪ͵saɪz] *v.* 批評；批判；苛求；非難

例 I always tell myself to listen to criticism but don't be crushed by it. 我總是告訴自己聽取批評意見，但不要被它擊垮。

❷ **unavoidable** [͵ʌnə`vɔɪdəb!] *adj.* 不可避免的

相關詞 **avoid** [ə`vɔɪd] *v.* 避開，躲開

同義詞 **inevitable** [ɪn`ɛvətəb!] *adj.*

反義詞 **confront** [kən`frʌnt] *v.* 迎面遇到；面臨；遭遇

例 I try not to be disturbed at trifles or unavoidable accidents at work. 我試著不為工作上的瑣事或不可避免的事故自尋煩惱。

❸ **constructive** [kən`strʌktɪv] *adj.* 建設性的；積極的；有助益的

相關詞 **construction** [kən`strʌkʃən] *n.* 建造，建設

例 I meant to provide constructive criticism, but he took it as a personal insult.
我的本意是提供建設性的批評，但他認為是對他個人的侮辱。

❹ **fulfill** [fʊl`fɪl] *v.* 完成（任務等）；實現

相關詞 **self-fulfilling** 自我實現的；實現自己抱負的
fulfilled 滿足的；個人志向得以實現的

同義詞 **accomplish** [ə`kɑmplɪʃ] *v.* **achieve** [ə`tʃiv] *v.*

例 I meant to provide constructive criticism, but he took it as a personal insult.
我的本意是提供建設性的批評，但他認為是對他個人的侮辱。

面試時別講錯

雖然我的主修不是應用英語，我在過去五年都在週末上語言中心的英語訓練課程。

（**✗**） Although I am not major Applied English, I the past five years on weekends attend language center English language training classes.

（**〇**） Though my major is not Applied English, I have been attending English language training classes at a language center on weekends for the past five years.

對照錯誤與正確的句子後我們可以發現英文與中文句子裡的地點時間排列方式不同。英文句子通常先寫地點，時間放在句尾。而中文句子通常先說時間再說地點。「我的主修」英文正確說法應為「my major」，有些人會說成「I am major」。「我的主修為~」可說「my major is~」 或「I major in~」。第一個major是名詞，而第二個major是動詞。「I am major in」是錯誤的說法。「語言中心的英語訓練課程」英文正確說法應為「English language training classes at a language center」而非照中文的邏輯思考講成「language center English language training classes」。

延伸說法

(1) Despite majoring in Electronic Engineering, I have extensive experience in business administration.
雖然我主修電機，但我在企管方面有很多經驗。

(2) In spite of being a newly graduate, I have worked part-time in related fields for four years.
雖然我是應屆畢業生，但我已在相關領域兼職四年。

Part

3

實際面試對答

Financial Analyst

銀行財務分析師

角色

H: Henry, the hiring manager. 面試官
F: Frank, the job applicant. 面試者

情景

Frank is applying for the financial analyst position at a bank.
法蘭克正在應徵銀行財務分析師一職。

對話

H：Tell me about yourself and your past experience.

說說你自己和你過去的一些經驗吧。

F：For the past ten years, I have worked for several companies in the financial industry. My current job is in investment banking, which I have been doing for three years. I am confident about my analytical mindset, and I have a background of solid accounting **principles**. I thrive on challenge and work well in high-stress environments.

過去十年我在金融業的幾家公司工作過。我目前的工作是投資銀行業務，這個工作我已做了三年。我對我的分析能力有自信，我也有紮實的會計原理知識。我善於應付挑戰，也能在壓力大的環境下有好的工作表現。

H：How would your boss describe you and your work style?

你的老闆會如何形容你和你的工作風格？

F：I guess she would say I have a lot of initiative. I see the big picture and I do what has to be done. I always meet deadlines. She would possibly also state that I have the ability to focus on what I am working on. That is, I am not easily **distracted**.

我想她會說我很積極。我顧全大局，會做完所有需要做的事。我總能在期限前完成工作。她可能也會說我能集中精神做事情。也就是說，我不會輕易被干擾。

H：If we offer you the job, which part of it would you find most challenging?

如果我們錄取你，這個工作的哪一部分你覺得最具挑戰？

F：My background and experience include working on a **variety** of projects and jobs in the financial industry. Most of my experience has been behind the scenes, doing the calculations. As a result, working with clients in person is quite challenging for me, but I take it as a chance for me to grow.

我的背景和經驗包括在金融業參與各項專案，做過不同的工作。我的大部分經驗都是在幕後做一些計算方面的工作。因此面對面和客戶打交道對我來說是蠻具挑戰性的，但我把它視為一個成長的機會。

H：Do you have any questions for me?

你有任何問題想問我嗎？

F：Yes, I do. What do you see as the future trends for the financial industry?

有的，你如何看待金融行業的未來發展趨勢？

Part
3

實際面試對答

273

🍎 單字

❶ analytical [ˌænəˈlɪtɪkəl] *a.* 分析的

相關詞 **analysis** [əˈnæləsɪs] *n.* 分析

analyze [ˈænˌaɪz] *v.* 分析

analyst [ˈænlɪst] *n.* 分析者

例 I think my boss will say that I have a clear analytical mind.

我想我老闆可能會說我頭腦清晰，善於分析。

❷ principle [ˈprɪnsəp!] *n.* 原則；原理

相關詞 **standard** [ˈstændəd] *n.* 標準，水準；規格；規範

principal [ˈprɪnsəp!] *adj.* 主要的，首要的；*n.* 校長

常用法 in principle 原則上

例 I always tell my subordinate that observance of the law is a matter of principle for us.

我總是告訴我的下屬：守法是我們的一個原則問題。

❸ distracted [dɪˈstræktɪd] *adj.* 分心的

相關詞 **distract** [dɪˈstrækt] *v.* 使分心

distraction [dɪˈstrækʃən] *n.* 使人分心的事物

常用法 distract from 使從…分心

例 I concentrate and don't allow myself to be distracted while working.

工作時我專心並且不允許自己分心。

❹ variety [vəˈraɪətɪ] *n.* 多樣化

相關詞 **various** [ˈvɛrɪəs] *adj.* 各種各樣的

常用法 a variety of 各種各樣的

例 Being a teacher, I try a variety of methods that help to liven up a lesson.

作為一個老師，我嘗試用各式各樣的方法來使課程更加生動。

📖 面試時別講錯

因此面對面和客戶打交道對我來說是蠻具挑戰性的，但我把它視為一個成長的機會。

（✗）So face to face working with clients is quite challenge, but I see it as a grow chance.

（○）As a result, working with clients in person is quite challenging for me, but I take it as a chance for me to grow.

「面對面」英文可說「face to face」或「in person」，但要注意要放在動詞後而非動詞前。也就是說，「面對面和客戶打交道」英文要說「work with clients face to face」或「work with clients in person」，而非「face to face work with clients」或「in person work with clients」。「成長的機會」英文要說「a chance to grow」而不是「a grow chance」。challenge 是名詞，指「挑戰」。「具挑戰性的」是形容詞，英文要說「challenging」。

🔗 延伸說法

(1) I have never involved in fundraising and therefore this job is quite challenging for me. However, this is also a chance for me to grow.
我從來沒有從事過募款，所以這個工作是蠻具挑戰性的。然而這也是一個成長機會。

(2) I am not afraid of making mistakes. I am only afraid that I can't learn anything from the mistake itself.
我不怕犯錯。我只怕我沒有從錯誤本身學習到東西。

Part

3

實際面試對答

Hotel Front Desk Clerk

3-5

飯店櫃台人員

角色

H: Henry, the hiring manager. 面試官
S: Sandy, the job applicant. 面試者

情景

Sandy is applying for the front-desk clerk position at Best Hotel.
Sandy 正在應徵倍斯特飯店櫃台的工作。

對話

H：Good afternoon. I'm Hank, and I'll be conducting your interview. Your resume is **impressive** and it's nice to see you in person today.

午安，我是 Hank。今天由我來面試你。你的履歷令人印象深刻，今天很高興見到你本人。

S：Thank you. I'm so happy to hear that. The pleasure is all mine.

謝謝，很高興您這樣説。這是我的榮幸。

H：First of all, your resume tells me that you have been a front-desk clerk for the past five years. Did you enjoy it and what have you learned from it?

首先，你的履歷告訴我在過去五年你擔任櫃檯人員。你喜歡這份工作嗎？你從中學習到甚麼？

S：Certainly I enjoy it, and these five years of working experiences have sharpened my **interpersonal** skills. I learned how to communicate with others effectively and how to provide good customer service to our guests. My English and Japanese communication skills also improved a lot.

我當然很喜歡，這五年的工作經驗磨練了我的人際溝通技巧。我學習到如何和他人有效率地溝通與如何提供優良的客戶服務給客人。我的英文與日文溝通技巧也進步很多。

H：What made you interested in working with Best Hotel?

你為什麼想在倍斯特飯店工作？

S：Best Hotel is a well-known international five-star hotel. I always wanted to work in such a famous hotel. In addition, I used to stay with Best Hotel in LA for two nights. I was very impressed with the excellent services you offer.

凱悦飯店是一個知名的國際五星級飯店。我一直都想在這樣著名的飯店工作。除此之外，我曾經在洛杉磯的倍斯特飯店住過兩晚，我對您提供的優質服務印象深刻。

H：Why do you want to leave your current position?

你為何想離開你現在的職位？

S：I have been there for five years and I think it's time for me to look for new **opportunities**.

我已經在那工作了五年，我想是時候尋找新的機會了。

Part

3

實際面試對答

單字

❶ impressive [ɪmˋprɛsɪv] *adj.* 予人深刻印象的

　常用法 impressive 是「予人深刻印象的」，而 impressed 是「對～感到印象深刻」，必須分辨清楚。

　　　　impress 是動詞，表「給……極深的印象」。

　例 I provide impressive services to every one of the guests who stay with our hotel.

　　　我提供予人深刻印象的服務給每個入住我們飯店的客人。

❷ sharpen [ˋʃɑrpn] *v.* 磨練

　相關詞 improve (v) 使分心

　例 Working in different departments sharpened my adaptability.

　　　在不同的部門工作磨練了我的適應力。

❸ interpersonal [ˌɪntɚˋpɝsən!] *a.* 人際的，人與人之間的

　相關詞 interpersonal communication 人際溝通

　　　　Interpersonal relationships 人際關係

　例 In my previous job, I've received extensive training in interpersonal skill.

　　　在我之前的工作，我受過廣泛的人際溝通技巧訓練。

❹ opportunity [ˌɑpɚˋtjunətɪ] *n.* 機會；良機

　相關詞 chance 機會

　　　　take the opportunity 藉機；藉此機會

　例 I always make myself prepared for any opportunity that comes.

　　　我總是為每個可能來臨的機會做好準備。

面試時別講錯

我曾經在洛杉磯的倍斯特飯店住過兩晚。

（✗）I ever lived two nights in LA's Best Hotel.

（○）I used to stay with Best Hotel in LA for two nights.

在飯店「住」過兩晚的「住」英文不說「live」而是「stay」。「live」指的是「你固定，長期居住～」，短暫停留的「住」英文要說「stay」。「洛杉磯的倍斯特飯店」很多人會直接說「LA's Best Hotel」。這是中文式思考。英文應把地點放後面，中間加介係詞 in。ever 表「曾經」時通常放在疑問句。英文中表示「你曾經做過～事」要說「used to +V.」。

延伸說法

(1) I stayed in the employee dormitory during my business trip in Shanghai.
我在上海出差時住在員工宿舍。

(2) I stayed in the employee dormitory during my business trip in Shanghai.
我在上海出差時住在員工宿舍。

Part

3

實際面試對答

Flight Attendant

3-6

空服員

角色

T: Tina, the hiring manager. 面試官
P: Patty, the job applicant. 面試者

情景

Patty is applying for the flight attendant position at China Airline.
Patty 正在面試中華航空公司的空服員的職位。

對話

T： Why would you like to take the flight attendant exam?

你為何想要參加空服員招考？

P： I like to travel, and I enjoy working with people.

我喜歡旅行，也喜歡從事與人有關的工作。

T： Aren't you concerned about air accidents?

你會擔心空難嗎？

P： Not really, because the accident rate for aircraft is the lowest of all modes of transportation.

不會，因為飛機的事故率是所有運輸工具中最低的。

T： What do you think is the desirable **characteristics** for a flight attendant?

你認為空服員應具備甚麼特質？

P：A good flight attendant should be friendly, polite, **tolerant** of people, and open-minded. He/She should be able to make the passengers relaxed and happy during the flight.

一個好的空服員應是友善的，有禮貌的，對人寬容，並且心胸寬大。他（她）要能夠讓乘客在飛行途中感到放鬆愉快。

T：What are the main responsibilities of a flight attendant?

空服員的主要職責為何？

P：Job duties include assisting passengers while entering or **disembarking** the aircraft; announcing and **demonstrating** safety and emergency procedures such as the use of oxygen masks, seat belts, and life jackets; checking to ensure that food, beverages, blankets, reading material, emergency equipment, and other supplies are aboard and are in adequate supply, etc.

工作職責包括協助客人上下飛機；宣布並展示安全和應急程序，如使用氧氣面罩，安全帶和救生衣；檢查並確保機上食品，飲料，毛毯，閱讀材料，應急設備和其他物資充足等。

Part

3

實際面試對答

單字

❶ **characteristic** [ˌkærəktəˈrɪstɪk] *n.* 特性，特徵，特色

常用法 characteristic of 是～的特色

impress 是動詞，表「給……極深的印象」。

例 Being humble is one of my characteristics.

謙遜是我的特性之一。

❷ **tolerant** [ˈtɑlərənt] *adj.* 忍受的，容忍的，寬恕的

常用法 ctolerant + of/ to/ towards 對～容忍

例 Being a supervisor, I always tell myself to be tolerant of different views.

作為一個主管，我總是告訴自己要容忍不同的意見。

❸ **disembark** [ˌdɪsɪmˈbɑrk] *v.* to get off a ship or aircraft 下船; 下飛機

反義詞 embark

例 One of flight attendants' job responsibilities is to assist passengers embarking and disembarking the aircraft.

空服員的工作職責之一是協助旅客上下飛機。

❹ **demonstrate** [ˈdɛmənˌstret] *v.* 示範操作，展示

相關詞 display, show, illustrate

例 In my previous job, I learnt how to demonstrate different products.

我之前的工作讓我學習到如何展示不同的產品。

面試時別講錯

不會，因為飛機的事故率是所有運輸工具中最低的。

（✗）Not really, because aircraft's accident rate is all transportation's lowest.

（○）Not really, because the accident rate of aircraft is the lowest of all modes of transportation.

「飛機的事故率」以中文的思考會說「aircraft's accident rate」，英文正確說法應為「the accident rate of aircraft」。「所有運輸工具中最低的」很多人會按照字面翻譯而說「is all transportation's lowest」，正確說法為「is the lowest of all modes of transportation」。

延伸說法

(1) Fight attendant is the job I want the most.
空服員是我最想要的工作。

(2) I was voted one of the most popular flight attendants.
我被票選為最受歡迎的空服員之一。

Part

3

實際面試對答

283

好書報報－職場系列

Best Publishing

國際化餐飲時代不可不學！
擁有這一本，即刻通往世界各地！

基礎應對 訂位帶位、包場、活動安排、菜色介紹...
前後場管理 服務生Must Know、擺設學問、食物管理...
人事管理 徵聘與訓練、福利升遷、管理者的職責...
狀況處理 客人不滿意、難纏的顧客、部落客評論...

120個餐廳工作情境
100%英語人士的對話用語
循序漸進勤做練習，職場英語一日千里！

作者：Mark Venekamp & Claire Chang
定價：新台幣369元
規格：328頁 / 18K / 雙色印刷 / MP3

這是一本以航空業為背景，
從職員角度出發的航空英語會話工具書。
從職員VS同事 & 職員VS客戶，
兩大角度，呈現100% 原汁原味職場情境！

特別規劃→
以Q&A的方式，英語實習role play
提供更多航空界專業知識的職場補給站
免稅品服務該留意甚麼？ 旅客出境的SOP！
迎賓服務的步驟與重點！違禁品相關規定?！
飛機健檢大作戰有哪些...

作者：Mark Venekamp & Claire Chang
定價：新台幣369元
規格：352頁 / 18K / 雙色印刷 / MP3

好書報報

Best Publishing

5★技巧，打造你五星級的餐旅英語實力!!
免訂位馬上享用!

★真實〔餐廳〕＋〔旅館〕會話，與客人寒暄零距離↓
　模擬真實情境，學習、練習 "聽" 與 "說"

★文法沒有這麼難，用一點點文法概念會講就好↓
　附簡單文法說明，用簡單的英文就能表達得很清楚。

★不冷場的實用句子，不管遇到哪國人都不怯場↓
　融入西式餐廳與旅館的服務內容知識，應對更有信心。

★簡單角色扮演練習，多練習英語口說更進步↓
　自己練習或者與同伴角色扮演練習口說，學習更佳。

★餐旅人不可不知職場專業TIPS!!中英對照實力加倍↓
　(一贏：加強英文閱讀能力)＋(二贏：入行需知)＝雙贏

作者：林昭菁、Jeri Fay Maynard
定價：新台幣369元
規格：312頁 / 18K / 雙色印刷 / MP3

行銷/公關/廣告人 有料必備! 加薪/升職/跳槽 捨我其誰!

在專業能力之外，語言能力的提升被視為職場競爭力的關鍵。
更應該知道要利用甚至創造各種機會來加強自己優勢的重要。

透過由資深媒體公關編寫成實用對話，透過實務常見的主題，
帶出品牌、行銷、廣告、媒體、市調與新品上市後的各種活動所必備的
專業知識與經驗分享!

◎本書特色
25個實用主題: 資深行銷公關執筆＝真實歷練＋職場百態
50篇情境對話: 專業外籍配音員錄製MP3＝聽說合一 效率學習
【主題對話】與主管、客戶開會、簡報、媒體採購、主視覺拍攝＝正式溝通 精彩有料
【延伸對話】與同事、外製閒聊哈啦＝非正式溝通 關鍵加分
【有料字彙＋句型】捨棄繁複文法分析＋不囉嗦直接給例句＝現學現用 立刻上手

作者：江昀璀、胥淑嵐
定價：新台幣32元
規格：272頁 / 18K / 雙色印刷 / MP3

好書報報

心理學研究顯示，一個習慣養成，至少必須重複21次!
全書規劃30天學習進度表，搭配學習，
不知不覺養成學習英語的好習慣!!

圖解學習英文文法，三效合一!
　　◎刺激大腦記憶 ◎快速掌握學習大綱 ◎複習迅速
英文文法學習元素一次到位!
　　◎20個必懂觀念 ◎30個必學句型 ◎40個必閃陷阱

流行有趣的英語!
◎「那裡有正妹!」
◎「今天我們去看變形金剛4吧!」

作者：朱懿婷
定價：新台幣399元
規格：368頁 / 18K / 雙色印刷 / 軟皮精裝

文法再弱也有救! 只要跟著解題邏輯分析句子，
釐清【文法重點】找出【判斷依據】並運用【關鍵知識】
《英文文法有一套》讓你一套走天下，三步驟有答案!

【一套邏輯】
　　文法重點＝常考、愛考、一直考的文法
　　判斷依據＝題目中足以判斷「文法重點」的依據
　　關鍵知識＝不受誘答選項影響，正確答案立即浮現的
　　　　　　　「關鍵文法知識」
【十大主題】
　　10大考官最愛文法主題 建立考生精準文法觀念
【三步驟解題】
　　先10題範例：3步驟 全面掌握解題邏輯
　　再10題練習：3步驟 完全熟練必考重點

作者：黃亭瑋
定價：新台幣369元
規格：372頁 / 18K / 雙色印刷

好書報報

Best Publishing

Leader 007

99%會問的百大企業英文面試題

贏得職場黃金入場券

作　　　者／王郁琪

封　面　設　計／Fiona

內　頁　排　版／菩薩蠻數位文化有限公司

發　　行　　人／周瑞德

企　劃　編　輯／徐瑞璞

校　　　對／劉俞青、陳欣慧、饒美君

印　　　製／大亞彩色印刷製版股份有限公司

初　　　版／2014 年 11 月

定　　　價／新台幣 360 元

出　　　版／力得文化

電　　　話／（02）2351-2007

傳　　　真／（02）2351-0887

地　　　址／100 台北市中正區福州街 1 號 10 樓之 2

E m a i l／best.books.service@gmail.com

港 澳 地 區 總 經 銷／泛華發行代理有限公司

地　　　址／香港筲箕灣東旺道 3 號星島新聞集團大廈 3 樓

電　　　話／（852）2798-2323

傳　　　真／（852）2796-5471

國家圖書館出版品預行編目(CIP)資料

99%會問的---百大企業英文面試題—贏得職場黃金入場券 / 王郁琪

作. -- 初版. -- 臺北市：力得文化, 2014.11

　面；　公分

ISBN 978-986-90759-6-1(平裝附光碟片)

1.英語 2.會話 3.面試

805.188　　　　　　　　　　　　　103021112

{ 即刻上 Facebook 搜尋【倍斯特出版】並加入粉絲團
{ 搶先新書內容第一手資訊與不定期好康優惠活動！
https://www.facebook.com/best.books.service